Also by the author:

Final Straw
Final Exam
Final Breath
Final Bid

Final Stretch

Final Stretch

Kathleen M. Fraze

To order additional copies of this book, contact:
Xlibris Corporation
1-888-795-4274
www.Xlibris.com
Orders@Xlibris.com
57985

To Patricia and Tim,
the original fan club

Prologue

Sunset was half an hour away, and the road running through the park was still bright with the golden heat of May. But back in the woods along the river, the trail had faded into cool grays and greens, and shadows hung over the path, masking the ruts and snake holes. It was the time of day when an inexperienced runner could snap an ankle or twist a knee.

But Carmen wasn't an inexperienced runner.

She knew the trail like she knew her own body—every turn, every rise, every rock. She could close her eyes and pinpoint by the sounds—the rush of the river, the creak of tree limbs overhead, the muffled growl of a car on the road—just where she was and just how much farther she had to go. She had been running the trail every day for two years, ever since she had been recruited by the university's track program. She ran through mud, through slush, through dry dust. Only the blizzards of winter hindered her, and then—well, then she ran in the road.

She was twenty years old, and next year, she was going to the Olympics. She'd told her coach so.

The run was five miles out and five miles back—nothing for a runner of her caliber. She needed a rougher trail, but in farm country, the path along the river was the worst she could get. She wished the park district would stop trying to *improve* the path. She needed the tough climbs. She didn't need crowds.

But it was getting dark now, and the old ladies strolling with their dogs had gone home. She had passed two runners from the high school team, and they had grunted to each other in recognition. They were serious boys, and it was okay. She didn't mind sharing the path with serious runners.

When the trail ended in a cornfield, she stopped and bent at the waist, spit into the grass, wiped sweat-soaked strands of hair off her forehead, then turned around for the five-mile run back. She felt the setting sun on her shoulders, then plunged into the woods and the cool shadows of twilight.

A mile from the turnaround, she passed a middle-aged man huffing and stumbling along the trail. His face was twisted in pain, and his bare chest and thighs were slick with sweat. He wasn't hard enough, she decided, and she didn't smile. He was taking up her space.

Two miles back, she passed a young man hunched over the rear wheel of his bicycle. He was swearing distractedly and didn't look up at her. Good, she thought. Bicyclists had no business on the trail.

She ran and felt her body release itself for the final push home. She felt strong.

She saw a brown wedge of gurgling river to her right, framed in soft green foliage, and her last coherent thought was how cool the water would feel on her hot, hot skin.

Then he grabbed her from behind and snapped her sweating neck.

Chapter One

On my fortieth birthday, I made a drunken promise to Dave that I was going to get myself back in shape. Not that I was a fat slob. My jeans were only one size bigger than the bellbottoms of my riotous youth, and if I didn't eat for a week, I could still squeeze into the uniform I used to wear on patrol. But gravity was doing distressing things to my bottom line. I occasionally sagged where I used to bounce. Dave assured me—just as drunkenly—that he appreciated every soft ounce.

But he's a man, and it's a constant challenge to keep his attention. So on the day after my fortieth birthday, I started hiking with the dog.

Barney is *not* my dog. He just showed up one day with Dave's son, Adam, and neither one has bothered to go home yet. As dogs go, Barney's not much trouble, but I still prefer the cats. They don't drool.

In the two months since my drunken promise, Barney and I had marched all over town, and when that got boring, we branched out into the country. Two or three times a week, I'd stuff Barney into the car, and we'd go exploring. Usually, we'd tramp up and down farm lanes, but there was one good park along the river, and on weekdays, it wasn't crowded. I could let Barney off the leash and be reasonably certain he wouldn't munch on a two-year-old for lunch.

I'd been on the afternoon shift all month and had slipped into the decadent habit of sleeping in until nine or ten. Logistically, it made perfect sense. Dave had to get up early to teach. Mother and Adam were both taking classes. It just cut down on the traffic jam in the bathrooms if I snuggled under the sheets until they were out of the house.

So on that particular Tuesday in May, it was nearly ten-thirty when I pulled off the road and parked in a small clearing next to the woods. The official entrance to the trail—with a paved parking lot and a unisex port-a-potty—was three miles down the road, but I'd discovered there were fewer people on this end of the path, meaning fewer mothers with little kids who wanted to pet the nice doggy. Barney wasn't a mean dog, but he didn't appreciate little hands tugging at his ears uninvited.

I opened the door, and Barney bowled over me and leaped to the ground before I could even unlatch my seat belt. I howled as one paw ground into my thigh, but Barney ignored me. He's a big mutt—eighty pounds, at least—and he's used to getting his way.

"You belong in the pound," I growled at him, but he was already watering the weeds and sniffing the wind.

The morning was overcast, and I shivered in my shorts and T-shirt as I locked the car. I should have worn jeans.

Barney veered off into the woods, and I slowly followed him. He knew exactly where he was. When I picked up the trail ten yards into the woods, he was nothing but a brown spot in the distance, merrily zigzagging from tree to tree.

I groaned and forced myself to pick up the pace. It was disconcerting how much forty-year-old muscles could stiffen over night.

It hadn't been a restful night to start with. It was finals week, and too many students were doing their cramming in bars. Detectives don't usually break up brawls downtown, but there had been so many high-spirited encounters that the patrols couldn't handle them all. The drunk tank had been bulging by the time I had clocked out.

Dave had stayed up late grading and, well, one thing led to another, and it was very, very late by the time we collapsed in a sleepy tangle of arms and legs. I think we might have discovered a new angle or two, because my hips were kind of stiff that morning, and I was having trouble finding my rhythm on the trail. I did not feel like a well-oiled machine.

The trail never wandered far from the river, but I noticed with surprise that the view was becoming obscured by vegetation. It had been cold, rainy April when Barney and I had discovered the trail, and the ground had been covered only by a moldy layer of brown leaves. But green things had sprouted up all over since then, and I could hear tiny creatures scampering through the undergrowth. Barney heard them, too, and was in a frenzy. By the time I hit the mile marker, he had covered at least four.

I plunked myself down on a hunk of tree that had conveniently fallen beside the trail and rubbed the thigh Barney had mangled. It was already turning blue. If I hadn't slept late, I'd have gone the extra mile to the end of the trail. But I *did* have to work and I *did* need time for a shower. So I sat on the log and let my mind drift over the cases waiting for me at the station.

A young woman jogged by and we smiled politely. I noticed there wasn't an ounce of fat jiggling on her thighs, and my smile frosted over.

Barney trotted out of the woods and poked a cold nose at my ankles.

"Have you been eating bunnies?" I asked sternly.

He rolled his eyes like he'd never dream of such a thing. Adam frequently gave me the same look. Sometimes I wished Adam and the dog would both go home to the boy's mother. But Dave had learned to live with *my* mother sleeping in the bedroom right above us, so I owed it to him to put up with his son for a while. But *damn*, the house was getting crowded.

I absently scratched the fur behind Barney's ears and acknowledged that the dog did have his good points. Sometimes, it's mighty lonely out in the woods, even for a tough cop like me.

"Let's go home," I said, and he shot down the path before I could haul myself off the log. Barney was distressingly energetic.

I could feel the morning slipping away from me, and I pushed myself a little harder on the hike back. The return trip was uphill, and I was pleased to note as I neared the turnoff to the car that I was *not* panting this time.

The dog had caromed off the path ahead of me, away from the river. I couldn't see him anymore, and I felt a twinge of irritation. It was just like the dog to disappear when it was time to go home.

"Barney!" I yelled, and spun myself around, looking for a telltale patch of brown among the green.

Nothing.

I stomped my foot on the trail as the clock ticked in my head. "Barney, come on! Heel!"

It always worked for Adam.

But all I got was a muted whine, off in the woods to my left.

"Barney?" I said uncertainly.

The whine rose eerily among the trees, and I had a sudden flash of the damned dog caught in a rusty trap. This had been private land before the park district had taken it over, and it had been a favorite haunt of hunters. The summer before, there had been a huge outcry when a little girl had wandered off the trail and had snagged her foot in a forgotten trap. Park rangers had combed the woods after that, searching for other implements of destruction. That had led to a finely orchestrated news conference, where the park superintendent had declared the trail *clean*.

But Barney's whine wasn't reassuring.

"*Damn* that dog," I muttered, and nervously plunged into the bushes. The place was probably crawling with poison ivy.

I pushed through the brambles, homing in on his strange whimpers. He had wandered beyond the turnoff to the car, and I finally caught sight of him circling in high grass a good twenty-five feet off the trail.

At least he wasn't dragging a trap behind him.

"What is your problem?" I demanded.

But Barney sidled away from me, then raised his head to the sky and howled mournfully.

It echoed through the woods like a primeval harbinger of death, and I hugged myself in fright.

The girl in the grass wasn't frightened. She was just dead.

Chapter Two

Doc Sweitzer squatted painfully in the weeds. He was getting too old for this crap, he told me, as though somehow it was my fault there was a body in the park. It wasn't my doing that he was the coroner. I'd been campaigning against him ever since I was old enough to vote.

He glanced up at me in irritation. "You disturb the body?" he demanded.

The deputies lurking behind me chortled. Like I didn't know how to preserve a crime scene, for Christ's sake.

"I checked for a pulse," I said stoutly.

"What the hell for?" Doc bellowed. "Any damn fool can see she's dead."

The woman was lying with her head twisted at an unhealthy angle, but this damn fool had still felt for a pulse. It's one of those things you do automatically. It didn't matter that there were flies dancing across her eyes. There's always the unacknowledged hope that maybe what you've stumbled upon isn't death.

She was young. I looked at her and immediately thought "girl," but she had probably been old enough to declare herself a woman. She might have been pretty, but her face was distorted from exposure and rigor. There were good running shoes on her feet and a T-shirt and athletic bra had been bunched up above her breasts, but her shorts and panties were missing.

Doc Sweitzer was on his knees, peering between her legs but delicately not touching her. It was a nauseating sight—that fat old man wheezing over her thighs—and I had to lecture myself that he was only doing his job. But I felt a flash of shame for the girl, exposed to all those men.

Ellen Graham was there, standing back in the trees and talking to a park ranger. I'd been a little annoyed with Herchek for sending Ellen as backup instead of Henry, but now it felt mildly comforting. The dead girl and I weren't so outnumbered.

There were a couple of deputies from the sheriff's office, but they were hanging around mostly for show. The park looked like it was out in the country, but through some creative politicking, it had recently been annexed to the city. I couldn't dump this body on the sheriff.

There were paramedics, too, and the state crime lab had coughed up a two-man forensics team to scour the body and the crime scene. It must have been a slow day for the state, because they'd shown up before Doc Sweitzer had come crashing through the woods. At least I could be reasonably certain of getting some decent reports from them.

Barney was pouting in the shade. I'd leashed him to a tree, and he was highly offended. But the last thing I needed was Doc Sweitzer bitching about the dog.

The coroner huffed and raised himself up on one knee. "I'd say she's been molested," he announced.

"*Molested?*" I repeated sarcastically.

"Well, now, I can't say rape till I get in to look at her, can I?"

That was a disgusting thought.

He grunted, and one of the deputies helped him to his feet. It was still cool to me, but Doc Sweitzer was sweating. "She's got some scratches inside her thighs, but no bleeding. I'd say she was killed first and *molested* later."

"How long ago?" I asked.

Doc Sweitzer was annoyed and looked at the deputy. "Isn't this your party?"

The deputy shrugged in embarrassment. "It's the city's jurisdiction, Doc."

The coroner tugged distractedly at his jacket, depositing all sorts of minuscule particles onto the body, and condescended to address me. "Twelve, fifteen hours. You want something better than that, you wait till I get her in the lab."

"Can I assume her neck is broken?" I asked testily.

"You can *assume* anything you damn well want," Doc huffed.

"Looks broke to me," the deputy offered.

Doc just glared.

I rolled my eyes and left it to the state lab technicians to ease Doc out of there.

One of the rangers, who had a better eye for that sort of thing, had spotted the mashed undergrowth where the body had been dragged back from the trail, and the deputies dutifully cordoned off the route so the techs could go over that, too. If we were lucky, they'd find a typed confession posted on a tree trunk.

Ellen waved me over to the ranger she had been questioning. Ellen had produced a baby daughter in February, and had been back at work for only two weeks. She had shed most of the weight she had picked up during the pregnancy, but she was not exactly in top form. She was almost ghostly pale, and there were deep circles under her eyes. Baby Amanda was not sleeping through the night yet.

But you didn't dare cut Ellen any slack because of it. The mere hint of it infuriated her.

Ellen introduced me to Ranger Larry, who apparently saw no need for a last name, and explained that he was in charge of the day shift in the park. He was about thirty, and he was much more interested in showing off his tan to Ellen than he was in talking to me. But he did have a pertinent tidbit to share.

"Ranger Larry thinks there's an unclaimed car in the parking lot," Ellen said. She said his name with a straight face. I would have giggled.

"What do you mean—unclaimed?" I asked.

The ranger reluctantly turned to me. I was getting a lot of that lately. And there I was, in skimpy shorts, too. "The park closes at dusk, but the night shift spotted a car in the lot after dark last night. They checked the trail for loiterers—usually, it's kids looking for a place to—um—you know—"

He blushed and I assured him that I knew what he meant.

"Normally, we run the plates, and if it's a slow night, maybe we even have the car towed," he said, "but last night the guys got a complaint about hunters on the other side of the river and—well—they kind of forgot about the car."

"It's still in the parking lot?" I asked.

"Well—" His blush deepened. "Yeah, it's still there. We had a bunch of school tours this morning, and no one got around to the car."

"Let's go," I said.

Ellen glanced at Doc Sweitzer, who was arguing with the state techs. "Shouldn't we stay with the body?" she asked.

"Oh, gee," I said, "we wouldn't want to get in anyone's way." And I waggled my fingers goodbye at Doc.

Ellen and I hiked to the road and our cars, with Barney meekly in tow. Ranger Larry was biking back along the trail to the parking lot. He promised to meet us there. He probably would have let Ellen ride on his handlebars, but she was wearing a skirt.

I backed out onto the road and drove the three miles to the parking lot. The river wound through the woods on our right; to the left, freshly planted fields peeked through the trees. Barney hung out the passenger side window, squinting as the wind flattened his ears to his head. Ellen drove sedately behind us.

There were a half dozen cars in the parking lot, but a ranger was posted at the entrance to turn newcomers away. He was a little skeptical about a woman in shorts, hauling around a mammoth dog and claiming to be a cop, but he took Ellen's word for it that we were respectable. I parked close to the trailhead and tied Barney to another tree. He eyed me like I was a traitor.

It took a few more minutes for Ranger Larry to show up, and by then two more cars had cleared out of the lot. I looked at what was left and bet on the rusty, dusty Cavalier. Ellen favored the sporty little Toyota.

Ranger Larry glided out of the trees and stopped behind the Toyota.

Ellen did not gloat.

The car was locked up tight, but I'm a cop, for Christ's sake. I can bust into a *car*. So while Ellen ran the plates, I slipped in a slim jim and popped the lock.

"You sure that's legal?" Ranger Larry asked.

"Oh, please," I said, and opened the door with a flourish.

The car was as neat on the inside as it was outside. The odometer read fifty-seven thousand plus, but someone had taken very good care of the merchandise. A warm-up jacket and sweat pants were lying across the back seat, and some kind of university parking pass hung from the rearview mirror, but there were no other personal items littering the interior. I crawled over the gearshift and jimmied open the glove compartment, but it was hardly worth the effort. The compartment held nothing but a Toyota owner's manual and two neatly folded maps.

Ellen stuck her head in the door and nodded as though that very neat interior suited her. Ellen's keen sense of order had not been shaken yet by motherhood. I couldn't wait until Baby Amanda started walking.

"The car's registered to a Carmen Martinez, Cincinnati address." And she rattled off a date of birth.

"Probably a student," I said, flicking the university parking pass with my finger.

"I already told dispatch to call the school registrar," Ellen said.

I did not make a face. I wanted to, but when you reach forty, you try to act with some kind of decorum.

So I wiggled in between the seats to the back and examined the jacket and sweat pants.

"Shouldn't we impound the car and let the state techs go through it?" Ellen asked pointedly.

"Oh, sure," I said. "But since we're already here—" And I jammed my hands into the pockets of the jacket.

"We're disturbing evidence, Jo," Ellen reminded me.

"She wasn't killed in the car, now was she?" I countered. Ellen always went by the book. And she got very good results, too. But sometimes, she just drove me crazy.

My hand closed around a billfold. "Ah," I said in contentment, and I settled back in the seat to pry through its secrets. Ellen shook her head and withdrew. She didn't want her fingerprints in the car.

The billfold was good brown leather, soft but utilitarian. I flipped it open and stared at the dead woman's face on the driver's license. The picture didn't seem to do her any more justice than death had. It was as unflattering as a mug shot—dark hair and eyes, complexion washed yellow by the flash. Her features were vaguely Latin, but maybe I was just associating the face with the Hispanic name. She looked hard in the photo, but I couldn't shake the impression I'd had back in the woods when I saw the body—that she might have been pretty in life.

The license had a Cincinnati address, and so did her insurance card, and her telephone calling card, and a very new looking VISA card. There was a university ID card, but no local address. Two snapshots had been stuffed behind the credit card. One was a fuzzy shot of an older couple—parents?—smiling obediently for the camera. The other was a shot of the dead woman, very much alive and standing next to a young man. He had an arm draped around her shoulders and was smiling directly at the camera. She had tilted her head to look up at him, and *there* was the spark I had missed before. She laughed for him, not the camera, and she looked very young and happy.

They were wearing heavy jackets, but both coats were hanging open. I could see bare tree branches behind them, but no snow. I was willing to bet the photo was only a few months old, taken while winter was still fighting for a hold against spring.

Taken while she was still nineteen.

I shivered and flipped the photo over. The name Jesse had been scrawled across the back. There were no cute little hearts scribbled alongside the name. I was pleased. Carmen had not struck me as a romantic.

I kept the picture but stuffed the billfold back into the jacket. It was official university issue, with the school seal emblazoned over the left breast pocket. The name Martinez had been sewn in felt letters across the back. Carmen, I realized, must have been somebody on campus.

I crawled out of the car in time to see Ranger Larry looking a little sick. "Oh, geez," he said to Ellen, "I think I know that girl."

"Whaddya mean, think?" I asked. "Didn't you look at the body?"

Ellen glanced at me in exasperation. It was the same kind of look I give Henry when he's being an oaf. It was downright insulting that Ellen was using it on me.

"I didn't want to get in the way," Ranger Larry said. "So, no, I didn't look at the body."

Right, I thought. He didn't look at a naked body. More likely, he didn't look at her face.

"But there's this girl," he said, talking to Ellen again, "she's out here every day, running the trail. Tough little girl. Doesn't talk to the guys. Just runs."

I shoved the snapshot under his nose. I'm usually a lot gentler with witnesses, more considerate of their feelings, but a grown man with no last name irritated me. And he wasn't paying attention.

"This her?" I asked.

He pulled his head back so he could get the picture in focus. He didn't want to touch it himself. But he recognized her, all right. The color drained from his face.

"Jesus," he said, "that's her."

"Can you tell us anything about her?" Ellen asked.

He shook his head sadly. "Nothing but she was good. She didn't come out her to fool around. She ran—hard. Guys used to make bets on whether she'd show up—you know, if it was raining or real cold. Never mattered what the weather was, she was always here."

"Same time every day?" I asked.

"Naw," he said. "She'd go in streaks—sometimes all mornings, sometimes all evenings. Must've had something to do with when she had classes. I haven't seen her much lately, so she must have been running in the evening."

"What about him?" I asked, still waving the picture. "You recognize him?"

Ranger Larry shrugged. "I don't know him."

Ranger Larry obviously didn't have an eye for men, I thought as I pocketed the photo.

"Did you see Carmen yesterday?" Ellen asked.

"No," he said. "But the night shift might have."

"We'll have to talk to them," Ellen decided.

Ranger Larry immediately offered to take her to his office, so they could go over the duty roster. Ellen was agreeable, but I had the dog, so I wasn't invited.

I got in one more question, though. "Have you had any complaints from people about anyone harassing them on the trail?"

"No one's been attacked," he protested. "This is a *good* park."

"I don't mean a physical attack," I amended, despite the fact that a dead woman was lying up the trail. "Anyone complain about people annoying them, getting in their way?"

His face twisted in thought. It was kind of cute—like a fourth-grader considering long division.

It was obviously just as taxing, too, because he took a long time thinking about it. "Well, you always got runners complaining about the cyclists, and cyclists complaining about kids getting in their way. Sometimes they get in arguments, but nothing serious. 'Course, if any of the guys heard about anything suspicious, it'd be in the logs." And he looked hopefully at Ellen.

"Better check those out, too," I said.

"I intended to," Ellen said. If I didn't know she was incapable of it, I'd have said she was insulted that I had felt the need to tell her what to do.

Herchek really should have known better than to pair us up.

The ranger's office was in a small building off the trailhead. I watched Ranger Larry lead Ellen up the path to the door, and noticed that even though it was only lunchtime, Ellen was dragging. I probably should have been kinder. If I tried really hard, I could remember the turmoil of motherhood.

Ellen just didn't make it easy.

"I'm a rat," I told Barney. And I settled myself on the grass beside him, to wait for the tow truck.

*   *   *

I had been a mother once, and it had been disastrous. My four-year-old daughter and my husband had died in a fire one night, and I had never had the courage to try motherhood again.

I had been twenty-eight when Elizabeth died. It was shocking to realize that if she had lived, she'd be looking forward to college about now. I had never really thought of myself as that old before, but the fact was, memories of my little girl were becoming fuzzier and fuzzier. Even the pain had become duller. It was always there, like a shadow, but I had learned to live despite it. And only rarely did the fiery nightmares return.

Dave, thank God, was always there to hold me and talk me through them. I had met him on a case six years before, and we had been together—more or less—since then. He had had his own nightmares—he would always need a cane thanks to a mine in the final days of Vietnam—but we had learned to fight off each other's ghosts. Dave taught political science at the university and, by nature, he distrusted cops. I, on the other hand, distrusted academics.

But we were very good in bed.

In between the fire and Dave, there had been Bradley, and he had made me a cop. He had been a detective then, and he had bullied me onto the police force before grief and self-pity could turn me into a drunk. He had probably saved my sanity, because I discovered that even though I had been a failure as a wife and mother, I was very good at being a cop. I had grown up in this town and was adept at learning—and keeping—its secrets. I didn't like much of what I saw each day—the pettiness, the stupidity and sometimes, the bodies—but I did enjoy piecing together the puzzles that came my way. I preferred order. Dave said it was my greatest weakness.

Bradley said it was my greatest strength. Bradley and I had been very good in bed once, too. But he was permanently married, and I was too selfish to share. Our affair had ended long before Dave had come along. But Bradley still knew me better than any other man ever would.

Bradley didn't like Dave. The feeling was mutual.

I had been a detective for eight years; Bradley had been the chief for five. We frequently got on each other's nerves. Which was probably why he scowled at me when I showed up in his office after the car had been towed. Certainly it had nothing to do with my shorts. Or Barney.

"Get the goddamned dog out of here," Bradley growled.

"He doesn't bite," I lied.

"I'm the fucking chief of police. What if the mayor sees a dog in my office?"

"I'll close the door," I said, and did so.

Barney promptly curled up in front of the door and closed his eyes. But he didn't fool me. He was playing possum.

Bradley snorted. He and Barney had a lot in common. Bradley was a big man, and a desk job had made him bigger. Back when he was a street cop, he was all hard muscle. He wasn't so hard anymore. But I wouldn't pick a fight with the man. If his fists didn't nail you, his eyes would. And he was still frightfully accurate with a gun.

Which was why I stood between him and the dog.

He took in the shorts and grunted. "You better run some more," he said.

"You don't like my legs, don't look."

"Hmph," he said. But he didn't turn away. I knew how to get Bradley's attention.

"We've got a dead woman in the park," I said.

He closed his eyes. "Don't tell me some school kids found her. I don't want to deal with hysterical parents."

"No kids," I assured him. "I found her."

He opened his eyes and looked at me speculatively. "You didn't kill her, did you?"

"No," I said, "I prefer to shoot people."

Bradley hesitated for just a moment. I *had* shot a man once, and it generally was not something I joked about. But this time, I hadn't even been thinking of the man I had killed.

And Bradley wisely let it pass. "Tell me about the body," he sighed.

So I plopped into a chair and told him what we had.

Bradley struck a lot of people as an impatient man, and when he was dealing with paperwork and politicians, he *was* impatient. As chief, he runs into a lot of both, and I frequently wonder whether it was a mistake for him to take the promotion. His best instincts are on the street. But the alternative would have been a bureaucrat in the chief's office, and given the choice, I'd rather answer to Bradley.

But I missed the way he evaluated a crime scene and talked people into revealing the most outrageous things. He could be a very good listener when it suited him.

He was listening very carefully to me. A dead woman in the park was not good for the city's image.

"What's your reading?" he asked when I was finished. "A stranger or someone who knew her?"

"It could be either," I admitted. "The location suggests a stranger—a lonely trail, a woman running alone, some pervert hanging around until the right victim wanders by."

"But?" he prodded.

"*But*," I said, stretching a little in the chair, just to keep him focused, "she was a regular on the trail. The ranger said she was out there every day. So anyone who knew her at all would know where to get her alone."

"We need to question the park staff," he said.

"Ellen's already on it," I assured him.

"And perverts in the woods."

"Ellen has started that, too."

"And the university."

I yawned. "I was thinking of wandering over there myself."

Bradley was staring pointedly at my thighs. "I assume you'll put some clothes on first."

"Well," I teased, "if you really think I should take the time."

"A shower, too," he sniffed.

Barney snorted as though he agreed.

"You are both insulting," I said.

Bradley shrugged. "The truth hurts."

I made a face and pulled myself out of the chair. Barney was on his feet like *that*, pawing at the door. My cats could sleep through a hurricane. I didn't think that dog ever stopped *listening*.

"You hike in the park a lot?" Bradley asked as I cajoled Barney back onto the leash.

"Couple times a week," I said.

"You always take him?" And he nodded at the dog.

I thumped Barney on the ribs. He slobbered in ecstasy. "Wouldn't leave home without him," I admitted.

"Good," Bradley said, and buried his nose in the afternoon paper.

I smiled to myself as we trotted out through the squad room. Barney had just been deputized by the chief of police.

Chapter Three

An hour later, I was in a respectable suit and on my way to the university. Out of deference to Bradley's ulcer, I left Barney at home to torment the cats.

The university sprawled across the northeast corner of town. It had been large when I was a student; it was twice as big now. It had gobbled up vast chunks of farmland and had sprouted all sorts of ungainly buildings where tomatoes had once grown. I preferred the original campus with its drafty yellow brick buildings surrounding a tree-studded quadrangle. But the university was partial to displaying it geometric fine arts building and its glass-enclosed science complex on the covers of its brochures.

Twenty thousand students descended on our town each fall, and because they kept half the city employed, there was an uneasy truce between town and gown. The townspeople viewed the campus as a necessary evil; it put food on their tables and paid the mortgage. The university viewed the town as a poor stepbrother—an ignorant one, at that. But the one couldn't survive without the other. That was the bottom line.

The student body tended to scare hell out of the straighter folks in town—all those kids meant a lot of energy bottled up in a relatively small area—but the campus really was no worse than any other community of twenty thousand. There were the usual drug problems, and brawls at the bars downtown. There were date rapes, there were robberies, and drunken accidents on the road. But it had been a while since there had been a murder.

The campus had its own police department, and normally I would have stopped in there first, as a matter of courtesy. Carmen Martinez had been killed on my turf, but she was a student, and that meant the university was involved. But Mike Edwards, who had been the campus chief longer than I had been a cop, had retired with the new year, and he had been replaced by a "security director" with whom I did not relate. Dave contends that I cannot relate to any female. I think he's wrong. I relate very well to Mother.

So even though it overlooked the quadrangle, I bypassed the security office and drove out past rows of dormitories to the field house, where the women's track coach had her office. The dispatcher, acting on Ellen's instructions, had not only verified that Carmen Martinez was a student, but had also picked up that she was one hot runner on the track team.

The sky was still overcast, but the afternoon had warmed up enough to draw dozens of students out to the track for a lap or two. I felt sorry for Dave, who was cooped up in a classroom giving a final. He would have enjoyed all those brightly colored short shorts and the firmly muscled legs pumping around the track. Even I took a moment to admire the backsides of the young men throwing themselves over the hurdles next to the parking lot.

But then Carmen Martinez's body flashed through my mind, and those trim butts didn't look so appealing anymore. I trudged into the field house.

The university had been politically correct when it had built the field house. The men's teams were housed down the right side, and the women's teams were down the left. Separate but equal. But I wondered perversely who got first dibs on the fine gym in the center.

I veered down the hallway to the left, looking for the track coach's office. It was easy to spot. It was the one where young women huddled outside the door, weeping quietly on each other's shoulders.

I edged around them to the door and got some very hostile stares for intruding. There were five women, all so trim and firm and unabashedly healthy that under normal circumstances, I would have been downright intimidated. They looked sleek enough to outrun bullets.

But they were also in shock, and it was sapping all that good health. One woman trembled so violently, I thought she was going to be ill.

A woman closer to my age was sitting at the desk in the office, and she was struggling with a conversation on the telephone. Her voice was pitched low, and she was speaking slowly and coherently, but I could hear the strain, like a scream begging to get out. She tapped the desk furiously with a pencil, and just as I looked in, the pencil snapped and splintered across the blotter. She irritably brushed the pieces onto the floor.

The office was small, and the cement block walls were covered with photos of women running and women accepting medals and women proudly holding trophies for the camera. There were a number of real trophies in there, too, perched on the desk, on the bookcase and on a small window ledge. I stared at them and eavesdropped on the young women mumbling behind me.

No one confessed to killing Carmen Martinez.

The woman at the desk abruptly hung up the phone and rubbed her temples in exasperation. I had the sudden eerie sense that she had been talking to Bradley. He had that effect on women.

She stared past me with reddened eyes, focusing on the students in the hallway. Then her brain registered a stranger on the premises, and she looked sharply back at me. "Who are you?" she demanded.

I flashed my badge.

She shuddered slightly. "Oh, God, it's true. Carmen's dead."

I nodded. And we stared at each other while the weight of it sank into her. Most people cringe when they hear of death, and for a moment, she looked like she was going to fold in on herself. But she was a tough woman. The extra years had rounded her out some, but she looked as strong as the younger women in the hall. And being a coach, she was used to taking charge. She allowed herself one moment to feel the pain, one moment when I could look into her eyes and see it throbbing, black and angry, then she shook her head and a mask fell competently into place.

She stood and walked past me to the door. She talked quietly but firmly to the students in the hall, and they reluctantly backed away. Then she closed the door and invited me to sit.

"I'm Pat August, Carmen's coach," she said as she sat again at her desk.

"Jo Ferris," I said as I pulled a notebook out of my purse. "Detective."

She looked at me with some anger. "I was just talking to your chief. He could have *told* me what happened to Carmen." And her tone said Bradley's behavior was inexcusable.

"We haven't reached Carmen's family yet," I said, trying to soothe her. "He won't discuss it with anyone until they've been notified."

"Notified of *what*?" she asked bitterly. "What *happened*?"

I tried to be gentle, but there's no kind way to describe murder. I told her simply what we had found, but even in its blandest terms, the effect was brutal. She gripped the edge of the desk and shook her head in shock, as though somehow she could chase it all away.

"Such a waste," she managed. "Such a goddamned waste!"

I sat quietly across from her and waited. I had learned over the years that silence brings out the worst in people.

Pat August swung nervously in her chair. "Do you have any idea who Carmen *was*? Do you know what she could *do*?"

I shook my head.

"She is—" Pat choked on her tenses, but quickly recovered—"she was the best runner this university has ever trained. She set five state records this spring and she was going to break them *all* next year. She was going to the Olympics. I swear to God, she was going to win the gold."

"This must be very painful for you," I said.

"For me?" she shot back. "My God, what about Carmen? Her *potential* was incredible. She had it all—the speed, the stamina, the determination. She could have been the pre-eminent runner of her generation. She could have shaped the record books for the next ten years. She was that good."

"Then why," I asked delicately, "was she here?"

Pat's face twisted in disgust. "She wouldn't have been here much longer. We have a good program, but not in Carmen's league. She had offers from the big-name programs, and she would have gone. Soon, as a matter of fact."

"So you were losing her regardless," I said.

"It doesn't matter what *I* lost," Pat snapped. "It's what the entire sport has lost." She tapped her fingers rapidly on the arms of her chair, and her eyes narrowed as a new thought occurred to her. "Do you think I killed her because she was leaving me?"

"Actually," I said carefully, "we suspect a man attacked her."

Pat blanched. "Oh, God, not that, too."

"She may have been—molested," I said, falling back awkwardly on Doc Sweitzer's term. "After she was killed."

Pat shuddered. "What kind of animal is out there?"

"We don't know," I said. "That's why we need your help. Who were Carmen's enemies?"

Pat's expression was puzzled. "Her enemies? I thought—the way you described it, I assumed she was just attacked by some stranger in the park."

"That's one possibility," I admitted. "It could have been a stranger. But it could have been someone who knew her habits, too."

"That's worse," Pat said. "That's much, much worse."

I wasn't sure I agreed. Death at anyone's hands seemed reprehensible to me.

Pat swung her chair around to a small refrigerator standing against the wall and she pulled out two bottles. "Apple or cranberry?" she asked abruptly.

I looked at her in consternation.

"I think better with a drink," she apologized. "Non-alcoholic."

"Apple," I said promptly.

And for the next few minutes, we slouched in our chairs and guzzled fruit juice. I studied the pictures on the walls—I recognized a few of Carmen and some of a much younger Pat August. Judging from the medals, she had a right to be a coach. And I wondered idly just how much it hurt a coach to see the best runner she'd ever train walk away to another program.

Pat, for her part, stared into her bottle, and her forehead furrowed as she thought. "Carmen was not a likable person," she announced after a while.

I raised an eyebrow.

"She was conceited, intolerant of weakness in others and driven only by one goal—her own success." Pat shrugged. "But she was an exquisite athlete."

"She must have made the other members of the team jealous," I said.

"Furiously jealous," Pat agreed. "I have some solid athletes this year, but it's been difficult for them to have a teammate of Carmen's caliber. No matter how good they were, Carmen was always better. She didn't go out of her way to antagonize them, but she made no attempt to help them, either. Carmen was not close to the other women. She was focused only on herself."

"But the others," I said, waving to the hall, "seemed upset."

"Of course, they were *upset*," Pat said irritably. "The sports editor from the campus paper came 'round just before you got here and said he'd heard Carmen was dead. The girls were frantic. *I* was frantic. It was the first we'd heard that anything was wrong." And she looked at me as though it was unforgivable that she hadn't been notified the moment we found Carmen's body.

"These other girls," I said, "did any of them dislike Carmen enough to hurt her?"

Pat's eyes narrowed. "I thought you were looking for a man."

"Men can be hired to do a woman's dirty work," I said.

"That's preposterous," Pat said. "My girls aren't that devious. If they had a problem with Carmen, they told her to her face. Frequently."

"But did any one girl have a bigger problem with Carmen?" I pressed.

"No," Pat said, and she snapped her mouth shut on any elaboration.

I sighed. The coach was not being helpful.

Pat drained her bottle and tossed it into the wastebasket. It landed with a thud. "You want a man who could have hurt Carmen, you should look up her boyfriend."

I pulled Carmen's snapshot out of my purse and passed it to Pat. "You mean him?"

She glanced at the photo and nodded. "Jesse Conklin. He was trouble."

"Did he mistreat her?" I asked.

"Oh, not in the traditional sense," she admitted. "He didn't abuse her—that I know of. He *distracted* her. He isn't an athlete. He's in engineering or something like that, and he didn't understand her commitment, her intensity."

"You don't approve of boyfriends," I said.

"That's not true," she objected. "A man who understood Carmen's drive would have been a great support. She needed an—an emotional outlet. But Jesse brought out her weaknesses. He eroded her dedication. He wasn't the right man."

Certainly not for Pat, I thought. But how had Carmen felt? And Jesse?

Pat was suddenly contrite. "I shouldn't have mentioned Jesse. He wasn't a good influence on Carmen, but he certainly wouldn't kill her."

"What about other men?" I asked. "Were other men pestering her?"

"Carmen wouldn't have noticed," Pat said. "She was oblivious to others."

"That could be infuriating," I said.

Pat nodded. "I suppose it could be. She could be so indifferent—I suppose if a man were infatuated with her and she didn't acknowledge him—well, it might make him angry."

"Did you know of any men like that?" I asked. "Old boyfriends? Boys who had a crush?"

Pat considered carefully. After condemning Jesse Conklin so quickly, she was reluctant to name any more names. "Jesse was Carmen's only real boyfriend. Before him, she just didn't take the time to date. Some of the guys on the men's team made passes, but they didn't connect. She wasn't interested."

I looked at my notebook. So far, there was only one name on it: Jesse Conklin.

"I'm not much help, am I?" Pat said.

"You've given me a better idea of what Carmen was like," I said truthfully.

"If you really want to find out whether Carmen had disgruntled admirers, you ought to talk to her roommate, Lisa. I don't think they were extremely close, but Carmen might have said something to Lisa—things she wouldn't necessarily tell her coach."

"The dorm is my next stop," I said as I snapped my notebook shut.

Pat stood to show me out. She had forced herself to deal with me calmly—hysterics didn't seem to be part of her nature—but now that the interview with the cop was over, she seemed to sag. Her strength had been focused on answering my questions. Now there was nothing to keep her from picturing her star runner frightened and dying in the park.

I wished I could tell her there had been no pain.

Pat asked me to call her if there was any news. I gave her my card in case anything occurred to her later that might be helpful. She absently stuffed the card into her pocket and turned to the window as cheers drifted in with the breeze. The office overlooked the track, and we could see clusters of students hanging around in their shorts.

"Is there a meet?" I asked.

She shook her head. "The season's over. It's probably just students challenging each other for fun. They never quit running, you know."

"Are they all on the team?" I asked, waving at the crowded track.

"No," Pat said. "Some just come out to watch. You know, fans. Others are doing a little running on the side to keep in shape. I'd say less than half of them are in the program."

"Any fanatic fans?" I asked.

"This isn't football," Pat said bitterly. "We don't have a booster club."

"No one out there makes you nervous, gives you a creepy feeling?" I pressed.

Pat shuddered. "After today, they *all* give me a creepy feeling."

"What about him?" I asked, pointing at random to a man resting on his bike near the track. "He ever pester your girls?"

"I've never seen him before," Pat said.

"Well, what about him?" I said, pointing to another young man sitting on the grass a few feet from the cyclist.

Pat just shook her head. "I know what you're trying to do, Detective Ferris, but I can't help you. No one was stalking Carmen. I wish I could point my finger at someone and say, he did it. *He* was after Carmen. But it just didn't happen that way. No one here is that sick."

Someone *was* that sick, I thought as I left her. Pat August just didn't want to admit it was in her midst.

*   *   *

The sun poked through the clouds as I stepped outside, and it was enough to lure me to the track.

The cyclist had pedaled off. The young man on the grass had been joined by a young lady, and they were nuzzling each other as though there weren't any overdressed 40-year-old cops around to notice.

There were two men racing each other down the track, and I forgot murder long enough to watch them go at it. They were young and lean, and it was pleasant to see the sun shimmering on their energetic thighs. Dave had nothing to fear, however. I was old enough to be their youngish aunt.

The spectators cheered as they dashed across the finish line, one just a hair ahead of the other. It was distressing to note that neither one was gasping.

"Excuse me," a voice said tentatively at my elbow.

I reluctantly turned away—I was prepared to perform CPR, in case either of the gentlemen was overcome by exertion—and was confronted by two young women in track uniforms. They were hugging themselves as though they were cold, and who could blame them, in those flimsy outfits? But I recognized them as two of the girls who had been hanging around Pat's office, and I knew they were fighting off more than a chill.

"Yes?" I asked.

"You're with the police, aren't you?" asked one girl, who would have looked downright wholesome except for her nose ring.

I tried not to gawk as I nodded. Mother had reacted much the same way the summer I had dyed my hair blond.

"Is it true someone attacked Carmen?" the girl asked.

"And she's dead?" her companion added.

I don't dance around death anymore. "Yes," I said, "someone killed Carmen in the park by the river last night."

The girls shuddered and automatically moved closer to each other. "Jesus," the one with the nose ring said. The other girl sniffed and stared vacantly over my head. She was tall enough to stare over many heads.

"Did—did you catch anyone?" the smaller girl asked. She had suddenly become so chilled, her lips were nearly blue.

"No," I admitted. "No one is in custody yet." And I stressed the "yet," to reassure them.

They weren't comforted. In fact, the taller one, who sported five rings in her left ear, plopped down on the grass beside the track and hung her head between her knees. "I told you," she mumbled as her friend patted her head, "I told you something was going to happen."

"We don't know it's him," her friend said.

"He's a goddamn creep," the girl sniffed. "I *told* you."

I felt out of the loop. "Maybe if you told *me*," I suggested.

The girls debated it as I passed out tissue from my purse. The one with the nose ring (she said her name was Marci) was reluctant to point fingers. The more traditional earrings (Elaine) believed in guilty until proven innocent. As they argued, I pretty much got what I wanted anyway. There had been a creep hanging around the track. Not a runner. Not the usual fan. Just a guy who'd shown up the last few weeks to leer at the women as they worked out.

Neither girl knew him. In fact, they couldn't even agree on what he looked like. He was young enough to be a student. His clothes were scruffy enough, too. He was probably white. His hair was just "dark." The short one said he was tall; the tall one thought he was short. He hadn't spoken to either girl. They had just noticed him at different times, standing back on the grass, and the way he looked gave them the creeps.

"Why?" I asked.

"He just stares," Elaine said. "You know."

"Like he can see through your clothes," Marci said.

And their faces twisted in distaste.

"Lots of guys look," I pointed out.

"His mouth hangs open," Elaine said. "Yuck."

I frowned. "You mean retarded?"

"No," Marci said quickly, "hungry."

Oh, I thought, *that* look. I might be battling flabby thighs, but I still knew the feeling when a man's look crossed over from healthy admiration to dark hunger.

Creepy.

"Did you complain to anyone?" I asked.

They guiltily shook their heads no.

"He never *did* anything," Marci said quickly.

"But I was going to tell Coach," Elaine said. "The next time he showed up."

"Has he been around today?" I asked.

They shrugged. "He might have been here yesterday," Marci said.

"Or maybe Sunday," Elaine said. "It's not like anyone *looks* for him."

"Has he ever talked to any of the other girls?" I asked. "To Carmen?"

Marci shook her head. "She never said anything if he did."

"She wouldn't," Elaine sniffed.

Marci shot her a warning look. Pat had been right on the money about the animosity toward Carmen. I could feel it smoldering beneath their comments, contained now because the woman was dead. But it wouldn't take much to fan it into red hot flames.

"Did you ever see anyone hanging around Carmen, maybe pestering her?" I asked.

"We really wouldn't know," Marci said delicately. "We didn't see her much outside practice."

"Would you tell me if you *did* know anything?" I asked.

Marci flushed furiously. "That's not fair at all. Just because we weren't good friends doesn't mean anyone wanted her dead."

Elaine looked like she wouldn't have minded maiming the girl, though.

"I mean, so what if she was a bitch?" Marci said. "No one had the right to kill her."

"Yeah," Elaine said, but without much conviction.

"Did she always run alone?" I asked.

"She didn't like company," Marci said. "In the winter, when it gets dark early, most of us work out together. But Carmen said we couldn't keep up, so she almost always took off alone."

"She was a fanatic," Elaine said. "Always talking Olympics, always talking gold. We weren't *good* enough to work out with her."

"Was it common knowledge she was a loner?" I asked.

"Well, all you had to do was watch her to figure it out," Marci said. "Even in practice, she was always off by herself, running her own laps. She never joked around with the rest of us."

Carmen, I realized sadly, had set herself up to be killed—the one woman on the team good enough for the gold, and the one woman who could easily be isolated from the rest of the pack.

"Look," Marci said, "we use that park, too. It's a real good trail. You think it's safe for us to go out there?"

I thought of Bradley, who was probably answering to the mayor at that very moment about death in the city parks. Bradley would never admit that his town wasn't safe. But image, thank God, was his problem, not mine. "The semester will be over in a couple of days," I said. "I'd stick close to the university if I were you."

Marci considered the options and decided the campus track didn't look so bad after all.

Elaine said there wouldn't be any problem if we'd just find the creep.

I fished my cards out of my purse and gave one to each of them. "If he shows up again, call me. Any time."

The girls nodded and stuffed the cards down their shirts. I had visions of them flopping all over the track.

"And don't run alone," I lectured them.

They gave me their solemn promise. And I figured they'd even keep it for a day or two. But they were young and invincible, and I knew it wouldn't be long before they'd go out running alone.

I'd bet Carmen had felt invincible, too.

Chapter Four

I went back to the field house to corner Pat August about the creep, but her office was locked. A note taped to the door said she was gone for the day. I couldn't blame her. If I'd just lost my best pupil, I'd probably crawl home and drink myself into oblivion.

But I was now officially on duty, so I drove instead to a cluster of dormitories within easy jogging distance of the track. The dorms resembled fairly comfortable apartment buildings on the outside, with neatly trimmed hedges lining the walks and a university maintenance man diligently weeding the flowerbeds. But inside, I was immediately accosted by the echoing voices and the drumming tape decks and the disinfectant odor of dorm life. I had lasted in the dorms just one semester when I was a student. I couldn't take all that giggling communal living.

A student at the main desk in the lobby solemnly inspected my badge, then just as solemnly directed me to the fourth floor. I thanked her for her assistance. She failed to smile. She really needed a course in customer relations.

I bypassed the elevator and bravely took the stairs. I was nearly knocked over by a young woman who was being chased down the stairs by a young man. She didn't look like she minded the pursuit, so I didn't shoot her pursuer.

I was *not* panting when I reached the fourth floor, and my leg muscles felt just fine, thank you. This business of turning forty was no big deal.

I stepped into the hall, and the guts of the dorm weren't nearly as inviting as the neat brick exterior. The fluorescent lighting picked up every scuff in the worn tile, every greasy spot on the walls and every scar in the wooden doors. It was a women's dorm, so there wasn't any underwear hanging on the doorknobs, but it still had the dingy look of transient housing.

It was finals week, so the noise level was in the bearable range, but I did pick out three different CDs competing for attention as I walked down the hall, and laughter spilled out of one door as I passed. In my sheltered youth, men weren't allowed in the women's dorms, but I noticed some decidedly male bodies sprawled around various rooms. A couple of them were even studying.

Carmen's room was halfway down the hall. I was diligently reading room numbers and had just picked out hers when the door was flung open and a young man barreled out, clutching a jacket to his chest.

"You pig!" a woman howled, and some books flew out the door after him.

The guy ducked and covered his head with one arm. It was a good thing, too, because one of the books would have brained him. It cracked him in the forearm instead. "Jesus," he croaked.

"You goddamned shit!" the woman yelled, and she tore through the door and flung herself at him, pounding his back with her fists. She was only half his size, but she was hammering him furiously. I dragged her off his back before he could belt her.

She tried to turn on me, but I had a good lock on her arms. I couldn't do anything about her mouth, though. She was spewing venom, and it was twisting her face into ugly, primitive shapes. The noise was drawing a crowd, too. People poked their heads out into the hall and wondered nervously whether they ought to do something about me. I was the stranger, and it looked like I was beating up on the home team.

The guy tried to slink away down the hall. "Stop right there!" I ordered. I couldn't bellow like Bradley, and the woman was squirming so much in my arms that I sounded a little breathless, but it was still enough to make him freeze in embarrassment.

"Let me go!" the woman hollered, and she tried to slug me.

I shoved her up against the wall. Not *too* hard. Just enough to press her nose firmly against cement block while she contemplated her future. I didn't leave *any* bruises.

Someone down the hall announced she was calling the cops.

"I *am* the police," I panted.

"Yeah," someone snickered, "and I'm the pope."

I held the little hellion against the wall with my hip and flipped open my jacket just enough to give the crowd a glimpse of my badge, which just happened to be hanging from my belt next to my gun. I don't always wear it, but this suit draped over it so nicely, I couldn't resist.

They got the point.

"You," I said to the guy, who looked very much like the man in Carmen's picture, "wait for me in the lobby."

"I got to study," he said sullenly.

"You can study in the lobby," I said sternly.

He wanted to object, but I *did* have a gun. He scowled and pushed his way past the residents to the stairway.

I eased up a little on the woman I was holding. "You going to behave?" I asked.

"I'm going to *sue*," she spat at the wall.

"Go ahead," I said, and stepped back from her. "I'm broke."

She shook herself free and stormed back into her room. She would have slammed the door in my face, but I was right on her tail. I caught the door with one hand and looked back at the kids still gawking in the hall.

"Party's over," I said. "Go home."

Then I slammed the door in *their* faces.

The woman—I assumed she was Carmen's roommate, Lisa—stomped to a desk under the window and began pawing angrily through a mess of books and papers. The room was standard university issue, a square box with dressers and closets built into one wall and bunk beds hugging the opposite wall. There was about ten square feet of open space in the middle of the room, and it had been covered with a very nice braided rug. Everything else was straight out of the university warehouse.

Lisa found what she was looking for—a pack of cigarettes—and nervously lit up. She really was small—she barely reached my shoulder—and the way she hunched over her cigarette, she looked even smaller. But I wouldn't call her defenseless. Perhaps it wasn't fair to judge her when her roommate had just been murdered, but she struck me as a tiny viper.

"I thought smoking in the dorm was banned," I said as I helped myself to a chair next to the door.

"Screw you," she said, and blew smoke across the room at me.

I ignored her poor manners and sat. "I'm Detective Ferris," I said. "You're Lisa what?"

"Spuhler, if it's any of your business," she snarled, and puffed hungrily on her cigarette. I wondered what Carmen, the fanatic runner, would have said about that.

"And who was the man you attacked?" I asked.

She rolled her eyes. "Oh, yeah, I attacked *him*. The pig."

"You were hitting him," I said.

"I should have *killed* him," she said.

"Why?"

"Oh, for God's sake," she said, and flopped into a chair across from me, "because he's a bastard, okay? Carmen's dead, he's supposed to be her boyfriend, and what does he do *first thing*? He comes over here and wants his jacket back. No 'Gee, Lisa, I'm sorry.' No 'God, I feel bad.' Just 'Give me the fucking jacket.'" And she furiously ground her cigarette into an ash tray.

"So you hit him," I said.

She looked at me with raw eyes. "Well, wouldn't you?"

I considered it for a moment, then nodded. "Probably," I said.

"Damn right," she said, and tapped her fingers angrily on the desk. She hadn't spent her rage on Jesse Conklin yet.

"Tell me about Carmen," I said.

"Why don't you tell me how she died?" Lisa countered.

"Fair enough," I said, and I gave her the PR version of what I had found in the woods. By police standards, it was mild, but just like Pat August, she seemed to shrink in on herself as I impassively spoke of death. Murder can still give me nightmares, but I deal with bodies often enough that I can speak of them without becoming nauseated. Sometimes I have to remind myself that corpses aren't the usual fare for normal people.

"Jesus," Lisa said quietly. "She was attacked last night? She was lying in the park all night long and nobody *knew*?"

"She was dead," I told her. "It wouldn't have made any difference *when* we found her. No one could have saved her."

Lisa shuddered and fumbled for another cigarette. "I should have known," she muttered as she shook one out of the pack. "When she didn't come home last night, I should have *known* something was wrong."

"Did she normally stay out?" I asked.

Lisa flashed me an angry look. "What? You think I should have called the police last night? Is that it?"

"I just asked a question," I said neutrally.

She furiously lit a match and sucked rapidly on the cigarette. "I wasn't Carmen's babysitter," she said through wisps of smoke. "She didn't come home, I figured she was with Jesse. It was her business, not mine."

"But you were surprised?" I pressed.

"She had a final today. I thought she'd come home to study." Lisa shrugged. "But she didn't. It wasn't *that* unusual."

"Was she supposed to be with Jesse last night?" I asked.

"You mean, like a date?" Lisa tapped her cigarette nervously on the ashtray. Smoke rose to the ceiling in angry spurts. "Well, no, she didn't *say* they were going out, but if she wasn't running and she wasn't here, she was with Jesse. She was totally hung up on him."

"And you didn't approve," I said.

She snorted. "He's a jerk. You saw him."

I'd seen a fairly good-looking young man, no more a jerk than the other young men raging around campus with their hormones making their decisions for them. Obviously, she knew something about Jesse that I didn't.

"Jesse," she said, as though reading my mind, "can't see past his own face. Carmen was a world-class runner. You ask anyone else, they'll tell you. She *had* it—you know, *here*." And she punched herself in the gut.

"There's this coach on the West Coast, he wanted Carmen to come out there. This is big time—guaranteed Olympics. Carmen was going to go, too, because the Olympics—that's what she *lived* for. Only Jesse—" and she made a face—"Jesse was making it hard on her. Said if she really loved him, she'd stay here with him. He was making her nuts."

"They were fighting about it?"

Lisa shook her head as she squashed out her cigarette. "There was nothing to fight about. She *had* to go. She was twenty years old, for God's sake. She couldn't wait for Jesse to finish school. Her time was *now*."

I felt ancient listening to her. As though Carmen was already a has-been.

"Carmen had her mind made up," Lisa told me. "She was leaving as soon as finals were over. But Jesse, the jerk, wasn't big enough to make it easy for her. He should have been *supporting* her, but all he could do was whine that she was leaving him. Like *he* couldn't adjust for *her*."

"Maybe he loved her," I ventured.

"Jesse Conklin loves himself," Lisa said. "There's no room in his head for anyone else."

"Do you think he killed her?" I asked.

"Maybe you ought to ask him," she shot back. "Ask him what *he* was doing last night."

"I intend to," I said.

She looked at me as though she had no faith in my intentions.

"Do you know if there was anyone else bothering Carmen?" I asked.

"Just Jesse," she said swiftly.

"Think about it," I said patiently. "Forget that you're pissed at Jesse and concentrate on Carmen. Did she mention anyone in the last few weeks who was pestering her? Any of her other friends?"

"I was her only friend," Lisa declared. "Everyone else was too damn jealous."

"Okay," I said, trying to swallow my exasperation, "everyone else was jealous of Carmen. That was the norm. Did any of these jealous people do anything different the last few weeks?"

Lisa frowned. "You mean, like stalk her?"

"That's a little extreme," I admitted.

"So is murder," she said.

I conceded the point.

Lisa was pleasantly surprised and agreed to consider the question. We sat for a long time in thought. My stomach was rumbling, and I focused on the dresser to keep my mind off hunger. The top of the dresser seemed to be crowded more with ointments and medicines than cosmetics. It was a glamorous life being a runner.

"She was having trouble with a psych class," Lisa finally announced. "Outside of Jesse and the move, that was bothering her the most. She wanted to transfer all her credits, but she needed a C in the psych class, and she wasn't sure she'd get it."

"Why not?" I asked.

Lisa sighed. "Carmen wasn't very word-oriented. She did okay on facts and memorization, but this psych prof liked essay questions, and Carmen just wasn't a writer. Her coach straightened it out, though. I think maybe she talked to the prof, 'cause Carmen stopped fussing about it a couple days ago."

"You know the prof's name?" I asked.

"It'll be in her records."

"It'd be faster if you'd just look for it."

Lisa shrugged as though it wasn't her problem.

I had to lecture myself that the girl was grief-stricken. Otherwise, I might have slugged her.

"How about her teammates?" I asked. "Anything unusual there?"

"The girls hated her and the guys were always hitting on her," Lisa said. "Same old, same old."

"Any of the guys particularly persistent?"

Lisa brightened. "There was one guy—Chuck something. He was actually *nice* to Carmen. He'd heard she was being recruited and he actually stopped her on the track one day and *congratulated* her. Carmen was floored."

How sinister, I thought, and wrote "Chuck" in my notebook.

"How about in the park?" I asked. "Carmen ran in the park a lot. Any trouble there?"

Lisa wrinkled her nose. "Just the bikers."

"Motorcycles?" I asked dubiously.

"No," Lisa scoffed, "*bicyclists*. God, there aren't any bike gangs on the trail."

"I should think not," I huffed.

"The cyclists drove her crazy," Lisa said. "They aren't out much in the winter, but they start crowding the trail in the spring. And they aren't very polite."

I raised an eyebrow.

"You know, they go so fast, they think they own the trail. They're always running people off the path."

"People like Carmen?"

Lisa laughed. "*No* one runs Carmen off. She wouldn't budge. Some idiot tried a couple weeks ago, but Carmen said she just stood her ground and *he* was run off. Right into a tree."

I didn't think it was nearly as amusing as Lisa did, but then, I'd probably seen a lot more bicyclists who had tangled with immovable objects.

"Was he hurt?" I asked.

"I dunno," Lisa said. "It wasn't like Carmen stopped and asked."

Nice girl, I thought.

I prodded some more, but Lisa couldn't think of anyone else who had been bothering her roommate. Carmen's world had clearly been limited to Jesse Conklin and the track. And even that world had been rigidly organized. Carmen worked out every morning, went to class every afternoon, ran again in the evening, and spent her nights either with Conklin or in the dorm with Lisa. During track season, her routine had been disrupted by meets, but Lisa suspected Carmen was just as predictable when she was out of town.

Carmen, I decided, was so focused, she had no imagination.

But that didn't mean she deserved to die.

Lisa was strung out, puffing her way through the interview, and her answers were getting shorter and sharper. She wanted me to go, and I was willing to oblige her. But I wondered fleetingly whether she had anyone to hold her once I was gone. Even vipers cry.

But when I tried to suggest that she find someone to keep her company, she scowled and purposefully opened the door. She was not a sociable animal.

She did, however, have a bit of a conscience.

"There's something you should know," she admitted as I was handing her my card.

"Yes?" I asked.

She looked at me defiantly. "Jesse Conklin is a selfish, narrow-minded beast, and if Carmen wasn't killed by some pervert, then I swear to God, Jesse must have done it. But—" and she took a deep breath—"I got to be fair."

"About what?" I asked cautiously.

"He called here last night, looking for Carmen." She blushed at the surprise on my face. "It was early—like maybe eight o'clock. I just assumed she was out running, and that's what I told him. Later, when Carmen didn't come home, I figured he'd found her."

"Jesse never called back?" I asked.

Lisa shook her head. "I mean, I *thought* it was all right. I *thought* Jesse had met up with her somewhere and everything was okay. I didn't know she was *dead*."

I patted her shoulder. "You couldn't have known," I assured her.

She twisted away from me. "It doesn't make any difference anyway. He's still a jerk."

And she shut the door in my face.

Chapter Five

I thought Jesse Conklin had bolted. There were no sullen young men pacing the lobby, and the girl at the reception desk stared at me in consternation when I asked if anyone had been hanging around, waiting for a cop. Of course not, she said. This was a *nice* dorm.

So I hustled outside, fretting because I'd spent so much time with Lisa, and there he was, sprawled beneath a tree on the front lawn, with his jacket bunched up under his head like a pillow. He looked like any other college kid, frittering away his afternoon when he should have been studying, and I felt a surprising stab of irritation. I must have absorbed some of Lisa's hostility: His girlfriend had just been murdered. How could he simply stretch himself out in the shade and nap?

But when I stooped over to nudge him awake, I saw the shiny track of one tear sliding from the corner of his eye and down his cheek. It was nearly dry. But I could almost taste the salt of it on my tongue, and I carefully backed away a few steps, suddenly embarrassed for him and for me.

"Jesse," I said loudly, and I purposely kept my distance as he started to attention. I focused on his feet as he swiped at his eyes with his shirtsleeve.

"Took you long enough," he said thickly. Maybe he had a cold. Maybe his voice was always gruff after a nap. Maybe I was just a sucker for a good-looking male, even one twenty years my junior. It happens.

"We need to talk about Carmen," I said.

I was standing just beyond the shade of the tree, and he had to squint to look at me. "Just who *are* you?" he demanded.

I introduced myself. If he hadn't already seen my gun, he might have been inclined to doubt me. Cops always look bigger on TV.

"What're you hassling *me* for?" he complained as he gathered his jacket and books and climbed to his feet. "Why aren't you out looking for the bastard who killed Carmen?"

"I need information first," I said reasonably.

"Like what?" he challenged.

"Like where you were last night."

He sucked hard on his teeth, as though he'd just been slugged in the belly. Apparently, it hadn't occurred to Jesse Conklin that the police might view *him* with suspicion.

"You got it all wrong, lady," he managed. "I'd never *ever* hurt Carmen."

"Some people think differently," I said, fishing.

His face darkened. "It's that bitch, Lisa, isn't it? She's been telling lies about Carmen and me, hasn't she?"

"I've been talking to a lot of people," I said vaguely.

"Yeah, right," he snarled.

We had moved off the grass and down the sidewalk toward the main campus. Jesse was walking quickly, as though he had a definite destination in mind—or maybe he was just trying to shake me. I doggedly kept up with him, even though my heels wobbled on the cement. Occasionally, a vile word or two slipped out of Jesse Conklin's mouth. I assumed he was thinking of Lisa, not Carmen.

"Last night," I reminded him as we slipped between two more dorms. "Where were you?"

"Studying," he said shortly. "At home."

"And where's that?"

He gave me an address a couple of blocks off campus, in a neighborhood of apartment buildings slapped together strictly for students. He had been there all evening studying, he said, and waiting for Carmen.

"Can anyone verify that?" I asked. "A roommate?"

"He was out," Jesse said. "Drinking."

Of course, I thought. It was finals week.

"How about callers?" I asked. "Anyone talk to you on the phone?"

"I called Carmen's room once," he said. Then he looked at me defiantly. "I bet Lisa didn't tell you *that*."

"You remember the time?" I asked, refusing to give him a direct answer.

"Eight-fifteen or eight-twenty. I remember because Carmen was late."

"You had a date?"

He shrugged. "She was coming over after she ran. We were gonna get a pizza or something."

Just what a runner needed, I thought.

"She should have been there by eight," Jesse said as we huffed around some dawdlers on the sidewalk. "She always ran the same route. Always finished the same time. You could set your watch by Carmen."

"So when she didn't show up, were you worried?" I asked.

He glanced at me irritably. "I called her room, didn't I?"

"Once," I reminded him. "She was missing all night, but you called only once."

"Yeah, well . . ." He stared up at the dorm to our left, and his voice trailed off. He could have been mesmerized by the ladies flitting by the windows, or he could have been imagining Carmen dead in the woods while he fumed because she was late. It would not have been a pretty thought.

"You might as well know," he said without looking at me, "Carmen and I were kind of arguing."

"Kind of?" I repeated gently.

His mouth twisted in embarrassment. "It wasn't major. We were gonna work it out. She wanted to transfer, and I didn't see the point. That's all."

That was *all*, I thought in a huff. Carmen was about to make the leap into big-time sports, and Jesse didn't think it was major?

I began to see why Pat August and Lisa Spuhler thought Jesse wasn't the best influence on Carmen's career.

Jesse turned away from the dorms and started walking across a parking lot toward a building that housed science labs. He had one hand jammed deep into a pocket, and he was staring hard at the pavement. His face was still very flushed.

"So we argued some," he said, as though he was working it out in his own head more than he was explaining it to me. "Couples argue all the time, right? Doesn't mean anything. So she didn't come over last night like she was supposed to. Okay, I made one call to find her, but when she still didn't show up, I said fine, screw it. I had to study. She wanted to make up later, she could call *me*."

"Weren't you worried?" I asked.

"Why would I be worried?" he countered. "She ran all the time. Nothing happened before. She didn't come to my place, I figured she went home to the dorm. She had finals, too, you know."

"And this morning when you didn't hear from her?"

He tried an elaborate shrug. It didn't quite work. "I thought she was still pissed. I didn't know she was dead." And his voice cracked a little on the word. "You didn't know Carmen. She'd get mad and go away. But then she'd cool down and she'd come back. She always came back."

"Until this morning," I said.

"Yeah," he said, "until this morning." He looked at me then, and finally there was desolation in his eyes. "We would have been married, you know. Someday." And he turned away from me abruptly and stomped up the steps to the science labs.

I didn't let him get away that easily. As Carmen's boyfriend, he should have been overloading my circuits with all sorts of information about her—friends, enemies, likes, dislikes, hopes, ideas. *Something* more than vague plans for a pizza after her run in the park. Instead, he was giving me nothing to work with.

So I grimly followed him inside and cornered him at the elevator. He blushed because there were other students hanging around and here I was, a strange woman, getting in his face. But the elevator was hung up somewhere on the floors above us, and I badgered him about people who might have been pestering Carmen.

Maybe it finally dawned on him that the best way to get me out of his life was to cooperate. Or maybe he was just afraid he'd miss the elevator, but suddenly he rattled off half a dozen names of people who liked to get in Carmen's way.

"These are all women," I said in exasperation.

He shrugged. "Women were jealous of Carmen."

"What about men?" I persisted.

He stiffened. "*I* was the only man Carmen cared about," he insisted.

I thought of all the male bodies I'd seen lounging around the track and decided it was rather odd Carmen hadn't taken up with one of them. At least they would have talked her language.

"How *did* you meet Carmen?" I asked as the bell dinged overhead and the elevator rumbled behind the doors.

Jesse's blush deepened as he edged toward the elevator. "What's it matter?" he asked.

"I won't know till you tell me," I said.

The door popped open and students squeezed past us, loading and unloading. Jesse stepped into the elevator.

I stubbornly propped open the door with my shoulder. Several fellow travelers groused loudly.

"Jesus," Jesse complained, "I went out a couple times with Lisa, okay? She introduced us."

"Ah," I said, and backed out of the door.

"The bitch," Jesse said, and slammed the controls with the palm of his hand.

The door slid shut, and I could hear the gears of the elevator grinding as loudly as the gears in my head.

Jesse dumped Lisa, because he loved Carmen.

Lisa hated Jesse.

But did she hate Carmen, too?

Too bad Carmen was killed by a man, I thought as I wandered back outside. So far, Lisa had the best motive for murder.

Chapter Six

Eddie Cochran, a campus cop, was idling his cruiser behind my car when I got back to Carmen's dorm. Cops don't get ticketed as a rule, and Eddie likes me, so he didn't even mention that I was parked in a handicapped spot.

"My boss wants to see you," he said cheerfully.

I thought of Sarah Tate, the new security director, and made a face. "Is that a request or an order?"

Eddie shrugged. "You don't want to check in with the lady, that's your business. I'm just delivering the message."

"What does she want?" I asked.

Eddie grinned. "Probably wants to know how the city let the university's star runner get murdered."

I grunted and leaned my butt against the trunk of my car.

"The administration's been on her case all day, Jo. Cut her some slack," Eddie advised.

"She's no Mike Edwards," I grumped.

"Nobody is," he agreed, and we both thought some of what we had lost when Mike retired.

"You got any suspects?" Eddie asked, popping us back to the present. We both judiciously ignored the driver who gave us the finger as he squeezed his truck around Eddie's cruiser.

"Everyone who ever met her," I sighed. "Carmen wasn't well-liked."

"Too bad," Eddie said. "She was something else on the track."

"You knew her?" I asked.

"I watched her," he corrected. "Girl was nuts, running all hours of the day or night. I'd keep an eye on her if she was out. Most of the guys did."

"And she was good?"

"She was lightning," Eddie said, smiling at the memory. If it'd been another man, I'd have called that smile suggestive. But Eddie's inclinations went the other way, so I chalked it up to pure pleasure in watching a fine piece of machinery in action.

I wished suddenly that I had seen Carmen run.

Another driver glared at us. Eddie obligingly put his cruiser in gear. "You better go see the boss," he suggested.

"Maybe you'd better check out the track," I countered.

Eddie raised an eyebrow.

"Coupla girls say there's a creep hanging around, leering at their shorts." Eddie frowned. "First I head of *that*."

"They were too embarrassed to report it," I said. "But after Carmen . . ."

"I'll swing by the track," Eddie promised.

"And I'll go be nice to your boss," I said. But as Eddie drove off, I couldn't help thinking he had the better part of the deal.

* * *

Mike Edwards had been an old-fashioned cop with a friendly interest in my anatomy. He had been an older, mellower version of Bradley, and we had worked well together whenever city crime spilled onto campus. He liked lady cops, but for politically incorrect reasons. I treasured his war stories. I actually cried at his retirement party.

Sarah Tate was nothing like him. She was hard and she was smart, and she had a list of degrees that made me feel like an ignoramus. But she had never actually been a cop. She was an administrator, and I just didn't trust her.

The feeling was mutual.

I used to be able to stroll into Mike's office, plunk myself down in a chair across from him and chew over a case until it started to taste right. But no one strolled into Sarah's office. She had a secretary.

Who kept me waiting in a cold little reception area for ten minutes until the director of security felt it was convenient to see me. I was pretty grouchy by the time the secretary escorted me into Sarah's office, and I failed to appreciate the dark circles under the director's eyes. All I saw was a large woman, about forty-five, with suspiciously blond hair frizzed and chopped very short. There was a slash of pink lipstick across the thin lips, and the eyebrows had been plucked into a look of permanent surprise. But there was nothing coy or soft in her demeanor. She stood in front of her window with her arms crossed beneath an imposing chest, and she came across as one intimidating woman.

I didn't sit. But I still had to look up at her. Her heels were higher.

"Is it correct you have been on campus questioning faculty and students about Carmen Martinez?" she demanded without so much as a hello.

"I certainly have," I agreed. "I'm investigating the Martinez murder."

"You have gone into academic buildings and dormitories to question people?" she asked.

"Wherever I could find them," I said.

"This university has a professional police force, Detective Ferris. When outside agencies venture onto this campus, I expect my department to be consulted and involved. I expect interviews to be conducted discreetly and without disruption. And I expect to be informed of all activities on my campus immediately. Do I make myself clear?"

I couldn't help myself. I chuckled.

Her eyes narrowed. "I don't believe I said anything amusing."

"Not amusing," I said. "Absurd."

Her cheeks bulged like two angry red balloons.

"I'm investigating a murder," I said, burning a big departmental bridge behind me. "And I don't need the university's permission to question anyone. That's a fact."

Sarah Tate should have been a real cop, because she had the bulk and the voice to squash any smart ass on the street, and she used both on me. She stepped in so close, I could taste her lunch, and her voice rolled over me like thunder. "It's a fact that the victim was a university student, and that makes her *my* business. If you expect to conduct any investigation on *my* campus, you will check in with *me* first."

I don't respond well to bullies. I should have backed off and tried to figure out what the hell was eating at the woman. It would have been much more constructive. But instead, I just lit another fuse. "You get in *my* way," I shot back, "and you'll be discussing obstruction of justice with the prosecutor."

"I'll have your badge," she hissed.

"Take it up with my chief," I said, and stomped out of there.

Check in with her first? I'd rather eat glass.

When I got back to the station, Bradley was ready to serve it to me straight.

Chapter Seven

"**O**bstruction of justice?" Bradley bellowed. "You threaten the campus chief of police with obstruction of justice? What the fuck are you *doing*?"

"She isn't the chief of police," I said as I primly crossed my legs. "She's the director of security."

"She's in Mike's office, she's the fucking chief," Bradley said, and pounded his desk with his fist so hard, his coffee splashed all over his papers.

I waited stoically in the chair across from his desk. The door from his office to the squad room was closed, but I was still relieved Henry was off duty. Henry enjoyed it immensely whenever Bradley tore into me.

Sarah Tate had wasted no time. It had taken me no more than fifteen minutes to get back to the station, and she had already blistered Bradley's ears by phone. He was livid by the time I walked in the door, and everyone else in the squad room was diving for cover. Bradley had never taken management courses or sensitivity training. When he was pissed, he let everyone know it.

I had lots of experience with Bradley's tantrums. Usually, it's best to just let him erupt. Because usually, there's some justification for it. So I sat there and let him chew my ass, and amused myself with thoughts of how he used to chew other things. It helped to pass the time.

"Give me one good reason why I shouldn't suspend you," he demanded. "Just one."

I could think of about a dozen, not the least of which being the department budget, which was half in my head. But I stuck to the Martinez case. "Ms. Tate says we can't interview anyone on campus without her say-so."

Bradley had been lowering himself into his chair, but that stopped him in mid-drop. "She said *what*?"

"She says we have to check in with her before going onto campus," I said calmly.

Bradley plopped into his chair with a thud that made the springs screech. "That's crap," he said.

"I thought so, too," I agreed.

"That's *bullshit*," he fumed.

"It's what she *said*."

"She can't bar my people from an investigation," he rumbled, and I could feel his blood pressure popping all over again. "That's fucking obstruction!"

I did not smile. I *wanted* to, but I behaved myself. "She's new," I said generously, dousing the flames a little. "She doesn't know how things work."

"I'll tell her how the fuck they work," Bradley threatened, and I let him vent some about town-gown relations. It took his mind off my sins.

"No one tells my detectives who they can interview," he growled. Then he looked at me suspiciously. "Who *did* you interview?"

"I don't think I can answer that," I said. "I've been suspended."

Bradley curled his lip.

I quickly straightened in my chair and gave him a stripped-down summary of my afternoon on campus, from Pat August to Jesse Conklin. He cooled down some as I talked, and I could almost see the gears in his head shifting from turf wars to cops and killers.

"You got shit," he said when I was finished.

I shrugged. I don't waste time debating the obvious with Bradley.

"Ellen struck out, too," he said in disgust. That was a big admission from him. Bradley was infatuated with Ellen and had sulked the whole time she was on maternity leave.

"No murderers among the park rangers?" I asked. I tried to sound sympathetic, but secretly, I was pleased. Ellen could solve her own homicides, thank you.

Bradley tossed some computer printouts across the desk. I assumed they were reports from the day shift. "She and Henry interviewed the entire park staff. Nothing. Henry thinks one of the rangers might be kind of hinky, but the guy was bowling all night with his wife."

"Kind of hard to sneak out between frames," I said as I thumbed through the printouts. Ellen's notes were concise and impeccable. Henry's were as horrid as the old reports he used to peck out on the typewriter. He still couldn't spell perpetrator.

"All the rangers know the girl," Bradley complained. "They see her every day on the trail. They make passes at her. They probably jerk off thinking about her. But you think any of 'em manage to *see* something when she gets killed? Nothing. Zero. Zip."

"They've got decent alibis, too," I sighed as I skimmed the notes. "Unless the two guys on the night shift did her and they're covering for each other with this poaching crap."

"Then they're making up citations, too," Bradley said, tossing more paper at me. "Two hunters caught on park land, trailing deer."

"That's sick," I said.

"Out of season, too," Bradley said. Like that made a difference.

"The rangers still could've done it," I said, reading the citations. "These hunters weren't caught until ten o'clock. Carmen was killed earlier than that."

"If two guys killed her, only one took the time to rape her."

I raised an eyebrow.

Bradley pawed through the files on his desk and came up with some notes from Doc Sweitzer. "Evidence of recent sexual intercourse . . . . Preliminary tests identify semen from one male . . . . Marks on the body suggest sexual contact after she died."

I sniffed. "Doc Sweitzer decided all that before he ever took a knife to her."

Bradley looked at me over his glasses. "Can you prove something different?"

I squirmed. "No."

"Then we assume she was killed first, raped after. Probably attacked on the trail, then dragged back into the woods for the fun and games."

I made a face.

"She was dead, Jo. The guy snapped her neck. She never knew."

"Doesn't make it any better," I said. And I purposefully focused on the notes from Ellen and Henry. I wasn't up to a debate with Bradley on the politics of rape.

"So we're looking for someone strong enough to break a woman's neck," Bradley said. "Strong, like the athletes she hung out with?"

"Or someone trained in hand-to-hand—" I stopped, distracted by Henry's notes. "Oh, my," I said.

"What?" Bradley demanded.

"The park has a flasher," I said, jabbing the notes with my finger.

Bradley was not impressed. "That was last fall," he said. "Months ago."

"So you want to flash in the winter?" I countered.

"It has its drawbacks," Bradley conceded. "Not that I have any personal knowledge."

"Not that you need any," I assured him. "But look at this—three reports of a guy popping up on the trail with his pants hanging open. Now *that's* interesting."

"You having problems with Dave?" Bradley asked.

"Dave's riveting," I said. "This doesn't begin to compare."

Bradley harrumphed.

"But look at the timing," I said. "All in the fall, after school started. Maybe a student. What do you think?"

"I think it's a big leap from flashing to rape and murder, especially with a whole winter in between."

"So maybe he just festered all winter and exploded into the big time with Carmen."

Bradley shook his head. "It's a stretch, Jo."

"We got anything better?"

Bradley reconsidered. "You put it that way . . ."

I folded the notes and put them in my purse. "I think I'll go look for a flasher."

"At the park?" Bradley asked.

"Where else?"

Bradley grunted and busied himself with paperwork. "Take the dog," he said. And he was only half-joking.

Chapter Eight

I detoured to McDonald's to pick up a cheeseburger, because even though I had vowed on my birthday to get back in shape, I hadn't promised to give up grease. And then, because it was still kind of early to harass the night shift at the park, I went to the hospital to see Mulhaney.

Mulhaney was a detective who should have retired like Mike Edwards. But Mulhaney's wife was dead and his kids were grown, and there wasn't much he wanted to retire *to*. In the winter, he'd come down with the flu, just like the rest of us, only he hadn't been able to shake it. He'd coughed and wheezed all the way into spring, getting paler and so thin, his butt disappeared. His doctor finally put him in the hospital and took out half a cancerous lung. The doctor was optimistically talking about chemotherapy. Mulhaney wasn't so sure.

I found him propped up in bed, staring at the TV mounted on the wall. His dinner tray—barely touched—had been pushed aside. People look ten years older when they're in the hospital, and I sucked in my breath as I came through the doorway and saw Mulhaney before he saw me. His hair seemed thinner and grayer, his eyes had sunk deep into bruised sockets, and his hands twitched fitfully on the covers like an old man's.

I wanted to duck out, because even though I had worked with him for the last eight years, I wasn't sure we were such good friends that I was entitled to see him this vulnerable. But he heard me before I could back out, and his face creased into a tired smile. I stitched a smile onto my own lips and forced myself to pull a chair up to his bed. I didn't have to stay long, I thought. And what was ten minutes out of my night?

It certainly made no difference to Carmen Martinez.

I asked Mulhaney how he was doing, and he launched into the only topic that really mattered to him at that point—his health. His voice wasn't strong, and the incision was still raw enough that he winced whenever he moved. But he was so happy for an audience that he plunged ahead, telling me things about his own body that he'd have never shared with me in good health. He'd lost a lot of inhibitions since his surgery.

He was still a cop, though, and eventually he asked what I was working on. I told him about Carmen Martinez.

He grunted, and that tugged at the hole in his chest, and that started a wave of coughs. I nervously held a water glass to his mouth, and in between coughs, he sucked weakly on the straw. His lips were so chapped, they had scabbed over.

Finally, he waved me away, and I sat down on the edge of the chair, wondering whether this visit was such a good idea.

But I hadn't realized just how bored Mulhaney was. His lungs weren't working too well, but his brain was focused on Carmen.

"You think it's a pervert?" he wheezed.

"It's possible," I said, and told him about the flasher.

Mulhaney nodded. "I remember that. I checked it out."

"You caught him?" I asked, suddenly very interested.

But Mulhaney said no. "I had an idea—a young guy hiked the park trail a lot—but I never got anything on him."

"Didn't he match the description from the victims?"

Mulhaney actually smiled. "The victims didn't remember much about his *face*."

"Oh," I said, and blushed.

"He coulda been the guy," Mulhaney said, "only the flasher gave it up when it got too cold, and I never got a good lead. Didn't even get an ID on the hiker."

That was quite a disturbing revelation from Mulhaney. I thought he knew everybody.

"So the case is still open," I said.

"Inactive," Mulhaney amended. "There weren't any other incidents after the fall, and other cases came along. You know how it is."

I knew too well. There were some major offenses sitting at the bottom of my "to do" pile, and not a single lead on any of them. Sometimes you have to satisfy yourself with the easy crimes and forget the rest.

Dave would have found the notion appalling.

"My notes are probably still in the computer," Mulhaney said. And he offered me his password so I could dig into his files.

I didn't tell him I already knew his password. I *was* a detective, after all.

A nurse stopped in to poke at his incision and fuss at him for not eating his dinner. I took the opportunity to escape. But I kissed his dry, stubbly cheek first and promised to come back.

He was flirting shamelessly with the nurse as I ran out. He wasn't dead *yet*.

* * *

It was dark by the time I got to the park, and there was a chain across the driveway to the parking lot. But there were several service roads into the park, and I eventually found the night shift camped out in a pickup truck on one of the tiny roads winding under the trees to the river. The truck had been backed into the woods so only its grill was visible from the main road.

The rangers were trolling for horny young high school students, they told me when I squeezed my car in beside them and the trees and flashed my badge. The night was chilly and they invited me into their truck for a chat. It was a tight fit. There were two rangers. Ray was about twenty-five and looked like a man who belonged outdoors. Joe was closer to thirty-five and was developing a bit of a gut. But I had learned to appreciate a man's *personality* since turning forty, so I ignored the belly straining his belt buckle and admired his strong hands.

The rangers were a little nervous at first. They'd already gone a round with Henry and weren't too pleased to be visited by the police twice in one day. But they were also shocked by the murder and were more than willing to speculate on the weirdos roaming the woods.

Ray scoffed at the idea of the flasher. "That was just some kid too scared to do anything but wag it at some women in the park."

"Sounds like he wagged it a lot," I objected.

Ray grinned. "Naw, two or three times was all. He was just gettin' his kicks. Puberty, you know."

"Did you ever see him?" I asked.

"I was on days then," Ray said. "I never had the pleasure."

"He always showed up around dusk," Joe said. "Always picked older ladies—not like that girl who got killed. He never tried to touch anyone. Just stepped out on the trail and showed his stuff."

"I don't remember hearing about it," I said.

"There wasn't much publicity," Joe admitted.

"Boss didn't want it," Ray put in.

"It would've been different if he'd been going after young girls," Joe said hastily. "Or if he'd tried to hurt anyone. But these were all ladies who'd seen it before. They didn't get hysterical."

"And no one was really in danger," Ray said.

I wondered about *that*.

Joe sensed my displeasure. "Hey, we didn't ignore the guy. We doubled our patrols on the trail and I staked out his favorite spots myself. Worked with one of your detectives a coupla nights. But nothin' happened. The guy just lost interest."

"Afraid of frostbite," Ray snickered. He reminded me a lot of Henry.

A car crept down the road in front of us, inching along without its headlights. Joe sighed and flicked the lights on the truck. The car's lights suddenly flashed on and it peeled out of there.

"Kids," Joe said in disgust.

"Studying mating habits," Ray chuckled.

"You get a lot of that?" I asked.

"Christ, all night," Joe said, and he rolled down his window to air out the cab. It was getting rather close.

Ray dug underneath the seat and came up with a thermos. Plastic cups, too. He poured, and we settled back against the seat, shoulder to shoulder, and sipped lukewarm coffee. I imagined the rangers hadn't been so cozy with Henry.

"What do you *do* all night?" I asked after we'd watched two more cars of kids tool by.

Joe shrugged. "Roust kids. Chase trespassers. Vandals. Poachers. When the weather's bad, we fight storm damage. The river can get nasty like *that*," he said, and snapped his fingers.

"Trail's caved in a coupla places already this spring," Ray said.

"Sometimes we lead night nature hikes," Joe said.

"*I* lead the hikes," Ray corrected.

"If I wanted to be a tour guide, I'd work days," Joe huffed.

"Joe really wants to be a cop," Ray chided.

"You get much trouble?" I asked, trying to steer them back to Carmen.

"Hey, this is a *good* park," Joe protested. "I know that girl got killed here, but it coulda happened anywhere."

"On campus," Ray said.

"Downtown," Joe said.

They reminded me sharply of Pat August, denying that anyone in their world could be bad.

But Carmen had died on *their* trail.

"If it wasn't the flasher, who could it be?" I asked. "Who else gives you trouble?"

"No one," Joe said stoutly. "'Least not murderers. You get fools trying to swim in the river and hikers bitching at cyclists—"

"Now *that* gets ugly," Ray broke in.

"But these are decent people out here," Joe insisted. "Most of 'em even clean up after themselves."

"Trash cans are full of condoms," Ray agreed.

Joe made a face.

The radio crackled, and Ray snatched it almost out of Joe's fingers. It kind of made me wonder just which one wanted to be the cop.

It was the sheriff's dispatcher, reporting hunters across the river. The mood in the truck suddenly picked up.

Joe switched on the engine. Ray made a move to let me out, then grinned. "You want to come along? Could be fun."

"Hunters have guns," Joe objected.

"So do I," I pointed out.

"Bet you can shoot, too," Ray chuckled.

Joe sighed and put the truck in gear. And we nosed out onto the main road.

I wasn't sure Bradley would approve of my tagging along, but there was nothing but paperwork waiting for me at the station, and it was too late to go calling on any of Carmen's friends. So I leaned forward in the seat and peered out at the dark woods streaming past us.

Joe drove north, beyond the turn into the parking lot, and onto park property that hadn't been opened to the public yet. About a mile past the main trailhead, we passed a cluster of bulldozers and tractors.

"Building a new picnic shelter," Joe said as he bounced around the ruts in the road. "New trails, too."

"Better build a *road*," Ray complained as we crashed around a yawning pothole.

I just gripped the dashboard.

The road deteriorated rapidly into a dirt lane so narrow that there was barely room for the truck. It had rained a lot that spring, and the road had fallen away in big chunks. Joe reluctantly slowed the truck, but the woods had closed in around us, and it was too damned dark to see every hole in time. I bounced toward the windshield, but Ray obligingly tugged me back. Didn't exactly let go of my arm, either. Maybe he fantasized about older women.

Joe took a sharp turn, and suddenly there were two pairs of eyes staring at us in the headlights.

"Jesus," Joe hissed, and he stomped on the brake.

The truck fishtailed, and I lunged into Ray's lap. We screeched to a stop just two feet from the deer. They didn't even move.

"Goddamn animals," Ray growled as he peeled himself off the door.

Two young does stood frozen in the middle of the road. We were so close, I could almost see the individual hairs of their rich brown coats fluttering in the night breeze. They stared at us with huge black eyes, and we gaped back like stupid humans.

"Why don't they run?" I gasped.

"Blinded," Joe grunted. "Dumb animals." And he laid on the horn.

The deer spun and darted into the woods. I saw a flash of white tail and delicate hooves as they plunged into the bushes, and then they were gone, just like that.

"God," I said, "they're gorgeous."

"They're pests," Joe said, and he irritably slammed the truck into gear.

"Over-populated," Ray informed me as we carefully rearranged ourselves in the seat. "They're protected in the park, and there aren't enough natural predators to keep 'em under control. That's why there's so many hunters. The deer have spread out into the farms. Into town. Too damn many of 'em."

"But what harm can they do?" I protested as we plowed ahead.

"Take out your front end," Joe said.

"You don't want to hit a deer," Ray said wisely. "Big-time repairs."

"They aren't Bambi," Joe lectured as he drove. "They aren't mean, but they do a hell of a lot of damage off park property. Can't blame some of these farmers for going after 'em."

"But not on *our* land," Ray said.

"Right," Joe said, and stopped the truck in front of a wooden barricade that had sprouted across the path. Ray popped open the door and jumped out to move the barricade.

The headlights cut through a narrow tunnel of green down to the river. I could just make out the black water splashing against the bank, and a narrow strip of bridge stretching out into the darkness.

"Jesus Christ," I said, "we aren't driving over *that*, are we?"

Joe shrugged. "Got to get across the river."

"There aren't any guard rails," I objected.

"Sure there are," Joe said. "Somewhere."

I could hear the river boiling over rocks and slapping the bridge. It wasn't a big river—maybe fifty feet from bank to bank—but my mother was younger than that bridge, and a hell of a lot sturdier. I thought the rangers were nuts.

Ray was grinning as he climbed back into the truck. "River's up," he said cheerfully.

I did not whimper.

Joe rolled the truck down to the bridge. I swear to God, it shuddered in the breeze.

Ray looked at me speculatively. "Pardon me for asking, but just how much do you weigh?"

I snarled at him.

Joe swallowed a smile and inched the truck onto the bridge.

It was a good thing it was dark, because I couldn't see the water swirling around the bridge supports or just how close the truck's tires were to the edge.

But I had excellent hearing, and I picked up every creak of wood as the truck crept out over the river.

"I don't think I've ever been on this bridge," I said bravely.

"Don't see why you would," Ray said. "It's been condemned."

I snapped my mouth shut.

Down river, some birds honked loudly.

"Don't they ever sleep?" I croaked.

"Something's disturbed them," Joe said absently. He was squinting out the windshield, concentrating on the bridge.

"Predators," Ray said, just to needle me.

I suddenly imagined bears. And other monsters of the forest. My little gun didn't feel so comforting anymore. I really should have gone back to the station, where a city cop belongs.

The headlights picked up the opposite bank, and I held my breath until Joe guided the truck off the bridge and onto muddy ground. Ray groused that we were going to get stuck. I didn't care if the truck sank into mud up to its axles. I was not going back on that bridge.

There was another barricade across the lane, and Ray got out to move it. While we waited, Joe explained that out "shortcut" put us between the hunters and the closest legal bridge out of the park. "We'll get 'em," he said confidently as he drove past the barricade and stopped for Ray.

We drove a couple hundred feet through dense woods, then popped out onto a more substantial road. Joe parked the truck across the road, neatly blocking both narrow lanes, then cut the engine.

"Now what?" I asked.

"Now we wait," Ray said, and dug out the thermos again.

"Aren't we going after them?" I asked, distinctly disappointed. I wanted a *chase*.

"You go crashing through the woods, they're gonna shoot *you*," Joe said reasonably.

"But what if they get some poor animal while we wait?" I objected.

"Better some animal than us," Ray said, and he slurped loudly on coffee.

I grunted and crossed my arms. Cops and robbers was much more fun than cowboys and Indians, I decided. Warmer, too.

We sat in the truck for maybe twenty minutes, listening for sounds of trespassers, but mostly talking quietly about Carmen and what kind of creep could kill a woman in the park. Ray confided that the park superintendent was so rattled, he was talking of having extra patrols. Joe grunted that the super would never cough up the dough. Ray thought maybe they should just close the trail until someone was arrested. Joe said that was bad PR.

I got the last swallow of coffee, and since they were being so hospitable, I answered their questions about the crime scene in a little more detail than was prudent. Ray lapped it up. Joe just shook his head.

The shot zinged off the back wheel. *Then* the buck crashed across the road and sliced into the woods. Joe and I instinctively ducked behind the dashboard. Ray gaped out the windshield like he didn't know any better.

And the silence of the night closed in around the truck just as quickly as it has been shattered.

"Goddamn," Ray said hoarsely.

Another shot slammed into a tree to our left, yards from where the buck had disappeared. And that made Joe mad.

"Fools are firing blind," he growled, and he lit up the truck like it was Christmas. Red lights twirled on the roof and the brights cut into the woods in two brilliant cones. It wasn't a smart way to take poachers by surprise, but they sure as hell couldn't mistake us for deer.

The hunters weren't too swift anyway. They stumbled onto the road and squinted at our lights.

There were two of them—teenage boys in denim and ball caps, each toting a shotgun. And they stood frozen in the glare, almost as mesmerized by our headlights as the deer had been.

Joe wasn't mesmerized. He was pissed. He jumped out of the truck and stomped toward the boys. I thought the odds weren't in his favor, seeing as how he was unarmed, and I scrambled out after him.

The boys weren't exactly intimidated by the two of us. One of them even grinned. But then Ray appeared from his side of the truck, and they decided to bolt.

"Police!" I shouted, just to make things clear.

They took off into the woods anyway.

Joe and Ray ran after them. I tried to keep up—after all, I was the one with the gun—but I was still in city shoes and it was very dark away from the truck. Just a few feet into the woods, my heels sank deep into the soft earth, and I fell hopelessly behind.

I stumbled ahead for a while, listening to the chase and glancing back every few steps to make sure I didn't wander too far from the comforting lights of the truck. Brambles snagged my hose and leaves slapped my arms and face. I yearned for ugly concrete.

I heard her wheezing softly before I actually stepped on her. There was half a moon, and I was far enough from the bright lights of the truck that the woods had taken on different shades of dark, and I could just make out a living shape lying a few feet in front of me. I had never hunted for pleasure, but I was a cop, and I knew the smell of blood.

She thrashed her legs at the sight of me, but she couldn't get up and run. I stood perfectly still and let my eyes widen in the dark, and eventually I could see the blacker black on her belly.

"Aw, shit," I whispered.

She stretched her neck in the weeds, and that was as far as she could get from me. Her only struggle now was to breathe, wetly in the brush.

Joe found me several minutes later, still standing over the doe, watching her die. He was breathing heavily, too, and he didn't have any trespassers in tow. But he did have a flashlight, and it glared on the bright red of blood.

"Gut shot," he said in disgust.

The doe didn't even turn her black eyes away from the light. She was quivering now as she breathed.

"You got your gun?" Joe asked.

I swallowed hard and nodded.

He held out his hand. He didn't try to talk me into doing it. I gave him the gun.

"You wouldn't want to leave her like this," he said.

"Right," I said, and turned back to the truck.

He fired before I was ten feet away. The shot echoed through the woods, then there was perfect silence. No thrashing. No wheezing. No rustling in the trees.

The night sucked.

Chapter Nine

Mother was camped in the kitchen, cramming for her last exam, when I got home. She took one look at my clothes and didn't bother to ask how my day had gone.

I grabbed a beer from the refrigerator and guzzled it at the counter. Dave was already in bed. Adam was out "studying" with his friends. Purrvis and Slash were out catting around, too. Only Barney was there to keep Mother company, and I wasn't exactly thrilled to see him. It was his fault we'd found Carmen's body.

Mother sighed and closed her textbook. After this semester, she'd technically have enough credits to be a senior, but she wasn't sure what she was a senior *in*. She had sampled half the departments at the university and was cheerfully planning to sample some more in the fall. Her grade point average was disgustingly high. I didn't think she had any intention of graduating.

She was seventy years old, and I couldn't stand living with her. Couldn't stand living without her, either. Sometimes, I thought she liked Dave best.

"You might as well tell me about it," she said as she neatly stacked her books on the table.

"Tell you what?" I asked peevishly.

"For one thing, why you look like you've been wrestling a bear."

I glanced down at my muddy shoes and made a face. "That isn't funny."

"It wasn't meant to be," she assured me. "Talk."

And I did, working my way through another beer and a sandwich as I hopped from Carmen Martinez to rangers in the woods, not exactly in chronological order but close enough that she got the gist of it. By the time I ran out of steam and appetite (Barney lapped up half the sandwich), I was slouched at the table across from her, the shoes were in a dirty heap on the floor and Mother had neatly homed in on my main character flaw of the evening.

"You're more disturbed by the dead deer than the dead girl," she said.

I stared moodily at the beer bottle.

"That's rather cold, don't you think?" she said.

I shrugged. "Never saw anyone kill a dumb animal before."

"But you've seen a lot of dead people," Mother said.

"More than a lot," I said.

"If I recall," Mother said, tapping the table with her forefinger, "it's what *you* decided to do with your life—chase the bad guys."

"Too many of them," I said, and drained the bottle. "Too damn many."

"So you're going to fret over a deer and block out this girl."

"It's a plan," I said defiantly. I shouldn't have indulged in the beer. I was getting flashes of Carmen's body in the tangled weeds and the doe thrashing in the darkness. All things considered, I preferred to be haunted by a deer.

"Not a very useful plan," Mother said as she walked to the door to check for the cats. Barney followed her hopefully.

"You ought to let him out," I groused. "Maybe he'll run away."

Mother glanced at me over her shoulder. "You'd be devastated."

I doubted it.

The cats slid in around her ankles, and Mother fussed around their food dishes. All of the animals got a midnight snack. The sounds of their slurping did not sit well on top of the beer.

Mother looked at me gagging at the table. "Go to bed, Jo."

It was the smartest suggestion I'd heard all day. I pulled myself up from the chair and aimed myself for the bathroom. Mother was toying with the dirty dishes on the counter. "Aren't you turning in?" I asked.

She shrugged. "I'm not sleepy yet."

I grunted and left her. She was sleepy, all right. She just couldn't rest until Adam was home.

Bad habits are hard to break.

Chapter Ten

Wednesday was a difficult day for small-town law enforcement. The murder had been all over the local news the night before, and Wednesday morning, Bradley discovered just how big a deal Carmen had been in the track world when the national networks started hammering him. I was still blissfully asleep when the CNN crew rolled into town, but there were TV vans all over the parking lot by the time I finally got to the station, and all sorts of strangers were crawling around the squad room. A razor-thin woman with too much makeup was batting her eyes at Herchek and trying to flirt her way around him into Bradley's office, but she was young enough to be Herchek's daughter, and wasn't getting much more out of him than an embarrassed blush. A young man with unmistakable TV hair had parked his butt on the corner of my desk and was jabbering into my phone, but I got rid of him with one growl.

I *hate* TV reporters.

Henry was leaning back in his chair, grinning as he cleaned his nails. He had three kids and was used to chaos. Henry was a couple of years younger than I, and he was everything Dave despised in cops. He was pushy, he was loud and he had never quite grown out of playing the bully. However, his badge kept him more or less in line. Sometimes, he was so crude, he even nauseated me. But he was the only man in the department I trusted implicitly on backup. Even more than Bradley.

"Shoulda worn blue, Jo," Henry said, nodding at my black jeans and striped top. "Blue looks good on TV."

"I will castrate anyone who comes near me with a camera," I said as I stuck my nose into a cup of coffee.

"Stripes'll make you look fat," Henry said. "But that gray in your hair will look real nice in the lights."

I snarled. I'd been living too long with Barney.

Henry smoothed his own hair, which was thinning out a bit at the temples but didn't have a strand of gray. "Maybe you should give me your notes and *I'll* talk to the cameras."

"Maybe you should give me *your* notes," I shot back, "and *I'll* go bust the son of a bitch killed Martinez."

Henry was unperturbed. "I got shit," he said pleasantly.

"Figures," I grumbled.

"Nothing compared to a dead deer," he agreed, and ambled over to the coffee pot before I could scratch out his eyes.

I grumpily signed onto the computer and scanned the updated file on Carmen Martinez. Berger, the detective who had the night shift that month because Mulhaney was sick, had created a masterpiece of a document on Carmen—computers really were Berger's thing—and I could see at a glance just where we were. Which was nowhere. Berger had plumbed the records for sex perverts, assailants and all-around bad guys, and he had put together a dandy list of people I'd never want to encounter in the park, even with Barney at my side. It kind of made me wonder why there weren't more dead girls on the trail.

Berger, of course, hadn't actually interviewed any of the people on his list. He doesn't put much effort into anything that doesn't involve a floppy disc. But Ellen, I noted, had spent the morning checking off suspects—in alphabetical order, of course.

There was an eruption of TV lights across the squad room as the door to Bradley's office opened. Bradley was leading out a grim-looking man about his own age, and they were immediately accosted by reporters who stabbed at them with their microphones. Herchek tried to herd the reporters away, but he's nearly sixty and they ran all over him. Henry ditched his coffee and waded into the pack, tossing reporters this way and that. So much for *his* TV debut.

Bradley got his guest out with a minimum of bloodshed, then stormed back to his office and slammed the door on another clutch of microphones. The damned things multiplied like rabbits. Henry, looking invigorated, retrieved his coffee and wandered back to his desk.

"Who was that with Bradley?" I asked as I reread Carmen's file.

"Dead girl's father," Henry said as he played with his own keyboard.

"Uh-oh," I said.

"You don't know the half of it," Henry said, enjoying the chance to gossip. "First the mayor is in here this morning, chewing on Bradley's ass for letting that poor little girl get killed in his park. Then the university president sails in with his hatchet-faced chief, and *he* chews on Bradley's ass for letting his track star get killed. Then the park super is in here, chewing on Bradley's ass for sealing off the best part of his trail. And then Dad shows up because Doc Sweitzer hasn't released the girl's body yet. And if that's not enough, Dad's some hotshot banker, and he says if Bradley doesn't mind, he's asking the feds to maybe take a look, because his daughter's an international celebrity and maybe she's been the victim of some terrorists or something."

"Terrorists?" I groaned.

"Honest to God," Henry said.

"Jesus Christ," I said, and cringed at the thought of the FBI coming to town. We had worked with the feds before, and it hadn't been pretty. No wonder Bradley was pissed.

"Dad says if the FBI won't help, he might hire some people of his own to investigate," Henry said.

My eyes narrowed. "How do you know that?" I demanded.

Henry shrugged innocently. "Hey, I've got my sources."

More likely, he was eavesdropping in the john, I thought irritably.

Henry grinned as he signed off with a flourish. It was quitting time.

"You're leaving?" I asked, appalled.

"I've been interviewing sex perverts all day," he informed me. "Kinda makes me want to go home to the wife."

That made me shudder.

The TV people were getting agitated because the afternoon was slipping away and they didn't have much for the evening news. They were pouncing on anything in uniform and driving poor Herchek to distraction. Herchek is the senior patrolman, and I've seen him juggle half a dozen calls from desperate citizens without breaking into a sweat. But the media unhinged him. Those pesky little reporters kept slipping behind the counter and poking their cameras and microphones into all sorts of private corners. They were noisy, too. I couldn't concentrate, and retreated to the electronic lair Berger had created for himself in another office. It smelled faintly of onions and Berger's aftershave, but at least it was off-limits to the press.

I didn't know how to operate half the gizmos in there (secretly, I wondered whether Berger even did), but I managed to retrieve Carmen's file again and opened up a neat little addendum that Berger had created when he should have been out nabbing felons. He had tapped into newspaper libraries around the state and had come up with dozens of stories that mentioned Carmen Martinez, the runner. They were in chronological order, too, which must have accounted for that hour of overtime I noticed Berger had turned in.

Most of the stories were brief accounts of track events, starting when Carmen was in high school. At first, she was only an afterthought at the bottom of the stories, a youngster barely worth mentioning. But after the first year, her name began appearing closer and closer to the top of the stories, and she sprouted adjectives—"fresh . . . promising . . . hot . . . determined." High school records started falling under her feet. Coaches suddenly noticed her. She was the youngest state champion in history, and she easily kept the title until she graduated.

There were brief biographies of her in national magazines, and a lengthy newspaper spread during her senior year in high school. I didn't know how much the reporter cleaned up her quotes, but she came across as an articulate, intelligent and very strong-willed young woman. There were no giggling bursts of teenage enthusiasm, no breathless desires to grow up to be just like Madonna. Carmen simply wanted to run faster than any other human being on earth, and by her own reasoned calculations, she was on track to do it. Her determination was almost tangible.

The writer made a stab at portraying Carmen Martinez at home—there was the father, who must have been a determined man himself to crack the banking establishment, and the mother, who had been a teacher but preferred to describe herself as a full-time mom, and a younger brother who chose the swimming pool over the track—but the picture I got from it was exasperatingly one-dimensional. Whether at school or at home, Carmen ran, ran, ran. Her life was built around training. I wanted to read that her secret passion was bingeing on chocolate chip cookies, but the writer let me down.

Carmen burst onto the college track and burned it up. I was still slightly surprised that a woman with her talent had ended up *here*, at a university with a solid program but not Olympic caliber. During her freshman year, a prominent sports columnist had toyed with the very same question. Carmen said she wanted to be close to her family. Her parents enthusiastically agreed. But the columnist clearly thought that Carmen Martinez, third-generation Cuban, had been stupidly overlooked by a racist sporting establishment.

If Carmen agreed, she didn't say. She simply ran, and chopped huge seconds off national records.

There were lots of stories from the last season, and blatant references to the next Olympic Games. And just the week before, another columnist had reported that California was primed to snatch up the state's premier female runner. Everyone but Jesse Conklin seemed to realize that Carmen Martinez was one hot property.

And now she was dead. Some monster had crept up on her in the park and snapped her neck in two, and all those dreams had vaporized like *that*.

I stopped fretting over the deer.

* * *

Henry is a loud mouth and Ellen is a pain in the ass, and some people say I'm about as open-minded as the Bible, but we're thorough. We couldn't make a splashy arrest in time for the evening news, but slowly over the next two days, we were able to reconstruct the last twenty-four hours of Carmen's life, and even the comings and goings at the park. Berger built an elaborate chronology for us in the computer, and though it had lots of aggravating blanks in it, it was a picture we could all share and flesh out with a detail here, a stroke of color there.

Ellen found the two high school kids who were running on the trail the night Carmen died. Henry found the pizza delivery boy. And I found the cyclist.

Ellen had taken a break from sex perverts to hang around the trailhead with Ranger Larry, checking out the park regulars. Ellen could have done it alone—in fact, she probably would have preferred to—but Ranger Larry had developed a crush and insisted on hanging around with her. She stopped dozens of people in one afternoon and finally turned up the two kids from the high school cross-country team. They admitted right off that they knew who Carmen was—even if they hadn't passed her a lot on the trail, they would have known *about* her. She was almost an idol. And since they had each other as alibis, they weren't afraid to own up to seeing her the night she was killed.

They said they had already run the length of the trail and were making good time back. Carmen was still on the first half of her run—hadn't even worked up a good sweat yet. She was running alone, as usual. Didn't say anything to them, as usual. The boys figured it must have been about seven-thirty when they passed her in the woods, near a bend in the river.

They were positive she was wearing new hot pink shorts. Ellen studiously made note of it.

Henry had taken a break from sex perverts to nose around Jesse Conklin's apartment building. He's always inclined to suspect the boyfriend, so he took it upon himself to check Jesse out. I would have objected, but the truth is, many times it *is* the boyfriend. So Henry questioned Jesse's neighbors, who were more than willing to gossip about murder. They just didn't *know* anything. After all, it was finals week. Half of them were busily moving out. Who had time to keep track of one guy in one apartment?

But just as Henry was leaving the apartment complex, a kid from one of the pizza shops drove up, and food being one of Henry's main passions, he started talking up the delivery boy. And the boy said, yeah, sure, he knew Jesse Conklin. Took a class with him, in fact. Hadn't seen him, though, since Monday night. About eight o'clock. Jesse was pulling into the apartment parking lot as the pizza boy was pulling out. They'd honked horns at each other.

It kind of blew Jesse's claim that he waited around the apartment all night, hoping for Carmen to show up.

Of course, he had an excuse. He'd run out to the drive-through to pick up a six-pack, and the clerk sort of backed him up. He remembered carding a guy who looked a lot like Jesse sometime Monday night.

It wasn't enough of a glitch in Jesse's story to haul him in, but we were keeping our options open.

I found the cyclist by accident. I'd gone through Mulhaney's notes on the flasher and had found one name—Dwayne. No last name, no age, no address—just Dwayne. I tried calling Mulhaney about it, but he'd just had his first round of chemotherapy, and wasn't up to talking on the phone. So I drove out to the park after my dinner break to find Joe, the ranger who had staked out the trail with Mulhaney.

It was about six o'clock on a Thursday evening, and the park was littered with people who were trying to work out the kinks from a day at the office. Some guys thought they'd seen a ranger down the trail, so I headed into the woods, feeling vaguely disoriented without Barney loping at my side. The damned dog had wormed his way into my brain.

I didn't find Joe, but I was nearly blown off the trail by a cyclist. It wasn't *entirely* his fault. The path curved up around the river bank and visibility was practically nil because of the trees around the water. And I was sort of in the middle of the path, gawking at two ducks who were diligently courting. I was distracted by thoughts of how ducks *do* it when the cyclist whipped around the curve. He swerved, and I jumped, and we just managed to avoid each other.

He swore and he probably would have zipped on by me, but I was in street clothes and definitely looked lost and bewildered in the wilderness. Certainly, it had nothing to do with the fact that I was twice his age and he felt sorry for me. He braked hard and looked back at me over his shoulder.

"You okay?" he asked, and his voice was a little breathless. From the strenuous ride, I decided. Not because he'd nearly flattened me under his wheels.

"I'm fine," I said hastily, embarrassed that I'd been caught ogling ducks.

The cyclist frowned at my feet. "You ought to get better shoes," he said, and started to pedal away.

But before he could pick up any speed, there was a screech and a clatter, and suddenly the chain was dangling from his bike.

"Shit," he muttered, and dismounted.

The ducks had fluttered away and Joe was nowhere in sight, so I toddled in my inappropriate footwear up to the bike and peered at the damage.

"Did I do that?" I asked.

The kid—he was about Adam's age, so to me, he was a kid—had squatted down beside the bike and was fussing with the chain. The evening was turning cool under the trees, but he must have been pushing hard on the bike, because his T-shirt was damp, and the back of his neck, just below the helmet, was beaded with sweat. I suspected if I took a deep breath, I'd smell his exertion.

The kid was irritated, but he was polite enough not to blame his troubles on me. "It's the bike," he said as he yanked off his helmet and a funny pair of gloves with no fingers. "The chain keeps slipping."

He went about fixing the bike like he knew what he was doing. I hovered uninvited. Since I couldn't find Joe, I had nothing better to do.

The kid gave me a peculiar look over his shoulder—okay, it was kind of weird for a forty-year-old woman in street clothes to hang around the woods hitting on young cyclists. So I flashed my badge, and he was properly impressed. His name was Rich, not Dwayne, and he admitted right off that he'd seen Carmen running on the trail. The night she died, in fact.

"Why didn't you tell anyone?" I asked in exasperation.

He sat back on his heels and squinted up at me. His skin was shiny with sweat, but it wasn't a bad face. Maybe the nose was a little too big, and the chin could have used some depth, but the eyes were good and the mouth had potential. If I'd been twenty years younger, I wouldn't have slobbered over him, but I might have given him a second look.

"I didn't tell anyone 'cause I didn't *see* anything," he said. "She was just a runner on the trail."

"But you knew who she was," I said.

"Everyone at school knows that," he said.

"And you knew she was killed."

"Uh-uh," he said, and shook his head. "Not till it was on TV."

"And you didn't tell anyone?" I asked.

He shrugged and focused on the bike. "Well, sure, I told my friends—I mean, everyone's talking about it at school—but what else was I supposed to do? It's not like I saw anything important."

"What *did* you see?" I asked.

He sighed and spun the pedals with his hand. The bike protested. So while he fiddled some more with the gears, he told me what it had been like that night—the woods just turning gray and cooling off fast because it was still only May, the trail a little rutted and muddy from the rain, the river churning loudly to his right, and the damn chain slipping again. It must have been getting late, Rich said, because he hadn't passed too many people on the path. Some joggers here and there. And Carmen.

"She was alone?" I asked.

"Guess so," Rich said to his bike. "I don't really remember. I was fixing the chain."

"No one else was hanging around, maybe following her?" I asked.

He looked at me in exasperation. "Hey, if I'd seen someone following her, I'd have told you first thing. I'm not *stupid*."

Maybe not stupid, I thought, but he seemed overly absorbed in his bike. He looked like a healthy male. If a good-looking woman trotted by, wouldn't a healthy young male take a little more notice? "You didn't talk to her?" I asked.

"You don't *talk* to runners," he said in disdain. "They're too busy *running*."

And cyclists are too busy cycling, I thought. And from what I'd learned of Carmen, she wouldn't have invited conversation anyway. She would have been focused on the trail, running around a disabled bicyclist as though he were just another obstacle in the path.

Rich twirled the pedals again and grunted as the chain hummed smoothly. He stood and gripped the handlebars to mount up.

I wouldn't let him get away without an address and phone number. He objected strongly—like it wasn't his fault some maniac was haunting the woods—but I insisted and he grumpily recited the numbers. He was homegrown, I noted. Not one of the transient hordes on campus who would disappear for the summer.

He swung his leg over the bike and I enviously noticed the taut definition of muscle in the thigh and calf. Maybe I ought to take up biking, I thought. Strangle Dave with my thighs.

Rich must have thought my stare was more accusatory than appreciative, because he tried to redeem himself before pedaling off. "Look, there were other people out here that night. Some guys in track gear, and some old guy jogging. You ought to hassle them, not me."

"What old guy?" I asked, ignoring the kids on the track team because Ellen had already found them.

"I dunno," Rich said, and pointed the bike with determination up the path. "Just some old guy trying to give himself a heart attack."

"How old?" I asked in frustration.

Rich shoved off with one foot. "Musta been as old as you," he tossed over his shoulder.

Then he sliced up the path and around the bend, and I was left alone in the woods, contemplating murder.

His.

Chapter Eleven

W e crowded around the television in Bradley's office about nine that night and watched as one of the all-news networks pretty much savaged us for failing to find the man who had killed a sure bet for the next Olympics. It was a slow night for war and pestilence, so the network devoted five whole minutes to the murder of Carmen Martinez. Most of it was file footage of Carmen at track meets and some scene shots of the university and the trail where she died. There were random interviews with students, an unflattering shot of the mayor ducking comment and a painful sequence with Carmen's father and Pat August. There was also a brief interview with Bradley, who said the only thing he *could* say—that we were developing several leads and hoped to make an arrest soon. I thought he carried himself very well and looked only a little bit chunky on television.

Bradley snarled and snapped off the TV. I shushed him. He was scaring the baby.

Ellen had gone home for dinner and had come back with her daughter. Ellen was mildly embarrassed. Her husband had been called out to *his* job, and she couldn't find a sitter. Henry scowled. If he wanted to be around screaming kids, he told me, he'd just go home to his own bunch. Herchek made goo-goo eyes at the baby and poked her belly with a fat finger, but that was about all *he* wanted to do with her. Bradley was speechless when he saw Ellen march in with a baby on one shoulder and a diaper bag on the other. It was a first for the squad room. But before he could rule on it one way or the other, the news had come on and we had all trooped into his office to see how bad it was.

We were a gloomy bunch of cops when the broadcast was over. Ninety percent of the time, you know right off who the killer is. Frequently, he's with the corpse when you get there. I've even seen husbands try to give their wives mouth to mouth after blasting them full of holes. It usually isn't any mystery who pulled the trigger or slashed with the knife.

But with the other ten percent, you're playing a different kind of game. Progress is measured in very small increments: a fact here, a fact there, nothing particularly significant by itself, but eventually, when you string all the facts together, a pattern starts to emerge, and if you're lucky, you nail the bastard.

Sometimes, it takes months of painstaking, tedious investigation before the picture comes into focus. Sometimes, it never happens. You just have to keep on digging and take your satisfaction in the small pieces of information that come your way.

Which was why we were mildly optimistic before the news. The attack on Carmen was slowly taking shape. We were pinning down the time frame. Alibis were either holding together or starting to crumble. We felt we were moving in the right direction.

Until one news team made us look like a bunch of boobs.

"Well?" Bradley demanded, but a decibel or two lower than usual in deference to the baby.

"Reporters are assholes," Henry said stoutly.

"Scum," Herchek agreed, and nodded vigorously.

Bradley glowered at me, expecting me to chime in.

"They've got to pick on somebody," I said bravely. "There's no suspect, so they're picking on us."

"And why the hell isn't there a suspect?" Bradley growled.

The baby whimpered softly on Ellen's shoulder. Ellen patted her diapered bottom and frowned at Bradley.

"We got the boyfriend," Henry jumped in. "His alibi is shit."

"It's shabby," I agreed. "But no one puts him at the park."

"We already know he lied," Henry said. "He didn't stay home all night like he said. And everyone says he was pissed off at the girl."

"Carmen's *roommate* says he was pissed off. But she's hardly objective. Jesse dumped her in favor of Carmen," I reminded them.

"She's got a grudge," Herchek said wisely.

"Big time," I said.

"Doesn't mean the boyfriend didn't do it," Henry reasoned. "If he's cold enough to dump one woman for another, he's cold enough to kill Martinez for trying to leave him."

"Give me some proof, Henry," Bradley grumbled.

Henry smiled weakly. "I'm workin' on it."

"Not hard enough," Bradley said pointedly.

"Right," Henry said, and he melted back against the filing cabinets for cover, just in case Bradley decided to throw things.

"I might have something interesting," Ellen offered.

Bradley focused on her, but not as warmly as usual. The baby had put him off.

"It's Carmen's shorts," Ellen said.

Henry rolled his eyes behind her back.

Herchek's cheeks reddened at the mention of personal clothing.

"Her shorts?" Bradley repeated.

"They're missing, you know," Ellen said earnestly.

"We noticed," I said.

"Pink shorts, the boys said," Ellen reminded us.

"Have you found them?" Bradley asked patiently.

"Oh, no," Ellen said. "But it might be significant that they're missing. I ran across a case—I don't remember the name—it's in my notes—" She stopped, suddenly flustered. Her hands were full of baby, and her notebook was buried in the diaper bag.

The men waited expectantly.

I sighed. I *knew* it would come down to this.

Ellen looked at me, and I wordlessly reached for the baby. As though no one else in the room was capable of holding an infant, for God's sake.

The baby squirmed and whined, and I almost lost her. It'd been *years*, damn it. I was out of practice. I'd forgotten how heavy a baby's head is, and how it wobbles on its tiny neck. I'd forgotten how easily the soft bones bend and how simple it is for arms and legs to pop out of the grip of big, adult hands. I'd forgotten it all over the years, and I awkwardly propped her against my shoulder. She flopped her face onto my blouse and drooled.

Ellen, the idiot, blithely assumed I knew what I was doing with her only child and dug through her notes without another glance in our direction. It'd serve her right, I thought, if I bounced her daughter on her head.

"Ah," she said, "this is it. James Battaglia. Sexual imposition."

And she smiled brightly at Bradley.

Bradley's patience was beginning to fray. Perhaps it was the sight of me cuddling a baby. "Did this guy know Martinez?" Bradley asked.

"He says no," Ellen said. "But he steals underwear."

Bradley gaped at her. Henry chuckled and stared at the ceiling. Herchek fidgeted.

"Underwear?" Bradley repeated.

Ellen nodded enthusiastically. "He was on Berger's list of sex offenders. Arrested five years ago down state. He cornered women who were out walking alone and made them give him their underwear."

Bradley blinked. "He stole their panties?"

Ellen nodded again.

"That's it?" Bradley asked. "Just their panties?"

Ellen blushed slightly. "Well, he did masturbate in front of them," she admitted.

"That's sick," Herchek said.

Henry was laughing into his fist.

I wanted to cover the baby's little ears.

"When the police arrested him," Ellen said, "they recovered half a dozen pairs of panties, all—um—unwashed."

Henry guffawed.

The baby jerked in my arms and nearly rolled off my shoulder. I glared at Henry and slapped the baby back into the curve of my neck.

Ellen was reading doggedly from her notes. "He kept the panties under his mattress. The arresting officer suspected he—um—slept with them."

Henry was nearly choking.

Herchek stared in painful embarrassment at his shoes.

"You talk to this pervert?" Bradley asked.

"Oh, yes," Ellen said. "I caught him at work. Fast food."

"Hope he washed his hands," Henry snickered.

I thought of the cheeseburger I'd grabbed for dinner and gagged.

"According to his records," Ellen said, "he served three months and was released into a counseling program. Completed it, too. He moved here about three years ago. Lives with his mother. Takes classes once in a while—"

Bradley suddenly looked interested.

"—single, works days, and swears he was home with his mother Monday night when Martinez was killed."

Herchek shifted uncomfortably in his chair. "He lives with his mother, maybe he's straightened himself out."

"He was living with his mother when he was arrested the first time," Ellen said.

Herchek frowned. "She must not be a positive influence."

Henry started to laugh, caught The Look from Bradley, and vigorously cleared his throat.

"You smoke too much," Bradley said evenly.

"You're right," Henry agreed, and thumped his chest. "I'll quit."

Bradley stared at him until he was reasonably sure Henry would behave, then transferred The Look to Ellen. "What's your point?"

Ellen was disconcerted. Bradley was seldom gruff with her. "It's the shorts. Martinez's shorts are missing, and this man has a history of taking women's underwear."

"Does he have a history of violence?" Bradley demanded.

"Well—" Ellen hesitated. "He's never actually hurt anyone, no."

"Has he been in trouble since he got out of jail?" Bradley asked.

Ellen frowned at her notes. "Well, no. He's been clean for five years."

"Is there any link to Martinez?" Bradley hammered.

"He goes to the university," Ellen managed. She glanced nervously at the baby, who was nesting comfortably on my chest, and rallied. "His history is significant," she said more firmly.

"It's pretty damned weak," Bradley growled.

"Christ, Brad," I said in exasperation, "it's a damn good lead."

Bradley looked at me in surprise. I wasn't in the habit of defending Ellen, but his attitude was irritating. Ellen hadn't parked her brains at the door when she'd trotted in with the baby, for God's sake.

"Carmen's shorts are missing," I snapped. "This man collects women's clothing. I think he's worth a look."

The baby fussed at the sharp edge to my voice, and I awkwardly tried to rock her. I caught a glimpse of Henry rolling his eyes again, and I curled my lip at him.

Bradley spread his arms innocently. "You ladies want to look at this pervert, by all means, look."

I transferred my snarl to him. The baby didn't like the vibes and spit up on my shoulder.

"Oh, my," Ellen said.

"Better pitch *that* blouse," Henry muttered.

I pried the baby off my shoulder and passed her, dripping, back to Ellen. Herchek kindly offered the box of Kleenex from Bradley's desk, and I absently blotted the goop off my blouse. Bradley watched the proceedings in consternation. He clearly wanted to bark, but how could he bark at a baby?

"I think Henry should keep on Jesse Conklin," I said, trying to wrap things up so Ellen could get her child out of there. "Ellen can check on Battaglia in the morning."

Ellen shot me a grateful look and began stuffing her notes one-handed back into the diaper bag. Henry liked the idea of squeezing Conklin, so he kept his mouth shut. Herchek was wrinkling his nose at the smell drifting off my blouse and scooted his chair toward the door, ready to escape. Only Bradley was dissatisfied.

"And just what are *you* going to do?" he demanded.

I shrugged. "Hang out at the trail and look for middle-aged joggers."

Bradley looked at me speculatively.

"Don't wear shorts," he said. "Might blind him with the glare."

I could have brained him.

Chapter Twelve

A week went by and nothing happened. Carmen Martinez was buried and most of the news crews went home. So did most of the students. Jesse Conklin took off for a few days, too, but Henry wasn't worried. According to the university, Jesse was enrolled in summer classes and he hadn't given up his apartment. Henry figured if anything turned up to bust Jesse's alibi, we'd find him soon enough.

Carmen's father was as good as his word. Two days after the funeral, Bradley got a courtesy call from the FBI. The agent was an older guy who had outgrown the need to shoot it out with terrorists. In fact, he was downright reasonable for a fed. He and Bradley spent a congenial afternoon going through the files, the agent made a lucid observation or two (he *really* liked the guy with the panties) and he and Bradley parted with vague talk about setting up a poker game. I wasn't invited.

We pretty much worked our way through the regulars at the park and Berger's list of sex perverts and even members of the track team, and except for James Battaglia, no one triggered that little tingle in the spine that says this guy is sick. Ellen dragged Battaglia into the station twice to question him, and, though he finally cracked and admitted to swiping ladies' underwear from the Laundromat, she couldn't shake his alibi for the night Carmen was killed. And outside of the fact that Battaglia and Carmen were both students at the university, Ellen couldn't find any link between the two. No shared classes. No mutual friends. Not even a hint that Carmen had ever stopped at the restaurant where Battaglia worked. Ellen finally sent Battaglia home with his mother, under stern orders to enroll him in counseling or else.

Barney and I haunted the park trail every day but encountered nothing but crabby cyclists and one hound in heat. Her owner lectured me bitterly for not keeping my degenerate animal on a leash.

"You should have stopped him," Mother said primly as we cleaned up after a late Sunday supper.

"Yeah, right," I said as I dumped dishes into the sink, "like Barney listens to *me*."

Adam chuckled into his dessert. There had been talk in the spring that he might go home to his mother's for the summer, but he'd just found a job clerking at a video store. There'd also been talk that he might get an apartment with one of his buddies, but I hadn't noticed him packing up any of his suitcases yet. I liked the boy, but our strange four-person household was getting a very permanent feel to it, and I wasn't sure how I felt about *that*.

Dave didn't talk about it much, but I sensed that after so many years apart from his son, he kind of liked having Adam around. I half-expected Adam's younger brother Josh to show up someday, too. I could just move out to the garage.

"It isn't civilized to let the dog have his way with anything in the park," Mother said.

"The little bitch wasn't exactly protesting," I said.

"They usually don't," Dave muttered to a slice of apple pie.

Adam snorted.

I glared at them both.

Mother patted my shoulder. "Just be firm with him, dear. When he misbehaves, tell him 'no.' It's always worked for me."

"Oh, for God's sake," I said as I dumped another load into the sink. "When did anything male ever listen to the word 'no'?"

Adam elbowed his dad. Dave's cheeks turned pink above his beard. It was mildly attractive.

The cause of all the fuss was stretched out on the kitchen floor, exhausted. His ears barely twitched as we talked, and he didn't seem to notice Slash sniffing at his food dish. At least Barney had had a productive day.

"What's the point of taking Barney anyway?" Adam asked as he helped himself to a second slice of pie. "No one's gonna mug you if you got Barney along."

"Precisely," Dave said without looking up.

"I'm not trying to get mugged," I said to the suds. "I'm looking for a witness."

"Who might really be a killer," Adam said.

"Right," I said.

"So he's not gonna show up if Barney's protecting you," Adam said reasonably.

"If he's innocent, he might show up," I said.

"If he's innocent, why bother with him?" Adam countered.

"Because he might know something," I said testily.

"If he knew something, he'd have already told you," Adam said.

"Right," I growled.

"I think you're irritating her," Dave warned.

Adam grinned. "You think?"

Dave nodded solemnly. "Trust me."

I vigorously scrubbed the dishes. Mother calmly wiped them dry and stacked them on the counter. "We've accounted for everyone in the park the night Carmen died except for the jogger, the one the cyclist saw."

"The old guy," Adam said.

I clenched my teeth. "Yes," I said, "the one my age."

"Really old," Adam said.

Dave, who is several years older than I, was no longer amused and grumbled a warning. I glanced at Adam out of the corner of my eye and decided he wasn't being obnoxious. He was being ornery. I'd seen the same gleam in his father's eye from time to time. With Dave, it was usually a prelude to a romp in bed. God knew what Adam was up to.

"What's your interest?" I asked as I tackled the pots and pans. "You know Carmen?"

"Naw," Adam said as he picked stray crumbs off his plate. "It's just cool, that's all."

"Murder," Mother said, horrified, "is *cool?*"

"Not murder," Adam said hastily. "That sucks. It's what Jo does. *That's* cool."

My jaw dropped. *No* one thought my job was cool.

I sensed Dave stiffening behind me. Despite the fact that he slept with a cop, he wasn't a big-time fan of law enforcement. He suspected we were all neo-Nazis.

"What, in particular, do you find cool?" Dave asked, and there was only the slightest hint of strain in his voice.

I found *that* remarkably cool.

Adam shrugged. "It's like a puzzle, you know? Pick out a piece here, a piece there, play around with them till they start to fit. I like that."

I shivered. It was as though Adam had been in my head.

Mother frowned as she shoved a stack of plates into the cupboard. "It isn't a game, Adam. Jo deals with pitiful, even dangerous, people."

Adam's eyes lit up.

"Mostly boring people," I said quickly.

Dave relaxed slightly.

"Yeah, like murder is boring," Adam said.

"High school shoplifting rings are boring. Check-kiting schemes are boring. Crackdowns on deadbeat days are boring," I said, ticking off the cases that had occupied my time before Carmen had managed to get herself killed.

"That's what I do most days—track down boring little people who don't even have the imagination to make their crimes interesting."

"Oh, sure," Adam said, "that stuff's a drag. But then someone whacks a big track star, and that's *sweet*, Jo."

"The big track star is dead," Mother said tartly. "That's not *sweet*."

"Well, right, not for her," Adam conceded. "But tell the truth, Jo. Don't you get a charge out of it?"

I carefully scrubbed a burnt piece of glop off a skillet. I could almost feel Dave holding his breath. I was certain he'd rather see his son invest in stocks and bonds and register as a Republican than show any hint of interest in police work. One cop was all he could handle.

But I wasn't going to lie, either. "Most times, it's a pain in the butt. Your cases drag in court. You deal all day with idiots who are too damned stupid or too lazy or too greedy to be decent, honest human beings. They lie to you. They whine. They cheat. They hurt other people for no good reason at all. They just irritate the *hell* out of me."

I balanced the skillet in the dish rack and turned to look at Adam. The ornery gleam had disappeared. He was listening carefully now, his face smooth and unlined, like his father's must have been once, before a land mine taught him he wasn't invincible.

I felt like a traitor as I wiped my hands on my jeans. "But you're right," I said. "When I finally nail some bastard, when I *know* he's going down and there's no way in hell he's ever gonna see the light of day again, it's like a bolt of lightning right up the spine."

Dave lowered his head angrily over his pie.

Mother snorted in disapproval.

But Adam just nodded thoughtfully. "I knew it," he said.

Chapter Thirteen

Late Monday afternoon, I was sitting at my desk, fondling a ruby red sherbet I'd snapped up at an auction that morning and mentally calculating my net worth in Depression glass, when Herchek steered a man in a suit in my direction. I don't usually get visitors in suits. Jeans and T-shirt are more my fare. But this man was in a very nice suit, and it almost disguised the extra ten pounds he was carrying.

"Yes?" I asked, reluctantly putting aside my new bauble.

The man cleared his throat and nodded at Herchek. "That officer says you're investigating the killing in the park."

"Carmen Martinez," I said helpfully.

"Yes, Martinez," he said, and his eyes darted nervously around the squad room. He was about my age, graying a little, sagging just a bit, but still worth looking at. I pegged him as a businessman, doing well if his suit was any indication, and uncomfortable at finding himself inside a police station. Mother would have liked him.

He took in the squad room—the battered metal desks and chairs and filing cabinets, the paper spilling onto the scuffed tile floor, the remnants of Henry's lunch, already drawing flies—and he breathed deeply, as though steeling himself. "I think I saw something," he said.

"You're the jogger," I said brilliantly.

"I run," he admitted.

"Let me get you some coffee," I said happily, and I settled the man as comfortably as possible at my desk and scurried around for a clean coffee cup. Witnesses don't usually drop into my lap. I was beside myself.

He sat awkwardly in the chair, as though there were a thousand places he'd rather be, and the coffee I gave him only tightened him up more. He suspected he was being ridiculous and wasting my time. I assured him I wanted nothing more than to hear what he had to say.

His name was Nieman, and he ran the local branch of the computer company that served the university. He wasn't local—he'd been transferred into town six months before, and I suspected this wasn't the last stop in his career. He had the air of a man still driving himself—seriously enough that he was doggedly fighting to keep the extra weight within bounds. I wouldn't have called the man over the hill by any means, but I could see how a brash young cyclist might have labeled him as old.

"I jog on the trail in the park," he said over his coffee cup. "A couple times a week. Whenever I can break out of the office for an hour or two."

"It's hard," I agreed.

He smiled ruefully at his waist. "Tell me about it."

I looked at my own thighs. I knew all about it.

He admitted he'd seen Carmen once or twice on the trail.

"You knew who she was?" I asked.

"Not at first," he said. "I just run for the exercise. I'm not in it for the sport, you understand. Track stars?" He shrugged. "Means nothing to me."

"But you found out who she was," I said.

He blushed slightly and put the cup on my desk, to busy himself. "I mentioned her to one of the rangers one day. She was a very attractive woman, good runner. You couldn't help but notice her. The ranger told me who she was."

"You talk to her?" I asked.

He laughed, more at himself than at me. "Talk to her? Hell, she blew me off the trail. I don't think I was in her league."

"Few people were," I said.

He shrugged again. "No big deal," he said. "We didn't know each other, but I knew who she was, and I guess I saw her on the night she died." He looked at me quizzically. "You knew that?"

"Some folks remembered seeing a jogger about your age that night," I said. "We've kind of been looking for you."

I waited for him to explain himself. After all, it had been a week since Carmen had been killed, and he was only now surfacing.

He had a very plausible excuse. He'd been out of town all week on business. "It's the end of my company's fiscal year. I was at corporate all week working on our annual report." He looked at me with wide brown eyes. "I never knew what happened."

"Kind of hard to imagine," I said. "It's been all over the news."

He uncomfortably flicked some lint off his trousers. "I left for Chicago the next morning, before anyone knew she was dead. And I wasn't on vacation. It was work. Sure, I heard talk about some girl getting killed, but I wasn't making the connection. I wasn't reading the papers from home and the TV news—" He hesitated in embarrassment. "I just didn't realize."

"A big track star dies in your town and you didn't figure it out?"

He smiled weakly. "It's the truth. I was tied up in meetings most of the time, and if it wasn't meetings, it was the computer. You know how it is."

I nodded like I understood annual reports.

"So I didn't get home until Saturday night and my wife mentioned it—because I run in the park, you understand—and she showed me the papers. And I recognized the girl's picture." His mouth twisted slightly. "Jesus, I must have seen her right before she was killed."

"So you figured this out Saturday night," I said. "Why'd you wait so long to come in?"

He looked at me in surprise. "It was the weekend."

I smiled brightly. "We never close."

"Um—well—" He shifted uncomfortably in the chair, and when that didn't ease his conscience any, he retrieved the cup from my desk and gulped some coffee. "I wasn't sure it was necessary to contact you. I didn't see that it would make any difference."

"It's difficult to get involved in a police investigation," I said sympathetically.

"Precisely," he said, pleased that I understood. "The publicity wouldn't be good for my company."

"Or your family," I said.

"Yes," he said, and perhaps we both thought of his wife.

We were silent as he placed the cup back on my desk. I wondered just how hard he had stared at Carmen's hot pink shorts. If he was anything like Dave, he had stared a lot.

"What changed your mind?" I asked. "Why are you here?"

He sighed unhappily. "I remembered something. Well, actually, someone."

I perked up. "On the trail?"

He shook his head. "In the parking lot."

"With Carmen?" I asked.

"No, no," he said impatiently. "If I'd seen anyone *with* her, I'd have called you right away. I'm not an idiot."

I valiantly made no comment.

He blushed as though I had.

"No," he said, "it was later, after I'd finished my run. I was coming off the trail, into the parking lot. You know where I mean?"

I nodded.

"It was getting dark, only a couple of cars left in the lot. I was just walking when—" He grinned at me sheepishly. "Okay, I was staggering, and I was still under the trees, so I guess he never saw me."

"He?" I prodded.

"A young guy," Nieman said. "He was jiggling the handle on one of the cars, like he'd locked himself out. Then he slammed his hand down on the roof, like he was mad."

"You say anything to him?" I asked.

Nieman twitched in embarrassment. "Well, no. In fact, I stayed under the trees. I was thinking, if he'd locked himself out of his car, he was going to want a ride and—I was on a tight schedule, I was leaving town in the morning, you see, and there were rangers around if he needed a lift."

"So you hung back," I said.

"I was cooling down," he said. "Stretching."

"Uh huh."

"And as it turned out, I was wrong," Nieman said quickly. "He wasn't stranded. He turned around and got into another car."

"By himself?" I asked.

Nieman nodded. "He sat behind the wheel, I figured it was okay, maybe he was just waiting for someone, and I went on into the lot and got into my own car. He was still sitting there when I drove out."

"The first car," I said carefully, "the one he was trying to get into. You remember what it looked like?"

"Red Toyota," Nieman said promptly.

Oh, yes, I thought.

"And the guy," I said. "You get a good look at him?"

Nieman hesitated. "It was getting dark." He stared unhappily at his coffee cup. "But I might recognize him."

I thought about it some, then I moved over to Henry's desk and rifled his drawers for snapshots from old cases. With my back to Nieman, I quickly snipped Carmen from the photo of her and Jesse Conklin, then went back to my desk and spread out five pictures, including Jesse, in front of Nieman.

"Any of these look like the guy?" I asked.

He studied them carefully, and even held a couple at arm's length and squinted at them because he wasn't ready to admit yet that he needed bifocals. I let him take his time.

Eventually, he sighed and looked up at me.

"It could have been him," Nieman said.

And his forefinger was clearly resting on Jesse Conklin's face.

Chapter Fourteen

"This is bullshit, man," Jesse protested as Henry led him into the interrogation room a couple of hours later.

Henry was on overtime and was grouchy. He'd been pleased when I'd called him at home and told him I had a witness who put Jesse Conklin at the park the night Carmen died, but then I told him Bradley wanted him to pick Jesse up, and he wasn't so happy anymore. I wasn't thrilled, either. I was big enough to bring Jesse in. But Bradley thought I might be kind of soft on the boy, and he sent Henry instead.

It was dark by the time Henry ran him down at a pizza joint, and the station was nearly empty when Henry brought him in. The civilians had gone home, and it was too early for the patrols to haul in the drunks. There were no reporters, either. Just Henry and me and the duty sergeant and the dispatcher. Bradley was out to dinner with the mayor.

Henry nudged Jesse toward a chair a little too vigorously, and Jesse shook his shoulders angrily. "You don't have to push, man."

"You want a lawyer?" I asked as I sat at the table.

Jesse transferred his glare to me. He was in jeans and a denim jacket, and they both fit him nicely. His face was flushed, and that was kind of attractive, too. Maybe Bradley had been right to send Henry.

"I don't need a lawyer. I didn't do nothing," Jesse objected. But he didn't look very confident when Henry closed the door and leaned back against the doorjamb, his arms folded grimly across his chest.

"There's been some mistake," Jesse said, but he sat anyway in the chair across from me.

"There *has* been a mistake," I agreed as I scanned my notes from our first interview. "You lied to us."

"Bullshit," Jesse said. But his eyes darted warily over the notes on the table.

"You said you waited at your apartment all night for Carmen," I said calmly. "That was a lie."

"You know I was there," he countered. "Carmen's roommate can tell you."

"Carmen's roommate can tell me you called," I said. "She can't tell me *where* you were when you called."

"I was home," he insisted.

"We know you went out," I said.

"Yeah, to get a six-pack. I already told *him* that," Jesse said, and he nodded sullenly at Henry.

Henry irritably drummed his fingers on his arms. He wanted a cigarette.

I paged through the papers and pulled out Henry's notes. "You know drive-throughs are computerized?" I asked, cheerfully making conversation. "A simple little drive-through in a town this size, it's got a computerized cash register. Guess you never noticed, huh?"

Jesse was too distracted to see where I was heading. "So?"

"So Henry had the store check its computer for the night Carmen was killed, and the times just don't match up. No one bought 'just a six-pack' during the time you say you were there. There was one six-pack sold at 7:05—it's right here on the computer tape—and a bunch were sold after eight o'clock, but nothing that matches up with your story that you ran out to pick up a six-pack right before eight."

And I smiled at him brightly.

Jesse squirmed. "Okay, so I must have been there at seven. So what?"

"But it was eight o'clock before you were seen returning to your apartment. It doesn't take an hour to drive five blocks from the store to your apartment."

"Maybe the computer's wrong," Jesse said defiantly.

"Maybe you're wrong," Henry grumbled.

Jesse shrank a little in his chair.

"You went from the drive-through to the park," I said. "Someone saw you."

Jesse blinked rapidly. "They couldn't have."

"They did," I said firmly.

"No way," Jesse said, and shook his head. "It was too dark."

And then he heard what he'd said and he sagged.

"Oh, man," he muttered.

Henry grinned at me.

I chewed on my lip and tried not to grin back.

"Oh, Jesus," Jesse said, and he held his head. "Oh, fuck."

"Maybe you want to reconsider a lawyer," I suggested.

But Jesse just rocked in his chair. "I didn't do anything, I swear to God. I never even saw her." And he rocked back and forth, holding his head.

Henry raised his eyebrows at me. We were getting too close to screw things up with a civil-rights violation. The kid needed a lawyer.

But he was also ready to talk.

"You Mirandize him?" I asked Henry.

"Trust me," Henry said.

Not in a million years, I thought.

"Jesse, you understand what's happening here?" I asked.

He raised angry red eyes to me. "Christ, I *loved* her. I'd never *kill* her."

"Then you'd better do some fast talking," Henry said, "because we got you in the park when the girl was killed."

"But I never even saw her," Jesse protested again. "I drove to the park—you were right. I was there. We'd had a fight the day before about her wanting to transfer, and she was avoiding me. I knew she'd be running at the park, so I went out there to catch her, try to straighten things out. If she'd just *talked* to me, we coulda worked it out."

I nodded encouragingly. Henry just grunted.

"There were only a couple cars in the parking lot, and no people," Jesse said. "I went down the trail a little ways, but I didn't see her and it was getting cold and it was getting dark, and I just said fuck it. I had studying to do, and if she wanted to run all night in the park, then screw it. I was going home."

"How far down the trail did you go?" I asked.

"Not far. I could still see the parking lot through the trees."

Jesse was not an outdoors type, I thought.

"So I went back to the parking lot and I thought maybe I'd wait in her car."

"You just said you'd decided to go home," Henry pointed out.

"So I changed my mind, okay?" Jesse flared at him. "I was pissed, but I thought maybe I should wait a few more minutes. Only her car was locked."

"You didn't try to break in?" I asked.

"No, I didn't," he said evenly. "I jiggled the handle, and maybe I *looked* mad, but I didn't do anything to her car. I just got in my own car and waited."

"How many cars were in the lot?" I asked.

"Just Carmen's and mine and—" He squinted, thinking back. "Maybe two others. But I think one of 'em might've left while I was waiting."

Nieman, I thought.

"What did the cars look like?" I asked.

"Jesus, how should I know?" Jesse objected. "I mean, if I'd *known* what was gonna happen, I'd've paid attention, but who memorizes a parking lot, for Christ's sake?"

"Did you see anyone?" I asked.

"You think I wouldn't have told you that already?" he demanded, exasperated. "You think if I'd seen anyone who might've hurt Carmen, I wouldn't have said so? Christ, I want the bastard who did this so bad, it's killing me."

And he was looking pretty awful right then. But how much of it was fear of getting caught rather than grief over Carmen?

"How long did you wait in your car?" I asked.

"I dunno. Maybe five minutes."

"Why'd you leave?" Henry asked.

"'Cause it was dark and it was cold and I was tired of waiting," he said sullenly.

"Your girlfriend was out running alone in the dark, and you just left her?" Henry asked.

"Look, she did it all the time, okay? She was a fanatic. Didn't matter if it was dark or wet or cold, if the clock said it was time to run, she ran. Didn't matter what I thought of it."

"And you weren't even a little bit worried?" Henry needled him.

"Jesus," Jesse shot back, "if I'd *known* she was in trouble, I'd have gone looking for her. Maybe I should've gone anyway. But I didn't, and now she's dead, and there's not a goddamned thing you can say to make me feel worse, okay?" And his voice cracked a little in guilt.

"If you didn't do anything at the park, why didn't you tell us you were there?" I asked. "Why did you lie?"

Jesse's face burned and he stared at his hands. "I was scared," he said quietly. "I was scared you'd think it was me."

"You got that right," Henry said.

I flipped back to the top of my notes. "Let's go over this again."

But Jesse shook his head. "Uh-uh," he said. "I want a lawyer."

Henry swore.

I sighed and got the kid a phone book.

$$* \quad * \quad *$$

Two hours later, Jesse was still closeted in the interrogation room, only this time with a lawyer who was hungry for a piece of the Carmen Martinez case, and Henry and I were in the squad room, squabbling over the last stale fries from our dinner. Bradley settled the argument by wandering in and scooping them up for himself.

We filled him in, and he brightened considerably at the prospect of wrapping up the case and getting the mayor off his back. Henry was pretty pleased with himself for pegging Jesse as the killer in the first place, and he was sprawled comfortably in his chair. I was almost ready to buy into it myself, but I was fretting a little over the time frame.

"What's the problem?" Henry scoffed. "He's got a great motive, and he was in the park when the girl got killed."

"He had to move pretty fast," I said. "Between the time Nieman spotted him in the parking lot and the time the pizza delivery boy saw him back at his apartment—that's not much of a window to rape and kill a woman and hide the body."

"It is if you're motivated," Henry said.

"I'm not saying it couldn't have been done," I said. "Nieman didn't exactly check his watch when he saw Jesse. He could've had maybe thirty, forty minutes to find Carmen and do it."

"In the dark," Bradley said.

"Plenty of time," Henry said.

And we stared at the clock and thought about it some.

"He could have done it *before* Nieman saw him," Henry said eventually. "That's why Nieman thought he looked mad. He'd just killed Martinez."

"That's even tougher," I said. "Get down the trail and kill her *after* Nieman sees her, then get back to the parking lot before Nieman does?"

"Nieman probably runs slow," Henry said, "if he's as old as you are."

I curled my lip."

"Cyclist should have passed him," Bradley said uncomfortably, "if he killed her first."

"Probably killed her later," Henry said.

"He could have," I said.

"You bet," Henry said.

And we stared at the clock some more, thinking about how long it takes to kill a woman with your bare hands.

The squad room was filling up some, with the night shift checking in and staring speculatively at Bradley. He wasn't usually in at night, and, though most of the uniforms liked him all right, it made them nervous if the boss was around when he shouldn't be. Even Quinlan, who wanted to make detective so much, he rarely missed a chance to suck up, steered clear of us and hustled on out to his cruiser.

Off to our right, in the radio room, the dispatcher was chattering into his headset. To our left, the door to the interrogation room was still firmly shut. Jesse Conklin was having a very long talk with his lawyer.

"I'm tired of this," Bradley said, pulling himself out of his chair. "Let's squeeze the kid."

"'Bout time," Henry grumbled.

The radio was squawking loudly. I half-registered the code for a coroner's case.

I stood and brushed the crumbs off my jeans. "You gonna handle Jesse?" I asked Bradley.

He grinned. "Might be kinda fun."

"Aw *right*," Henry said, and he rubbed his hands together.

I rolled my eyes. *Boys.*

The radio room was erupting with rapid-fire transmissions. Heads were turning in the squad room.

"Let's do it," Bradley said, and he started for the interrogation room.

I was bringing up the rear, and the duty sergeant managed to catch my eye and wave me over. I reluctantly detoured to his desk.

"We got a situation here," he said, raising his voice above the radio.

I glanced at Bradley and Henry. They were waiting for me impatiently at the door to the interrogation room. "What?"

"Looks like a woman got mugged," the sergeant said.

"Send a cruiser," I said.

"Aw, Jo," he said reproachfully, "I already done that. It's just this woman—she got mugged at the park."

"Don't tell me that," I said, shaking my head.

"She's dead, Jo."

"Well, fuck," I said.

We sent Jesse Conklin home.

Chapter Fifteen

She lay crumpled in the young green growth several yards off the trail, just at the edge of the woods. In a couple more weeks, no one would have been able to spot her from the trail, especially at night. But now the delicate wildflowers were barely thick enough to cover her ankles.

The patrols had hauled in some lights, and her body shimmered in pale white and blue, with a gash of red where her shirt was rolled up around her armpits. Her breasts sagged apart like melted candle wax, and a dark smear of blood stained her thighs.

Her head was twisted as she looked toward the woods, and I couldn't see her face. But the hair was dark and streaked with gray. She was not a young runner like Carmen.

She had been attacked about half a mile from the parking lot, at a point where the trail curved so far from the river, you couldn't even hear it anymore. Carmen had been killed a good two miles farther down the trail, where the trees were thicker and the cover was better. Apparently, the killer hadn't felt as great a need to conceal himself this time.

Bradley and I stood at the edge of the trail, outside the pool of light. Since she was obviously dead, we were leaving her alone until the state techs could get there. The ranger who had found her—Ray—had already done enough damage trampling through the brush.

There was an unclaimed car in the parking lot, and Henry was off running the plates.

And there was a little, curly-haired dog, yapping frantically where the other ranger, Joe, had tied it to a tree.

Bradley hunkered in his topcoat, his head jutting up from the collar like a rough block of granite. His voice was just as friendly. "You got any thoughts on this?"

I shivered in an unlined denim jacket. It must have dropped down to forty degrees, and the wind was slicing raucously down the trail. The dead woman looked very cold.

"It wasn't Jesse Conklin," I said through blue lips.

"Good thing you had him locked up," Bradley said, "or you wouldn't know that much."

"Probably wasn't you or Henry, either," I said.

"Or the mayor," Bradley said.

"Damn," I said, "we're making progress."

There were dark shapes trudging down the trail behind flashlights. One of the shapes separated itself from the others and joined us. It was Joe, and he had a Thermos of coffee.

I would have hugged him if Bradley hadn't been there. Instead, I took the Styrofoam cup he offered and made introductions while Joe poured some coffee for Bradley and himself. He steadfastly stood with his back to the body.

"You know this woman?" Bradley asked, pointing at the body with his cup.

"I've seen her around," Joe said, without turning to look at her. "Don't know her name. She was out here a lot with the dog last summer. Haven't seen her much this spring. Too cold."

Bradley scowled at the dog. It barked right back.

"Dog was how we knew something was wrong," Joe said. "It wandered back to the parking lot, dragging its leash. Coupla joggers caught it and brought it to the office. Ray and I figured either the dog got away from its owner and she was still on the trail looking for it, or she'd fallen and *couldn't* go looking for it, you know?"

Bradley nodded over his coffee. I cupped mine to my face and hoarded its warmth.

"It happens a coupla times a year," Joe said. "Owner slips and falls and bam—the dog's gone." He looked at me speculatively. "You ought to keep that in mind."

"I don't hike in the dark," I said primly.

"Neither did she," Joe said. "It wasn't dark yet when they found the dog. Wasn't even that cold. She'd have had plenty of time to get back to the parking lot if she'd been all right."

"So you went looking for her?" Bradley asked.

"Me and Ray did. All the way down the trail. That's five miles, and we didn't see a sign of her. By then, it *was* dark, so we radioed the rescue squad to get some extra guys out here. We have a rescue plan to follow when a hiker's missing. It's not like there's a bunch of amateurs tearing up the park. There were half a dozen other guys out here looking, all trained for this kind of thing. Only it was dark."

Bradley looked over Joe's shoulder at the body. "She's not that far off the trail."

"Well, that's not quite how Ray found her," Joe said. "She was shoved in under the bushes more, but Ray pulled her out some, to see if she was alive."

"Christ," Bradley muttered.

"He didn't know any better," Joe said. "And if she *had* been alive—well, she wouldn't even be here now, would she? She'd be at the hospital, and your crime scene would still be messed up."

Bradley grumbled about disturbing the evidence. I thought it was rather rude, considering Joe had brought us coffee.

"How *did* Ray find her?" I asked, just to shut Bradley up.

"He let the dog find her," Joe said. "We'd locked it in the office at first, 'cause it's kind of an annoying mutt. Never figured it as a tracker. But when the other guys came up empty, Ray thought, what the hell, he'd get the dog. And the little guy led him right down here. Bit Ray in the ankle, too, when he started tugging at the body."

The dog was running around in little circles, growling and snapping at its tail. It was fifteen pounds of furious fluff.

"Psychotic dog," Bradley said.

"I wonder if he bit the killer," I said.

Both men looked at me as though I'd spoken in tongues. But then Joe nodded. "I bet he did."

Bradley grudgingly told me to check the hospital and the clinics for dog bites.

"Anything else happen today?" Bradley asked Joe. "Any complaints, any trouble?"

Joe shook his head. "Not since I came on duty. We had a pretty good crowd here today. Wouldn't know it now, but it was nice and warm this afternoon. Lots of cyclists. Lots of joggers."

"And dogs," I said.

"Bad as the deer," Joe said. "Only the deer keep their mess in the woods." And he looked pointedly at me again.

I felt myself blushing. Barney was not a fastidious dog.

The dead woman's dog had collapsed in a shaggy little heap under the tree, its tongue hanging out as it panted.

"Too bad dogs can't talk," Joe said. "He knows who did it."

Bradley crumpled his empty cup and shoved it into his coat pocket. "Maybe your mutt ought to visit with this mutt," he said to me. "See if he can get the dog to talk."

"Hey, now, that's productive," I said.

"'Bout as productive as everything else we've tried," Bradley said, and he turned morosely back toward the parking lot.

And I was so strung out, I looked at the dog and wondered whether Bradley might have something there.

* * *

An hour later, I was sitting in a tidy little living room, tearing John DeMarco's life apart.

Henry had traced the license plates to John and Judy DeMarco, who lived in a quiet neighborhood on the west side of town, away from the university and only a ten-minute drive from the park. He was an ad salesman for the local newspaper; she was a secretary at the junior high school. They had two boys, one in college and the other in the Army. The house was nearly paid for, the kids had pretty much moved out. They were planning a trip to Europe in the summer. And now Judy was dead.

"I mean, Jesus," her husband said, running his hands through his hair, "there's got to be a mistake."

He was sitting on the edge of an overstuffed armchair, and a neighbor woman was standing behind him, ineffectually patting his shoulder. Other neighbors were clattering around the kitchen, doing all those things neighbors do when there's a crisis.

Henry and I sat on the couch across from DeMarco, feeling pretty much like shit.

It was past midnight, but, of course, we hadn't gotten him out of bed. When it had gotten dark and Judy hadn't come home, he'd gone out looking for her. He'd driven around town, but he hadn't gone to the park, because he'd told his wife not to walk the dog there after Carmen was killed. It never occurred to him that she wouldn't listen to him.

When he didn't spot her in town, he came home and started phoning around. The neighbor woman came over because she and Judy were best friends, and a couple of other neighbors started driving around looking for her, too. They thought that maybe her car broke down, or maybe she stopped back at the school or ran into friends. They were only just starting to think that John might want to call the police when Henry and I pulled into the driveway.

The house was a neat, carefully maintained Cape Cod. The kids were grown, and the battered furniture of childhood had been replaced with good pieces, tastefully chosen and tastefully arranged. Except for stray wisps of dog hair and an unfortunate scratch or two on the woodwork, the housekeeping put me to shame. Even the neighbors hadn't made much of a mess.

John DeMarco was a wreck. He was about fifty, soft in the gut, losing his hair, but the face might have been attractive if it hadn't been so ravaged. It could have been an act, but he was doing a damned good job of convincing me that I'd just given him the worst news of his life.

"She can't be dead," he kept saying to me, his eyes wide and red. "You've got it wrong."

And I kept pounding him over the head with it: Judy is dead. Judy is dead.

She was forty-six years old. She was in the choir at church. The school board had just named her secretary of the year; the newspaper had run her picture. John dug a copy of it out of his wallet for me, and I looked at a nice woman with a round, pleasant face and no-nonsense glasses, framed by short hair styled appropriately for a school secretary. Her smile for the camera had been slightly nervous, as though she was much more comfortable dealing with twelve-year-old kids.

She certainly didn't look like someone who deserved to have her neck broken in a quiet corner of the park.

"When did you see her last, Mr. DeMarco?" I asked as I handed back the clipping.

His hands shook as he folded it and put it back in his wallet. "We ate dinner and she was washing the dishes. I said I was running out to the hardware store. We got a leak in the washer. I was gonna fix it. She said she was gonna finish up the dishes and walk the dog. It mighta been six-fifteen, six-thirty."

"She was still here when you left?" I asked.

"Right there at the sink," he said, pointing to the kitchen. "She said to take my time. She was gonna walk the dog." He looked at me miserably. "That was the last thing she said to me."

Christ almighty, I thought. What was the last thing I'd said to Dave that morning? Something like pick up your own damned socks.

"Did she normally walk the dog in the evening?" I asked.

"If she didn't have choir practice. It was her exercise, she said. Kept her from getting fat." He looked guiltily at his neighbor. "I never told her she was fat. It was all in her head."

"Of course, John," the neighbor said, and squeezed his shoulder. She was pretty teary-eyed herself and poked at her nose with a Kleenex whenever he wasn't looking.

"Did she normally walk in the park?" I asked.

DeMarco's eyes flashed angrily at me. "No, goddamn it, no. I told her, stay away from the park. I didn't want her anywhere near the park after that girl got killed."

"But she went there tonight," I said.

"I told her not to," he said, his voice rising. "I *told* her."

"She went because of the dog," the neighbor said.

DeMarco looked up at her incredulously. "What the hell for—the dog? The dog didn't tell her what to do."

The neighbor nervously stepped back from him. "You know how he is, John. He snaps at people. Judy took him to the river so she could keep him away from kids."

"He can't hurt anybody," DeMarco protested. "He's a runt."

The neighbor looked uncomfortably at me. "He bites," she said. "Judy liked to go to the park so he wouldn't bite people."

"For God's sake," DeMarco said.

"It's what she *did*," the neighbor said defensively.

"Jesus Christ," DeMarco said. And if the dog had been in the room, he might have wrung its neck.

"Did your wife say if anyone was bothering her?" I asked. "Hanging around the house or following her when she was out with the dog?"

"How would I know?" he asked bitterly. "I tell her not to go to the park, she goes to the park. How the fuck should I know?"

The neighbor cringed and moved back another step.

Henry had been slumped on the couch, grumpily listening to us and trying not to yawn. But he perked up when DeMarco lost his manners.

"You got a receipt from the hardware store, Mr. DeMarco?" Henry asked.

DeMarco's eyes darted to Henry. "What the hell for?"

"Just to prove you were there," Henry said equably.

"Whaddya mean, prove? What the hell are you trying to say?"

Henry shrugged. "Just covering all the bases."

DeMarco looked at me. "What's he mean?"

"He means," I said carefully, "can you prove you weren't at the park when your wife was killed?"

"You son of a bitch," DeMarco growled, and he lunged from his chair. I wasn't sure whether he meant to come at me or Henry, but it didn't really matter, because the neighbor woman grabbed his arm, and before he could throw her off, other neighbors ran in from the kitchen and backed him up against the wall. DeMarco was howling and swinging his arms, but he wasn't in any kind of shape to do serious damage. The men shielded him from us as he flailed frantically, and the neighbor woman disentangled herself from the mess and suggested breathlessly that we ought to leave.

Henry lit up as soon as we stepped outside. He ground the match out on the concrete stoop and watched the first lungful of smoke drift out into the night. "Stirred things up some, huh?"

"Not sure what good it did," I groused. It wasn't as cold and windy in town as it had been out in the woods, but I still shivered. If Henry hadn't been smoking, I'd have hustled myself into the car.

"We ought to find out what her old man was up to tonight," Henry said as he studied the cigarette in his fingers. "Make sure he didn't do it."

"You don't buy his story?" I asked. Henry never believed husbands. I never believed wives.

Henry took another drag on his cigarette. It visibly relaxed him. "Let's just say he coulda been out killing his wife instead of just looking for her."

"And he just happened to break her neck, the same way someone broke Carmen's."

Henry shrugged. "Why not? It isn't any secret how Martinez got killed."

I frowned at my shoes. DeMarco hadn't impressed me as a man devious enough to copy another killer or slick enough to pretend such shock when we told him his wife was dead. But what did I really know about him?

Henry flicked an ash into a freshly mulched flowerbed. "It'd take balls," he admitted. "Someone could have seen him at the park."

"I suppose we could ask around," I conceded. It was the right thing to do. I just wasn't too thrilled by the extra work.

The door rattled behind us, and the neighbor woman nervously stepped outside. She was holding a small brown paper bag in her hand. She looked at Henry, but something in the way he looked back intimidated her. She turned to me and offered the bag.

"Maybe this will help," she said, and she slipped back into the warm living room.

The bag was empty except for a cash register tape from the hardware store. It was stamped with that day's date.

"DeMarco went to the store, like he said."

Henry took one last puff on his cigarette and mashed it with his foot. "Doesn't prove anything. He still had time to kill his wife."

"You don't want to let him off the hook," I said.

"And you want to think there's a serial killer out there," he countered.

"I want it to be simple," I said wearily. "It's simpler to chase after one bastard."

Henry grinned as he steered me off the stoop. "Haven't you figured it out yet, Jo?" he said. "We're all bastards."

Chapter Sixteen

Gene Emery, the publisher of the local newspaper, rousted me out of bed the next morning to blister my ears for harassing his ad salesman. Gene was usually a pretty sensible guy, even though ownership of the paper sometimes made him think he owned the town, too. When he wanted something, he usually squeezed Bradley. He rarely slipped down the food chain to my level. But he must have missed Bradley that morning, so he gnawed on me instead.

It was barely light out and I was groggy. I'd had only a couple hours' sleep and didn't appreciate waking up to Gene's bitching about our insensitive treatment of the bereaved. I probably snarled more than I should have, and Gene snarled right back. We hung up on each other.

But I was too irritated to go back to sleep. I tossed around, but it was disturbing Dave. If I'd been in a more congenial mood, I might have tried to toss him around with me. Instead, I groped around for some clothes and stumbled down the hall to the bathroom.

Barney charged after me, tail wagging and ears twitching. He assumed I existed solely to take him for walks.

I squinted at him through bleary eyes and thought, why not?

Adam's butt was sticking out of the refrigerator as I passed through the kitchen to pick up Barney's leash. "You're up?" Adam croaked, his head still buried in the juice bottles.

"*Your* dog needs a walk," I said as I lifted a jacket off the coat rack.

Adam didn't believe in ownership. So he let that crack slide right off his back. But he disentangled himself from the leftovers and smiled at me. "You want company?"

"You aren't going back to bed?" I asked as I slipped on my jacket.

His smile broadened. "Haven't been there yet."

I looked at his rumpled shirt and jeans, which I was sure he'd been wearing yesterday, and harrumphed—just like Mother. He'd been to bed, all right. He just hadn't been in *his* bed.

But he was wired, and it was a foggy dawn, so I let him tag along. It wouldn't hurt to have company.

It was chilly and gray, and I needed the headlights as we drove through town. Barney rode with his nose plastered to the back window. Adam slumped in the front seat and appeared to doze as I told him about the late Judy DeMarco. It was highly unethical to tell an outsider about working cases, but Adam had learned the rules of the house quickly. He didn't tell Dave's students what was going to be on their tests and he didn't tell his buddies whom I was busting next. In exchange, he got free room and board. So far, he hadn't screwed up.

I pulled into the empty parking lot next to the trailhead and killed the engine. The trees rose in black spires out of the fog, and the trail disappeared in a swirl of white. The park looked no friendlier now than it had at midnight. I had been nuts to think of coming out here alone.

Barney whined to get out. Adam roused himself and opened the door. Barney climbed over him and disappeared into the woods with a joyful yelp.

Adam looked at the leash lying on the console between us and grinned sheepishly. "Oops," he said.

"He mates with a pedigreed poodle, you get to explain it to Mother," I said, and hauled my butt out of the car.

The mist wrapped itself around me, slipping under my collar and up the sleeves of my jacket. I stuffed my hands into my pockets and started down the trail. Adam quickly caught up with me, and we walked side by side, silently watching for tree roots that might leap out and grab our ankles. The fog deadened sound so we could barely hear the river to our left. I assumed the thrashing to our right was Barney, introducing himself to a chipmunk.

Or maybe a wild boar.

We wandered along in a cushion of white, concentrating so thoroughly on our footing that we came up with no warning on the spot where Judy DeMarco had died. I knew the yellow crime scene tape would be there, but it still startled me when it popped up out of the fog at the side of the path.

Adam sucked in his breath. "That's it, huh?" he said.

I shivered and nodded. "That's it."

Except for the tape, it really was an unremarkable sight. The technicians had gone during the night, and all that was left was a wide patch of brush trampled down into damp earth. Judy DeMarco had bled very little, so there were no pools of blood to turn the stomach and no spare body parts left behind to rot. The techs had carted away their evidence, and now there were only shredded leaves and a footprint or two where DeMarco's body had lain just a few hours before.

Yet the knowledge of death made the spot gruesome. Adam wrinkled his nose, almost as though he could smell her dying.

"He broke her neck?" Adam asked.

"Just like Martinez," I said. "Grabbed her from behind and snapped it."

"Strong guy," Adam said.

"Or very excited," I said.

And we stared at the spot in silence. I was wondering what kind of man could kill a woman like that, then have sex with her. Adam was thinking more practical thoughts.

"He must have come down the trail the same way we did," Adam said.

I looked at him quizzically. "Why do you say that?"

"Look at the trail," Adam said.

The path curved slightly just a few yards behind us and meandered back into the trees toward the trailhead. Ahead of us, the path was more or less straight for about twenty yards before it veered toward the river. There was good visibility ahead of us, if you discounted the fog. There was very little behind us.

"The guy comes around the bend and grabs her before she has a chance to see him. Wham, it's over," Adam said. "He comes the other way, she's got too much time to see him and maybe run."

"I don't think she ran," I said.

"So he must have followed her from the parking lot instead of coming the other way."

I nodded thoughtfully. Not that it made much difference which direction he'd come from. It didn't help identify the guy. But I was pleasantly surprised that Adam was sorting it out so logically.

Dave would have been appalled.

"Even if you're right," I said, "I still can't believe she didn't hear *something*. Or that the dog didn't react. She *should* have had enough warning to at least yell."

"Naw," Adam said, "not if he was fast."

I shook my head. "I can't picture it. She should have struggled."

"Would you?" Adam asked.

"Damn right," I said stoutly.

"Uh-huh," Adam said, and he dug into the cinder path with his toe.

Barney trotted out onto the trail below us and paused to gnaw at something on his leg. I had the leash and decided to mosey on down toward him and see if maybe I could trick him back onto the chain.

And while I moseyed, I tried to picture how it could have happened to Judy DeMarco. The fog surely reduced my visibility as much as the twilight had dimmed the path for her. The woods must have been just as quiet then as now. Ahead of me, the trail was empty except for Barney chewing on himself. Judy DeMarco could have been walking just like this, looking absently at the wild things sprouting along the path, stopping now and then to listen to the squirrels chattering in the trees, or the geese honking on the river. Maybe she even talked to the dog, the way I sometimes caught myself talking to Barney, as though he could understand.

I shook my head again in frustration. Damn it, the woman had been only a couple of years older than I. She hadn't been carrying that many extra pounds. She should have been able to run.

Barney raised his head and tilted it, his eyes focused just beyond me.

I heard a whisper of rubber sole crunching cinder. I stopped and felt him exhale on the back of my neck.

His arm whipped around me and locked around my throat. I tried to jerk away, but his other arm snaked around my chest and yanked me back against his body. I gagged and clawed at the arms squeezing the breath out of me.

"See," Adam whispered in my ear, "it's a snap."

Chapter Seventeen

I charred Adam's ears all the way back to the car. He was chuckling because he'd proved his point—if you weren't expecting trouble, *anyone* could be taken out, even a cop. I was furious that I'd let him catch me off guard, and I was furious over the icy fear that had immobilized me just long enough for the boy to crush his arm across my throat. And even though I had realized almost immediately that it was only Adam, the fear was still churning in my gut long after he let me go, and that infuriated me even more. God damn it, I was a *cop.* Young men weren't *supposed* to take me down.

Adam was contrite by the time we got home, and he was apologizing profusely as we stomped through the back door. Dave raised an eyebrow over his coffee cup, but we ignored him. Dave wisely chose to stay out of it, assuming it was a quasi-stepmother thing. It was better if he didn't know I had taken his son out to play cop.

It was better if Bradley didn't know, either, but I was still so angry over my own momentary vulnerability that I made a pretty loud case that afternoon for shutting down the park. I was in his office and the door was closed, but I could see Herchek watching us curiously through the window as I paced in front of Bradley's desk, and I imagined other heads were turned our way, too. Dave would have said I was shrill. I thought I was just forceful. Bradley simply listened with the bemused look men get when a normally sane woman raises her voice, and when I was spent, he patted my shoulder and said, "Okay, Jo, I'll see what I can do." And he hastily shoved me out of his office before I could get revved up again.

People in the squad room got real busy as I marched to my desk, and they stayed pretty much out of my way the rest of the afternoon. I didn't see *why.* It was a police station, for God's sake. Why shouldn't I shout?

So I huffed and puffed around the coffee pot and the locker room and my desk, and when I'd done a thorough job of chasing everyone out of my way, I planted myself in front of my PC and pounded on the keyboard. No one else felt like talking to me, but the computer had no choice. I punched the right buttons, and it spewed out the DeMarco file, without making one snide remark about the time of the month.

Ellen had spent the day canvassing Judy DeMarco's neighborhood, and had entered screen after screen of precise notes from her interviews. Her prose wasn't gripping, but the woman was thorough. It took the better part of an hour to scroll through it all, but by the end, I grudgingly admitted to myself that Ellen had pieced together a damned good profile of the victim.

And Judy DeMarco wasn't anything at all like Carmen Martinez.

Carmen had been young and full of herself. Judy had been twice her age and, by everyone's account, was a woman who gave naturally and seemed to expect nothing in return. She was the mom who attracted all the other kids in the neighborhood, patched up their scrapes and bumps, mediated their squabbles, swatted whoever acted up and hugged them all when they cried. As her own boys grew up, she had transferred her mothering to the kids at school. Children gravitated to her. Mrs. DeMarco always had time to listen.

Other mothers spoke of her in some awe, some with a hint of resentment. They weren't quite sure how Judy related to the adolescent monsters their children had become, but the smart ones were grateful.

The men in the neighborhood were more vague. She was a nice lady, they said. She was helpful. She was friendly. Ellen surprised me by asking the men whether they were attracted to Judy DeMarco. Ellen's mind didn't usually run in sexual channels. But it was a smart question. And she got dumb looks in response. Judy DeMarco didn't radiate sexual energy. She was a *mother*.

The men were a little more specific about her husband. He was a salesman, more adept with his speech than with his hands. He was a sociable guy, good for a beer, pleasant company at a game, but a spectator, not a player. He liked to look at the ladies, but, hell, didn't any normal guy? There had been talk years ago that John DeMarco fooled around, but it couldn't have been serious. He was over fifty now and pretty much settled down. Neighbors basically agreed, Judy's death was tearing him apart.

Did the DeMarcos get along? The neighbors thought so. Sure, they had their spats. John always had been a workaholic, and Judy was left to raise the kids, but it must have suited them, because after so many years, they were still together, weren't they? These days, that meant something. And as proof, they rattled off their own divorces.

Had anyone been bothering Judy?

The men didn't have the foggiest idea. The women talked uneasily of Carmen. Well, of course, her death had bothered them, and it had bothered Judy, too. But not so much that they were fixated on it. After all, Carmen had been a student, a young girl who maybe invited that kind of trouble. Certainly, the sort of man who would attack Carmen wouldn't be attracted to a woman like **them.**

So Judy had shrugged off her husband's warnings and had taken the dog to the park.

And had died for it.

I thought of Adam with his arm wrapped around my neck, and shook my head. Judy DeMarco had been a short-sighted fool.

*　　*　　*

Mulhaney was watching a baseball game on the tube when I stopped at the hospital on my dinner break. He guzzled the Coke I brought him, but politely declined the french fries. He'd been throwing up all day.

He was very pale, and his face and hands were puffy. He said he was losing his hair. I couldn't see much difference. He was propped in his own bed instead of watching the game in the lounge, where other patients were taking a livelier interest in the game. But his voice was strong, and his eyes were sharp.

"They're sending me home tomorrow," he said.

"Safer for the nurses," I said as I hauled a chair to the side of the bed so I could watch TV, too.

"They have good hands," Mulhaney admitted.

"And pure hearts," I said.

Mulhaney belched softly into his fist. I wasn't sure whether that was an editorial comment or not.

We watched half an inning in silence while the good guys struck out, but when the bad guys came up to bat, Mulhaney's eyes darted from the screen to me and he asked about Judy DeMarco.

I had lived with Dave long enough to learn how to pace my narrative around the pitches. Mulhaney didn't miss anything important—not in the game or in the DeMarco case.

When a commercial blared onto the tube, Mulhaney hitched himself up onto his pillows and sucked on the Coke. "Sounds like something Ernie Nash'd do," Mulhaney said, then wiped his mouth with the back of his hand. "Only Ernie's dead."

I raised an eyebrow.

"You remember Ernie," Mulhaney said.

I chewed on a fry and admitted I didn't have a clue.

"He hung around the Laundromat," Mulhaney said. "You gotta remember him."

"Must not have been my case," I said diplomatically.

"Couldn't have been more than fifteen years ago."

I just gave Mulhaney a look.

He grinned sheepishly. "Maybe before your time."

I huffed and rearranged my skirt. Mulhaney noticed it.

"Ernie was a young guy, not built too bad, not too bad looking, either, but he was twisted—you know, up here," Mulhaney said, and tapped his head.

"You mean retarded?" I asked.

"Naw, he was a smart guy. But he was a sick bastard—mean. First time I took him in, he was barely more'n a kid. Beat the shit out of a neighbor boy. Stomped him with his boots."

"Effective," I said.

"With the right boots," Mulhaney agreed. "Ernie got off, though—first offense. But he was always gettin' in trouble after that. Hurtin' people, mostly."

"Why didn't we lock him up?"

Mulhaney grunted. "He was a juvenile. Court kept tryin' to rehabilitate him. Never did any good. Turned eighteen, he was still a mean bastard, only by then, folks were leery of pressin' charges. Too scared."

"So he kept on doing it," I said.

"Yep," Mulhaney said.

We watched another half inning in silence, and when the commercials blared back on, Mulhaney picked up the story as though he had never stopped. "Ernie started attackin' women at the Laundromat—usually picked students who were dumb enough to go there alone at night. At first, he just beat 'em up, then he got into rape."

"Jesus," I shuddered. "Why didn't we stop him?"

"Gotta have proof, don't you?" Mulhaney asked reasonably. "I thought it was him early on—it just smelled like something Ernie would do—but there was nothing to nail him with. He was a sneaky son of a bitch. He always grabbed the women from behind, and he usually knocked 'em out before they could see anything. He kinda liked his women unconscious so they couldn't object to what he was doin'."

"Dead women don't object too much, either," I said to the TV screen.

"Yep," Mulhaney said, "though I never did understand the attraction. Touchin' a corpse, I mean."

I unconsciously patted his hand, which was warm and dry and very much alive, despite the disease that was eating at him. His fingers closed around mine.

"But you did get him," I said.

"Yep, we did, but not before he bashed a girl in the head so hard, he turned her into a vegetable." Mulhaney sighed and reluctantly withdrew his hand. He needed both hands to hold the Coke.

"He got careless. Someone saw him tryin' to dump this girl off the road, and we got a good ID. The judge was pretty sick of Ernie by then, and he piled on the sentences so thick, Ernie was gonna be an old man before he got back on the street. Turned out, he never got out anyway. Someone knifed him a coupla years after he got sent up."

"And the girl?" I asked. "She's still a vegetable?"

Mulhaney shook his head sadly. "She died, too, after a few years. Held on long enough to bankrupt her folks with the bills, then she just slipped away. You know how they do."

I nodded. Even when you nail the bastard, you don't always get a happy ending.

The good guys bobbled a double into a run for the bad guys, and Mulhaney groaned painfully. "What made you think of Ernie?" I asked, more to take his mind off the pain than anything else.

"Two things," Mulhaney said as he shifted uncomfortably around the bed. "Your guy's grabbin' women from behind, just like Ernie did. The MO's a little different. Ernie knocked them out; your guy's breaking their necks. But the effect's the same—the victims are unresponsive."

"Passive," I said.

"Dead passive," Mulhaney agreed.

"And the other thing?"

Mulhaney's eyes hardened, and you could almost see the cop he had been long before I had joined the force. "Ernie Nash was a cold-hearted son of a bitch. And so's this guy doin' your ladies. They got the same kind of twisted psyche. They don't see these women as people. They aren't even victims. They're just things that animals like Ernie use up and throw away. Ernie couldn't feel anything for any other human being. Their suffering meant nothing to him."

I stared back at the TV. The good guys got lucky and ended the inning with a double play. I stood for the seventh inning stretch.

"He's gonna do it again, isn't he?" I said.

Mulhaney looked at me sadly. "As sure as I'm dyin'."

Chapter Eighteen

Judy DeMarco's underwear was missing.

I didn't know how we overlooked it. I mean, even if we hadn't all been gawking at the body, shaking our heads over the abused corpse, it was right there in the inventory from the autopsy and in the crime lab report. The body had been delivered to the morgue with one red T-shirt, a bra, denim shorts, a pair of sweat socks and one worn pair of tennis shoes. No underpants.

The FBI agent noticed it first thing.

He wandered back to town the next afternoon because Carmen Martinez's father was still complaining bitterly of terrorist plots and a racist police department. Judy DeMarco's death kind of shot the terrorist theory full of holes, because there was no reason on earth for terrorists to target an Olympic-caliber runner *and* a junior high school secretary from the Midwest. But the DeMarco murder did raise the possibility of a serial killer, and that kind of thing made the FBI nervous. So the agent dropped by Bradley's office to "consult," and he politely pointed out that no one could account for DeMarco's underwear.

Bradley was acutely embarrassed. After all, he'd been at the crime scene, too, and hadn't noticed the lack of panties. So he compensated by bellowing at me to haul that pervert James Battaglia in right *now*.

"Shouldn't Ellen bring him in?" I suggested. "She knows him."

"Ellen," Bradley snarled, "is home with a sick baby. Bring him in."

I decided not to argue. But I took Henry with me, just in case Battaglia got any ideas about *my* underwear.

We found him at home, still in his restaurant uniform, and he was pretty scared to see cops at his door again. But he didn't fight the trip to the station. Maybe if his mother had been home, we would have had a problem, but Battaglia didn't seem capable of saying no to the cops. He struck me as a guy with a permanently guilty conscience. I just wasn't sure what he was guilty *of*.

He was about twenty-five and just as big as Henry, but he wasn't in nearly as good a shape. Henry's bulk was in his shoulders and chest; Battaglia's had settled in his stomach and butt. Henry packed him into the back seat, then grinned at me over the roof of the car. "Scary dude, Jo."

I made a face and slid into the front seat. So Battaglia didn't look scary. He still liked other people's underwear.

We set him up in the interrogation room, and just to be friendly, bought him a Coke. He guzzled it and watched us warily. The FBI agent—his name was Beck—strolled in and settled himself at the table for some friendly observation. Since he had pointed out the missing underwear, I didn't think I could ask him to leave.

Henry leaned back against the door and folded his arms. He was content to let Beck and me wrestle over Battaglia. Frankly, I wasn't in the mood. Battaglia was Ellen's find, not mine.

But everyone was watching me like it was my show, so I sat across from Battaglia and asked him what he was doing while Judy DeMarco was getting killed.

Battaglia's eyes shifted nervously from Beck to me. "I didn't do anything to that lady. No way. Not me." And he sucked hard on the Coke.

"Where were you?" I asked.

He belched and wiped his mouth with his hand. It was dimpled with grease burns from the grill. "What time?" he asked.

I smiled pleasantly. "Say, six o'clock? Seven?"

"Well, which?" he asked peevishly. "'Cuz maybe I was doing one thing at six and something else at seven."

Henry chuckled.

Beck stared in boredom at the wall.

My pleasant smile frosted over. "Six," I said evenly.

Battaglia considered his Coke. "Probably watchin' TV at home."

"And at seven?" I asked.

Battaglia shrugged. "Still watchin' TV."

Henry chortled.

The corner of Beck's mouth twitched.

I silently damned Ellen and her sick baby.

"Can you prove you were watching TV?" I demanded.

Battaglia smiled and rattled off the plots of three sitcoms. Big deal. They were all reruns in syndication.

He started to quote some dialogue—in simpering falsetto—but I cut him short. "Was anyone with you?" I asked.

"Well, sure," he said, like I was some kind of dope. "My mom."

Of course, I thought. He was always with his mom.

"She comes home from work and makes dinner, and we eat in front of the TV 'cuz she says why mess up the dining room for just the two of us?" Battaglia looked earnestly at Beck. "You don't miss nothin' if you eat in front of the TV."

Beck grunted. He was having trouble staying awake.

"You can miss the funniest parts if you eat in the dining room," Battaglia said. "'Course, you can always turn up the TV, but my mom doesn't like it too loud. She doesn't want to disturb the neighbors. She's afraid they'll call the cops."

Then he shrugged. "'Course, the cops always come around anyway."

"Why is that?" I asked.

"'Cuz of me, I guess, and my problem." He sounded resigned to the fact that his penchant for underwear made him a handy suspect for any kind of sex crime.

"Do you normally spend your evenings watching TV?" I asked.

Henry yawned widely.

Beck nearly snored.

But Battaglia was happy to talk about himself. "If I'm not workin' nights. Sometimes I gotta work nights 'cuz people get sick and the boss needs me to help out, but mostly I work days 'cuz I got seniority. So, yeah, I watch TV with my mom 'cuz she likes the company. And it makes her feel safer if I'm at home."

Where she could keep an eye on him, I thought.

"'Course," Battaglia said, warming up to the conversation, "two nights a week, I go to school. Boss says I gotta work on my math if I want to get promoted." He grinned. "I could be manager someday."

Henry gagged.

Beck chose not to notice.

"But you weren't in class when Mrs. DeMarco was attacked," I said.

"Nope," Battaglia said firmly. "I was watching TV. Ask my mom."

I was beginning to see why he frustrated Ellen. Every answer seemed to wind up with his mom.

Beck finally roused himself. "Did you know Mrs. DeMarco?"

Battaglia almost jumped. I'd been lobbing pretty easy questions at him. Maybe he thought he could handle me without Mom's assistance. But Beck was an unknown. Battaglia looked at Beck and his eyelids twitched. "Maybe I did. I dunno."

"Yes or no," Beck said dispassionately.

"We get a lot of customers," Battaglia protested. "I don't know their names."

"But you know their faces?" Beck asked.

"Well—" Battaglia swallowed hard. "Yeah, sometimes, if they come regular like. Some folks come same time every day, order the same thing, so, yeah, you recognize 'em. Doesn't mean you *know* them."

Beck looked at me. "You got a picture?"

I pawed through the file, bypassing the autopsy photos, and came up with the same snapshot that had been used in the newspaper. Beck flipped it over to Battaglia. "Know her?"

Battaglia looked at the picture and promptly recited, "Double cheeseburger, hold the onions, small fries and a medium vanilla shake."

I tried not to gape.

Henry grunted in approval of Beck's style.

Battaglia heard his own words echoing in the room, and he seemed to shrink into his chair.

"So you *did* know her," Beck said.

"I said I might," Battaglia said feebly.

"How *well* did you know her?" Beck pressed.

"I didn't do nothing to her," Battaglia protested. "She comes in a coupla times a week for lunch. Always gets the same thing. I just take her order. That's all." And he looked at me in desperation. "Honest, she's just a customer."

"And now she's dead," I said.

Battaglia pushed himself back from the table. "Not my fault. Ask my mom."

"Your mom's not here," Henry said.

Battaglia's eyes shifted to Henry. "You got no reason to hassle me for this. Lots of people musta known her. Just 'cuz I got a problem, you got no business comin' after me."

"Let's talk about your problem," Beck said.

Battaglia's head swiveled back to the table. "What about it?" he asked warily.

"You steal underwear," Beck said.

"I never hurt nobody," Battaglia objected. "Check my file. Nobody hurt. *Never.*"

"But you steal underwear," Beck persisted.

Battaglia stared at Beck, and I could smell the sweat breaking out under his shirt. He was getting scared, and I wondered suddenly whether we had blown it by taking his mother's word for it that he had been with her when Carmen Martinez was killed. If Ellen had pushed for a search warrant, would we have found Carmen's hot pink shorts stuffed under his mattress? Could we have cornered him before Judy DeMarco died?

My stomach was suddenly in knots.

But then, damn it, James Battaglia smiled. "Is *that* all? You think someone took that lady's panties?"

Beck nodded solemnly.

Battaglia threw back his head and laughed. It was a big, ugly laugh that wobbled the gut beneath his stained uniform, a laugh as twisted as his perversions. Even Henry looked at him as though something slimy had just slithered into the room.

"You think that's funny?" Beck asked sternly.

"Oh, man," Battaglia wheezed, "that's too much. You got me in here 'cuz you think I took her panties?" And he laughed some more and wiped his eyes.

"This is a serious charge, Mr. Battaglia," Beck said.

"Yeah, right," Battaglia chuckled. "Serious charge, theft of underwear. Only your *lady* never wore none to steal."

I thought Beck's jaw dropped. I know Henry and I just stared.

Battaglia grinned back at us, enjoying himself. "Take my word for it. I *notice* them things. Miz DeMarco didn't wear underpants."

I recovered a little faster than the men did—maybe because I wasn't trying to picture a forty-six-year-old school secretary sans underwear. "You have—um—proof of that?" I managed.

Battaglia spread his hands. "No panty lines. What can I say?"

Beck looked at me. "You better check it out."

So I did.

*　　*　　*

John DeMarco was drunk. He'd just bought a five-thousand-dollar casket for his wife and paid fifty bucks to have her dog put to sleep. He was hunched over his kitchen table with a beer can in one hand and a lot of empties stacked around him. The neighbor women tiptoed nervously through the kitchen, wishing his boys would get home and take charge. John DeMarco was a nasty drunk.

I'm not intimidated by drunks. And I didn't bat an eye when he threw his beer at me. But I didn't get anything coherent out of him, either, least of all his wife's clothing preferences. I tried to broach the subject delicately, but he was too drunk to get my drift. So then I put it in simple, one-syllable words, and he got it, all right. He told me to go fuck myself.

So I left him and was standing in the driveway, wondering whether I could really ask the DeMarco boys about their dead mother's underwear habits, when one of the neighbor women—the one who had given me the shopping bag the night DeMarco died—slipped out the door after me.

She was embarrassed—she hated to talk about Judy's personal hygiene—but she'd heard my questions and, well, **someone** ought to set the record straight. Judy wasn't a loose woman, the neighbor assured me, and she certainly wasn't trying to tease other men. She was just pleasing her husband, who **detested** panty lines. So Judy never wore panties.

"Never?" I asked in disbelief.

"Not even after she put on a little weight," the neighbor said. "John liked it that way."

"Even in jeans?" I asked.

The neighbor nodded solemnly.

I squirmed. "Oh, yuck," I said.

"She loved him," the neighbor said.

Love hurt.

Chapter Nineteen

We spent the next week methodically tracking down everyone we had questioned in the Martinez case, looking for a connection to Judy DeMarco. Despite the brilliant spreadsheet Berger created, we got nowhere. The track coach, Pat August, went to DeMarco's church. One of the men on the university track team had a little brother who attended the school where DeMarco worked. And the park rangers, of course, recognized both women. But outside of that, nothing but coincidence tied Martinez to DeMarco. They both happened to use the park trail, and they both died there.

We spent a good amount of time tracking DeMarco's acquaintances and neighbors, and struck out there, too. The woman had been a saint. No one disliked her. Carmen, at least, had been disagreeable enough to make a few enemies in her life, but Judy DeMarco apparently hadn't offended a single soul in forty-six years. It made me nuts.

Berger amused himself by casting a wider and wider computer net for sex perverts. He accidentally cleared a child abuse case that way, and the victim's mother was tearfully grateful, but none of the files he pulled got us any closer to the killer. There were some really sick people buried in the records, and a few were perfectly capable of snapping someone's neck for the hell of it. But they had good alibis for the murders. It's hard to kill a woman from a prison cell.

The state techs had found a nice shoe print beside DeMarco's body, but the brand was rather common. Ellen made a stab at tracking shoe sales and tediously eliminating the shoes worn by the dozen or so men who had tramped around DeMarco's body after it was found. Frankly, a footprint wasn't going to get us anywhere until we had a suspect, but Ellen diligently added her findings to the growing file.

The techs also lifted a fingerprint from DeMarco's glasses. *That* got people excited for a while. The only problem was, we didn't hit a match in anyone's files. Like the shoe print, it would come in handy once we had a suspect, but until then, it was just a tantalizing morsel. It didn't come with a name.

Henry made the rounds of all the hospitals and clinics in the area, but didn't come up with anything like a dog bite. If Judy DeMarco's dog had nipped at the killer, he had treated the wound himself. And a fat lot of good it would have done us if Henry *had* found anything. DeMarco had pretty much destroyed that line of investigation when he'd destroyed the dog.

The park superintendent kept the trail closed for a week, but even with the parking lots barricaded and rangers patrolling the woods, people started sneaking back onto the path. Sheer fright had kept the park deserted for the first few days, but spring exploded overnight into summer, and fear couldn't compete with cloudless blue skies and cool breezes drifting through the trees. At first, only men ventured back onto the trail, because no one was breaking *their* necks. But then the women began showing up with them, and by the end of the week, joggers and cyclists were openly defying the cops and hitting the trail. The superintendent finally gave up and reopened the park with double shifts of rangers.

And no one else died.

Each morning, I lay in bed beside Dave, waiting for Bradley to call and tell me another woman had been found dead in the woods. Some mornings, while I waited, I amused myself with Dave, but even then, part of me was listening for the phone. Dave didn't appear to mind. But Bradley never called.

Each afternoon, I slipped into the station, bracing myself for the news that another woman's neck had been snapped. But the only thing snapping was Bradley's temper. City Hall was squeezing him. Reporters were sniping at him. And Concerned Citizens were berating him daily about his ineffective police force. He responded by squeezing, sniping and berating us, but that did nothing except raise everyone else's blood pressure.

No one ran in to confess.

Each night, I listened in dread as the dispatcher fielded calls, afraid that every mugging would turn into a death. But the university was in between sessions and only a fraction of the usual troublemakers were in town. Crime settled in to the homegrown variety—domestics and burglaries and high school kids on drugs.

No one was raped.

No one was murdered.

Eventually, the reporters went home.

Chapter Twenty

On a damp Saturday morning in June, I hauled my butt out of bed while Dave snored blissfully in tune with the fan, dressed in the bathroom and slipped out of the house alone. Barney whined when I left him behind, but I was on a mission that did not allow dogs, not even dogs deputized by the chief of police.

The rain was so gentle, it was really just a mist, certainly nothing strong enough to make me turn back. It was about eight-thirty, but the sky was so thick with clouds, I needed my headlights as I backed out of the drive. The county map was spread out on the passenger seat beside me. My pockets were stuffed full of dollar bills. And the auction ad that promised a treasure in red glass was fluttering on the dashboard.

I hadn't hit a sale in more than a month—not since Carmen Martinez had died. Bradley had pushed us so hard that on most days off, I barely had the energy to keep up with the household chores. But I was getting antsy. I'd missed three good sales in as many weeks. Mother thought that was fine—we were running out of places to put all the junk that I brought home. But I needed a fix.

I splashed through McDonald's to pick up coffee and didn't even shiver as the radio predicted an unseasonably cool day. Rotten weather would discourage the competition. Only idiots like me would be willing to get soaked for a few pieces of glass.

The auction was in a poor corner of the county. The house, occupied until recently by a widow with no family, was small and shabby. The paint was peeling, rusty spouting drooped from the front porch, and a thick layer of moss carpeted the roof. The widow had probably died destitute. But old women stash all sorts of prizes in their basements. And the ad had promised red glass.

I had become hooked on auctions by accident. Dave and I had stopped at a sale one afternoon because we had nothing better to do. I thought at first that it was rather grotesque pawing through a dead person's belongings, but then I had seen red, and I had been haunting auctions ever since. Dave occasionally accompanied me, but his interest was flagging. Mother saw no point in buying something old when you could just as easily buy new. And Adam was dreadfully bored by it all. But I still felt a buzz every time I dug through musty cardboard boxes and pulled out a brilliantly colored piece of glass.

As I told Dave, cops need something to do when they aren't abusing a mugger's civil rights.

I parked on the berm a few houses from the sale and strolled down the road, sipping my coffee. If you accept the fact that you're going to get wet, there's no point in running through the drizzle. The sale would last for hours. I would be drenched long before it was over. So I strolled.

The furniture was lined up in the front and side yards, and the auctioneer had draped plastic sheets over the better pieces. But lots of battered chairs and tables were sitting uncovered, and water had beaded on their scarred surfaces.

The junk dealers I knew wouldn't really mind.

I registered for a bidder's number with a clerk who had blocked the driveway with her van, then wandered down to a small garage where the "good" items had been laid out on folding tables. There was still half an hour to go until sale time, and the crowd was small. I recognized a dozen or so auction regulars, people who stocked their quaint shops with things they picked up at sales like this one, and I knew most of them could be vicious bidders. But I saw no one who dealt in my kind of glass. The muscles in my shoulders relaxed. I smelled an easy kill.

And I smelled old age and poverty. The garage floor was oil-stained dirt, and it was covered with rotting boxes and rusted tools and yellowed stacks of newspapers and magazines. There was barely room to maneuver around the tables, and I had visions of smashing the china with my hip or snagging a lampshade with my sleeve. I hugged my coffee cup to my chest and tiptoed into the gloom.

Daylight barely penetrated past the entrance, and the windows were so thick with grime, they were useless. Someone had had the bright idea of lighting one of the old oil lamps sitting on a table. It scared me silly.

Dealers in rain-spattered flannel and denim leaned over the tables and squinted at the collection of old watches and costume jewelry and trinkets that had been old when I was a child. There was a lot of china and pottery scattered around the tables, but so far, nothing red.

I was fingering a worn pink creamer when a familiar voice said behind me, "Miss America, Anchor Hocking. Not your kind of thing."

I bristled and tried not to show it. The voice belonged to a dealer who could afford to be choosy because a trust fund paid most of his bills. He leaned more toward furniture than glass, but he frequently bid against me just to be ornery.

"It's listed in the books for fifteen dollars," I said as I carefully placed the creamer back onto the table and glanced up at him.

Anthony Kirby smiled engagingly. "You'd never sell it for book value."

"*I'd* never buy it," I said, and edged down the table to some perfectly dreadful vases.

He stayed right with me. He was about fifty, looked forty and hid any depressing layers of flab under clothing so artfully casual, it had to be outrageously expensive. His reputation as a dealer was scrupulously honest, but with women, it was a bit shadier. He was occasionally married and continually looking. I had been deflecting his passes for almost a year now. He was never offended.

I suspected if I ever gave in, we'd both be disappointed.

He stepped in too close to examine the vases, and I could smell the soap from his shower. I liked it better on Dave.

"This is junk," I said to the vases.

"This lady's head will get forty dollars," Kirby said as he idly fingered a ceramic figure with a gaping hole in her head.

"It's gross," I said.

"It sells," he said, and he stuck by me as I browsed deeper into the garage.

"Are you here on business or pleasure?" he asked. His definition of my business meant glass; pleasure meant him. Police work didn't even enter into the equation.

"Strictly business," I said, and carefully studied a garishly striped pitcher.

"Of course," he said, and lazily inspected an equally revolting ashtray.

He followed me through the entire garage, examining bits and pieces of an old woman's life along the way. I didn't particularly encourage him, but I did pay attention as he talked because he did know the business and occasionally he saved me from impulsively buying junk. I also paid attention to the pieces he ignored. Sometimes I learned more from what he didn't tell me.

By the time we had circled the tables, I was certain he was angling for a celluloid dresser set. He hadn't so much as glanced at it.

And I was certain the auction ad had been mistaken. I didn't see any red.

Kirby stood in the doorway and turned up his collar. His hair curled rather provocatively in back.

He grinned at me, and I was glad I had Dave to keep me focused.

"It's in the box under the sewing machine," he said, and ambled out into the rain.

I abruptly elbowed my way back into the garage, to a treadle sewing machine jammed into a corner. There were boxes stacked all around it, most of them packed with old linens and shoes and the odd Christmas ornament. But one box stuffed with newspaper had the heavy feel of glass, and I anxiously squatted down beside it, ignoring the cobwebs and the spiders that certainly came with it.

I pulled yellowed newspaper off the top piece and, glancing around to make sure no one else was watching, quickly held it up to the glow from the oil lamp. The saucer burned red in my hand, and I grunted in satisfaction and quickly shoved it back under the newspaper.

It was a bubble pattern that I seldom found at any auction. When I did, it was always out of my price range. I nervously felt around the inside of the box, and I figured there were enough pieces wrapped up in there for a complete dinner set for four, plus a tumbler or two. *Damn* Kirby for finding it first.

I packed some more newspaper around the top piece, sprinkled the box with some dirt from the floor, just to discourage the overly fastidious shopper, and carefully pushed the box back under the sewing machine.

And then a big butt bumped into mine and I cringed as my precious box rattled.

"'Scuse me," the owner of the big butt mumbled, but she didn't exactly get out of the way. She was bent over a box across from me, and all I could see was about an acre of denim.

I thought of saying something rude, but I didn't want to draw attention to *my* box.

She was digging through a box of Christmas decorations, her arms buried to the elbows in tinsel. If she'd been nice, I might have steered her down the row to a box of really old ornaments. Decorations in good condition can draw big bucks.

But she had been clumsy and had touched me with her butt, for God's sake, so I backed out of the corner without saying a word.

And bumped *my* butt into Eddie Corrigan, the patrolman from the university.

We did the usual embarrassed double take—you just don't expect to find people you know digging through junk with the same malicious glee on their faces—and then we chattered loudly while he nonchalantly replaced the mustache cup he had been fondling and I turned my back on my box of glass. Eddie was a nice enough guy, but there was no sense in advertising what I was after.

We gabbed about the weather and the strange characters in the crowd. Eddie admitted that he didn't make a habit of scouting out auctions, and when I pressed him about giving up his Saturday morning for this sale, he just shrugged and mumbled something about a friend. I glanced around the garage, trying to pick out the likeliest "friend," because Eddie had impeccable taste.

And then the owner of the big butt straightened up and looked at Eddie with the grim intensity of a collector who had made a gut-wrenching find, and I groaned. It was his boss, Sarah Tate.

"We're staying," she said to Eddie.

Eddie was blushing like he'd just been caught playing with himself. I couldn't tell whether it was because he'd been caught with me, or because I'd caught him being nice to the boss. Maybe it was a little of both.

He uncomfortably cleared his throat. "Um, you remember Jo?"

Sarah Tate looked straight through me. But at the mention of my name, her eyes shot back to my face. "What do you collect?" she demanded, without so much as a hello.

She caught me by such surprise that I did the unthinkable. I told her.

She dismissed my glass with a shrug of her heavy shoulders. "I buy Santas," she said. "Celluloid Santas. If you see any, they're mine."

She said it with a perfectly straight face. But the corners of Eddie's mouth twitched, and mine might have too, if any other adult had made the same claim. But this was Sarah Tate, the woman who dared to replace Mike Edwards, and nothing she could say would ever be amusing, endearing or remotely humanizing. So I clamped my lips shut and said nothing.

"We need to register," Sarah said to Eddie in a tone that was clearly a command.

And Eddie hopped to it, like it wasn't his day off at all. He nodded to me, then hunched himself deeper into his denim jacket and trotted out into the drizzle. Maybe he *was* toadying a little, getting himself wet while his boss stayed dry in the garage, but I couldn't fault him for it. I had been known to behave just as foolishly for Bradley.

Sarah bullied her way around the garage, squishing people against the wall but delicately sidestepping the merchandise. I was afraid that since we were off duty and on neutral ground, she might try a little girl-to-girl chitchat, but I held myself in too high a regard. She forgot me as quickly as last night's supper.

So I wandered out to the lunch wagon parked on the edge of the road and warmed up my coffee. The rain had slowed to the point where you couldn't even feel it under the trees. I backed my butt up against the trunk of a maple tree about fifteen feet from the auction block, and that was where I stayed for the next two hours, shuffling from one foot to the other and feeling my hair curl up in the unrelenting damp. I am cursed at auctions. No matter who is running the sale and no matter what I am trying to buy, it's never put on the block early. In January, I court frostbite while waiting; in August, I broil. On a wet morning in June, I felt fungus taking root in my Reeboks.

Eddie Corrigan eventually drifted to my tree. His boss was planted in a lawn chair between me and the auction block and couldn't see Eddie making nice with the city cop. I would have ragged him about it, but he had hot coffee and was willing to share.

Eddie asked how things were going with the Martinez case. I made a face in the steam rising from my cup.

"That good," Eddie said.

I grunted while keeping an eye on the auction block. There was no sign of my box of glass.

"I heard the feds were involved," Eddie said. I knew he was pumping me, and anything I said to him would get back to Sarah Tate. But I didn't see any harm in admitting that the FBI had paid a call or two.

Eddie chuckled and told a story about the first time he had ever worked with the feds.

I sniffed and told a story of my own.

There was still no red glass on the block.

Eddie shook his head as a Barbie doll, in its original package, went for a hundred fifty dollars. He crushed his Styrofoam cup in his hand and looked for a place to toss it. "I've been checking the track," he said as he scanned the crowd the way a cop does, "but I haven't seen anyone bugging the girls."

"There aren't any girls in town to bug," I said. "It's summer."

"Oh, there's some," Eddie said, "keeping in shape and stuff." His eyes did *not* slide to my stomach.

And I did *not* suck in my gut.

"Coupla girls said there was a guy hanging around in the spring, staring at them while they ran. He never said anything to them, though. Never made a move. And they don't remember seeing him lately."

Despite the buzz in my head from the auction, I felt a vague disappointment. "What do you think?" I asked.

"I think I'll keep checking the track," Eddie said, his eyes on his boss's broad back, "but I don't think I'm gonna see that particular creep until fall."

I swallowed some coffee as I thought it over. "You think this guy went home for the summer?"

"Yep," Eddie said.

"Judy DeMarco was killed after everyone cleared out of the dorms."

"Yep," Eddie agreed.

"Then this creep didn't kill DeMarco," I said.

"Probably not," Eddie said, "but he's still scaring nice young ladies."

"You can bust him for that," I said.

"I intend to," Eddie said, and he nodded goodbye as he drifted away.

I chewed on my lip as a toaster was put up for sale. Whoever had killed Carmen Martinez had killed Judy DeMarco, too. If the creep at the track hadn't killed DeMarco, then he couldn't have killed Martinez, either. So forget the creep.

I brightened as one of the auctioneer's helpers walked out of the garage with The Box. Not only had I eliminated a suspect in the Martinez/DeMarco murders, but I was also going to make a killing on some ruby red glass. Life was good.

I stepped away from the tree, into the auctioneer's line of sight.

The man with the box began to lift it up to the auction block.

Sarah Tate straightened up from a box of wreaths she had been examining and her shoulder butted the man's upper arm.

The box wobbled on his upraised palms for one long moment. I heard glass clinking against glass, and I moaned.

The box crashed to the driveway, and the crowd went "Oh!" as my priceless glass shattered.

I plotted ways to kill Sarah Tate all the way home.

Chapter Twenty-One

It was a muggy morning in July when I decided that Barney and I really needed to find more challenging trails. Neither Dave nor I had slept well. The night had been too humid, and we had been lying too close, baking in each other's heat. When Dave crawled out about six o'clock to use the bathroom, I woke up, too, and stretched in the suddenly empty bed.

Which was how I noticed that my thighs were looking a little—well—thick these days.

I raised my right leg, pointing my toes at the ceiling, and fingered the tight muscles in back. They had hardened since Barney and I had started hiking, but I could still feel a lumpy layer of fat. Gross.

I dropped my right leg and lifted my left. Which was about the time Dave stumbled back from the bathroom. He stood in the doorway, absently scratching his chest and tilting his head so he could get a better view of the proceedings.

"Whoa," he said.

"Don't you mean, 'Giddyup'?" I asked.

"Got to mount up before you can giddyup," he said, and he nodded happily at the sights.

I primly lowered my leg.

Dave pouted.

I straightened the tank top I'd worn to bed. It didn't cover much.

Dave cheerfully crawled over the footboard and hovered over me.

"Whoa," I said.

Dave looked like a little kid whose lollipop had been snatched away. "Whoa?" he repeated plaintively.

I slid a finger under the waistband of his Jockeys (which he wore only because Mother sometimes wandered in) and tugged at the elastic.

"Wouldn't you rather ride bareback?" I asked.

Dave was vastly relieved and showed it. "If I'm to ride bareback," he countered, "wouldn't you be the one with the bare back?"

I considered this at great length. Dave didn't seem to mind. Eventually, I conceded it wasn't clear who should be bare, so we both stripped. It was much cooler that way.

Well, in the beginning, at least. But nature being what it is, things heated up, and we were both in a lather by the time we galloped to the finish line, and Dave hollered, "Yee haw!"

Mother was annoyed.

*   *   *

We were both drifting in that twilight after sex when the phone shrilled in our ears. Dave groaned and buried his head under the pillow. No one calls a college professor at six-thirty in the morning, so he didn't even try to answer it. I wanted to bury my head, too. No one calls a cop with good news at six-thirty in the morning.

I growled hello.

Henry, who had moved to the night shift, growled right back.

"Oh, Christ," I said, "now what?"

"The park," he said.

I shook off the pleasant remnants of the romp with Dave and stared wide-eyed at the ceiling. "What have you got?"

"One jogger," Henry said, "dead."

"Broken neck?"

"I'd say so."

"Raped?"

"It appears that way."

I shivered. Dave reached over and squeezed my thigh. "What's her name?" I asked in a low voice, afraid this time I'd know her.

Henry hesitated, and I could almost hear him lighting up. "Well, that's the funny thing, Jo," Henry said, but his voice wasn't amused at all. "The victim's a guy."

Chapter Twenty-Two

I didn't take time for a shower (Dave thought that maybe I should), but I did stop at McDonald's for a bucket of coffee, and while creeping up to the drive-through window, it occurred to me that perhaps middle age had finally caught up with Henry and he really needed glasses. I even suggested as much to him when he met me at the trailhead and I handed him some coffee. He just grunted and led me down the trail.

This body was only fifty yards down the path, barely around the first turn from the parking lot. The path curved close to the river there, and the body had been tossed down the bank and onto the pebbles at the river's edge. The victim was naked from the waist down, and he was definitely male. No problem with Henry's eyesight.

Bradley was standing on the edge of the bank, staring down at the body five feet below. I'd brought him coffee, too. He'd have confiscated mine if I hadn't.

The state techs were already working around the body. They looked up hopefully at the smell of coffee, but I hadn't brought *that* much. They grumbled and waded out into the river to get a look at the body from that angle. Two ambulance attendants sat on the rocks upstream and smoked cigarettes while they waited. The sun was just below the trees on the opposite bank, and the woods were still fuzzy with mist and shadows.

I wished I was back in bed with Dave.

Bradley was shaking his head as though he couldn't quite believe what he was seeing. I couldn't blame him. What kind of killer raped and murdered women *and* men?

I stood beside Bradley. Henry climbed down the bank to bum a smoke from the ambulance attendants.

Bradley sipped his coffee and made a face. "Where the hell is the sugar?"

I smiled sweetly.

Bradley blushed. The past occasionally took him by surprise.

"Techs found a university ID in the victim's pocket," Bradley said, stiffly steering us back to the problem at hand. "Name's Seth Schirria."

"Local?" I asked obediently.

"Don't know yet. Herchek's trying to run the name through the registrar's office but—" Bradley looked with disgust at the shadows of night still lurking in the woods—"they don't open this early."

Must be nice, I thought, stamping my feet against the chill, to have a job with regular hours.

I looked at the body—a dead weight sagging into the damp shoreline. He looked *small* for a university student, but it was tough to judge the size or age of the dead. They seemed to shrink in on themselves, taking their wrinkles and blemishes with them. This body could have been a hot twenty-five or an awkward fifteen. I couldn't tell anything other than, like Judy DeMarco and Carmen Martinez, his head was tilted at an impossible angle.

I sucked on my teeth. "You ever seen anything like this, Brad?"

"Like what? Attacking different sexes?"

I nodded. "It's comforting that he's an equal opportunity rapist, but have you *ever* seen a serial killer who goes after men and women?"

Bradley shrugged. "There was a case once I heard of—guy killed a couple of people, men and women, and did his wife in the middle so police would think it was a psycho serial killer instead of the cold-blooded murder of his wife." Bradley frowned. "'Course, *he* didn't rape *his* victims. Would've had to be a little kinky for that."

As though killing wasn't kinky enough, I thought.

"And political killings could be male or female," he said.

"I don't think our guy is making a political statement."

"Maybe," Bradley said, "maybe not."

We watched as one of the techs slipped in the mud and nearly dumped his camera into the water. Henry and the ambulance attendants razzed the guy, who responded in kind. Bradley glared at the whole crew, and they immediately shut up.

Bradley sipped some more coffee and pointed at a damp roll of cloth around the dead man's ankles. "Underwear," he grunted.

"Jockeys," I noted.

"Why didn't the killer take them?" Bradley asked.

"Maybe they weren't as pretty as Carmen's," I said.

Bradley's expression was disappointed.

"What's the difference?" I asked hastily. "We decided after DeMarco that underwear wasn't relevant. She never wore any."

"Maybe we were wrong," Bradley said.

"About what?" I asked in exasperation.

Bradley crumpled his coffee cup, stuffed it in his jacket pocket and turned back toward the trailhead. "Maybe," he said over his shoulder, "we were wrong about everything."

*   *   *

Seth Schirria should have been sitting in a computer graphics class that morning instead of lying dead next to the river. He should have been sweating because his girlfriend was two weeks late. He should have been making excuses because he'd forgotten his mother's birthday. He should have been scheming ways to buy that new bass in the window of the music store downtown.

Instead, he went running along the river, and it turned out to be the worst decision of his life.

The university registrar said Seth Schirria was twenty-one, a graphic design major with just enough credits to make him a junior and just enough C's to avoid flunking out. His test scores said he was a smart guy, but he was enjoying college life too much to get smart grades. He lived with a dozen other guys in his fraternity house and he made some extra bucks delivering pizza on slow weeknights.

His real home was in a town seventy-five miles away, where Dad sold insurance, Mom clerked part-time at a department store and two younger sisters were flirting their way through high school. Seth, his mother said, was a good boy. He just hadn't learned to take his responsibilities seriously.

Seth had planned to spend his summer at home, with his family. But he hadn't been able to find a summer job there, so he had come back to town, enrolled late in the summer term and picked up the pizza job from a friend. His father said maybe the boy should have joined the Marines.

Seth, I thought, would have been a rather diminutive Marine. Pictures at the fraternity house showed a slim young man with a rather plain face—plain except when the camera caught his rakish grin. Then it was easy to see why Seth had been having such a hard time concentrating on school. The grin said feed me, play me, stroke me, fuck me. There was nothing in it about midterms and grades and bachelor degrees.

His body was found at dawn by the ranger Ray. Seth was last seen alive about two a.m., when he left one of the student bars downtown. He'd had a little too much beer, he admitted to one of his fraternity brothers, and he was going out to the river to run it off. No one pointed out that the park closed at sunset or that he could hurt himself running drunk in the dark. No one thought to warn him about the crazy man stalking the trail. After all, Seth was safe. He was a *guy*.

This particular guy had had his neck snapped in two just like Carmen Martinez and Judy DeMarco, and he was sexually assaulted. According to the preliminary autopsy report, he'd been so drunk at the time, he may have died more surprised than frightened. There were no signs he had put up a fight.

"Nothing?" I asked in disbelief. I had stopped by the morgue to pick up the report, and unfortunately, Doc Sweitzer was still there. He didn't actually do autopsies in homicides anymore; he hired a forensic pathologist from the university instead, and our evidence held up much better in court. But he still watched the autopsy if the case was big enough, and Seth Schirria qualified as big.

So Doc Sweitzer was still in his office when I got there, and under the chain of command, I had to get the report from him.

"No struggle," Doc said as leaned back in his chair and clasped his hands across his belly. "You can take that to court."

I wouldn't take anything Doc said to court unless it was backed up by three expert witnesses, and he knew it.

"There are no marks on the body indicating the boy tried to defend himself," Doc huffed. "He's just like the others."

"He is **not** like the others," I said testily. "He's a man."

"And his neck was broken just like the others and he was violated just like the others," Doc said. "Same maniac killed all three."

I frowned at the report. "You're sure he was 'violated'? There's no evidence of semen here."

"The anus was penetrated," Doc said impatiently. "There are tears."

"But no semen?" I persisted.

"He's a tidy rapist," Doc said. "He used a condom."

"Never did that before," I said.

"Never raped 'em anally before, either," Doc said, daring me to take it further. I didn't.

"The killer's experimenting," Doc said. "He had a pretty young girl, a mature woman who knew a thing or two, now a young man. Who knows what he'll do next?" And Doc raised his eyebrows at the macabre possibilities.

"You don't think it's a copy cat?" I asked as I slipped the report into my shoulder bag.

"'Cause he suddenly shifted to boys?" Doc asked.

I nodded.

"He's a copy cat," Doc declared, "he's a damn good one. Sex is different, but they all three had their necks snapped the same way. And that's not something every man can do well. Lots of folks don't have the inclination. It's too personal."

I looked at Doc in some surprise. Anatomy was his field, not psychology.

"This fella isn't in a rage," Doc said, nodding as he thought about it. "He's a hunter. He stalks 'em, he kills 'em quick and clean, and **then** he does what he wants with 'em. You find yourself a hunter, Jo. Then you'll have your man."

I should have listened to Doc.

Chapter Twenty-Three

I found Seth Schirria's drinking buddies from the night before sprawled around a table in a dark little bar downtown. By my clock, it was still a little early for serious drinking, but as one of Seth's friends pointed out, it had been a bad day.

There were four of them, all fraternity brothers, all somewhere in their early twenties. One of them might have been under age, but given the circumstances, I didn't card him. Two had lived in the fraternity house with Seth; the other two shared an apartment nearby. Like Seth, one of them had been officially enrolled in summer classes; the other three had stayed in town over break to keep their part-time jobs. There wasn't any work for them back home.

When the bartender pointed me to their table, they were horsing around like young guys do when the air is hot and the beer is very cold. There were three young ladies at the next table, and the young men knew it. But there was an extra edge to their voices. Something that was more than hormones, something that warned of violence, raised the hairs on the back of my neck, and I approached their table cautiously.

The first one to notice me leered like he thought he was old enough.

The second one caught the look and leaned back in his chair to enjoy the show. The other two flirted with the girls at the next table and ignored me.

The first one hooked his thumbs in his pockets. It drew attention to the snug fit of his jeans. I'll admit, I was impressed. But then he had to open his mouth.

"Hey, Mama," he drawled.

I looked at his buddy, the one who was probably a few months shy of legal. "Did he say 'Mama'?" I asked.

His buddy just grinned.

The first one snagged an empty chair with his foot and dragged it up to the table. "Why don't you plant it right there?" he said, and patted the seat with his palm.

The other two had taken notice and snorted at their friend's great wit.

The girls at the next table looked at me as though afraid I might be their future.

I sighed and pulled out my badge.

It put a whole new perspective on the evening.

The flirt, who was named Don, flushed a deep red and hid behind a cigarette and his beer. The two who had been trying to pick up the girls next door sat at attention and became very earnest. Their names were Dennis and Brad, and they both declared they were ready to disembowel the son of a bitch who had killed Seth. The fourth one, Ryan, just smiled and every so often, nudged his beer closer to Don so maybe I wouldn't think it was his.

I did plant it in the chair Don had offered, but he was careful to move his knees away from mine. To set a good example, I ordered a tall Coke.

I got everyone's name, rank and serial number. They got mine. And then they asked whether I'd arrested anyone yet.

I said no.

Dennis and Brad erupted into more vile descriptions of what they'd do if they ever got their hands on the killer.

"I'll rip his tongue out," Dennis said.

"And pound nails into his eyes," Brad said.

Dennis reconsidered. "I'll twist his balls off," he said.

Brad glowered. "And stuff 'em down his throat."

I heard the same kind of talk every weekend from the drunk tank. It barely registered. I turned to the flirt, hoping his excellent taste in women signaled a somewhat higher intelligence level.

"Were you with Seth last night?" I asked.

He still wasn't ready for eye contact, but he nodded as he worked on his beer.

"Was it some special night out, or do you fellas normally end up here?"

"Hey, this is *our* bar," Brad broke in, thumping his chest. "Phi Sigs. Ask anybody."

"Yeah," Dennis said. And belched.

Don winced.

I smiled brightly. "So you were doing what you normally do on Monday night?"

There was loud agreement all around.

Except for Don, who was squinting at the label on his beer bottle. "Seth shouldn't have been here," he said, so quietly that I almost missed it.

I leaned a little closer. "Pardon me?"

Don picked at the label with his thumbnail, tearing loose little wet scraps of paper. "Seth usually worked Monday nights," Don said. "Usually had the late shift."

"That's right," Ryan said, forgetting for a moment that he didn't want to be noticed. "Seth always worked Mondays. Always bitched about it, too. Said it was the worst night of the week for tips."

"So why didn't he work this Monday?" I asked.

"He traded days with somebody," Don said. "Did somebody a favor at work."

Ryan shook his head. "Geez, that stinks. Maybe if he'd have worked like usual, he wouldn't be dead, huh?"

Don cuffed him on the head. "Stop talkin' like that, okay? It'll make you nuts, you start talkin', 'If only he'd have done this. If only he'd have done that.' Seth's dead. Get used to it."

"Sure, Don," Ryan said swiftly, and he scooted his chair a little closer to Brad.

"So," I said to the table in general, "no one who knew Seth would have expected to find him here last night, right?"

Three enthusiastic nods.

Don finally decided to look at me. His eyes were doe soft but rimmed in red. "What difference does it make what anyone expected? Seth was killed by some nut in the park, wasn't he?"

"He was attacked in the park, yes," I said.

"So what does it matter where he was before?" Don asked.

"Well," I said, "it'd help if we could figure out how Seth ended up being a victim. Why did the killer pick him?"

"He was in the wrong place at the wrong time," Don said.

"But why was he there?" I asked. "It was two o'clock in the morning. Why'd he try to sober up in the park?"

"Lotta guys go there," Brad said.

"Yeah," Dennis said. "Alla time."

"At two a.m.?" I persisted.

Ryan tried to shush them. He'd had less to drink than the others and was tracking quicker. But Brad and Dennis plunged ahead, intent on convincing me that it was no big deal for a guy to be out in the woods, miles away from the campus and the bars, in the middle of the night.

"He wasn't poaching, was he?" I asked, remembering the two hunters.

"Oh, hell, no," Brad laughed. "Not poaching."

"More like tokin'," Dennis chortled.

"Ah," I said.

Silence descended rapidly on the table. Silence except for the sound of Brad whipping his ball cap off his head and slapping Dennis with it. Ryan sat back with his arms crossed and an I-told-you-so look on his face. Don was blushing again and absolutely mesmerized by the inch of beer left in his bottle.

The girls at the next table decided it was time to leave.

"So you all are familiar with the park," I said.

They made rumbling, grumbling noises.

I leaned into the table. "I didn't get that."

"Some of the guys go out there," Brad said. "I never liked it much."

Dennis started to laugh, then checked himself.

"They'd go at night?" I asked.

Small nods around the table.

"To get high?" I asked.

Even smaller nods.

"And the rangers never caught on?"

Loud protests this time. No one ever got busted at the park. Never. We weren't talking major crime here, they assured me. All the guys were honest, God-fearing, mother-loving genuine Americans. So, no, ma'am, they never got picked up by the rangers.

"Now how'd you manage that?" I asked.

Brad looked nervously at Dennis, and Dennis looked nervously at Ryan. Don just looked at his beer bottle. "Might as well tell her," Don said. "Gone this far."

So they explained—hypothetically speaking, of course—how to do dope in the park without running into the law.

"You gotta go late," Brad said. "Real late."

"Like maybe three or four in the morning," Dennis said.

"And you keep the group small," Brad said.

"Two-three guys at the most," Dennis said.

"And don't damage anything," Brad said.

"So they don't have any reason to come looking for you later," Dennis said.

"No littering," Brad said.

"No girls," Dennis said.

"Well, usually no girls," Brad amended.

Dennis turned on him. "You takin' Jen back there?" he demanded.

"It's not Jen," Ryan said to the ceiling.

Brad blushed.

"Jesus," Dennis sputtered. "You take *girls* back there, you're gonna ruin it."

"It's already ruined," Don said flatly. "We can't ever go back there now."

And they all pondered the inconveniences of death.

Don drained his beer and leveled his gaze on me. "Everybody in the fraternity knows about the park. Any one of them coulda been there last night. But none of 'em killed Seth."

"Damn straight," Dennis said.

"He was our brother," Brad said.

I could see them closing ranks against me, so I steered their animosity in other directions.

"Who else could have known Seth was going out to the park last night?" I asked.

Don spread his arms wide. "The whole damn bar. Seth didn't make it any secret where he was going."

The other guys nodded.

I looked around me. There weren't even a dozen people lounging at the tables or leaning on the bar. But it was early. Most folks were still at home, chewing on their dinners. In another hour or so, the booths would start to fill up, the owner would crank up the stereo and the air would thicken with smoke and sweat. Even on a Monday night, this bar did a good business, and lots of people would have been around to hear Seth announce his intentions.

"Who else was here last night?" I asked.

"We already told you," Brad said. "This is *our* bar. None of the brothers would hurt Seth."

"Humor me," I said. "Name names."

Brad glanced sideways at Dennis.

"Aw, hell," Dennis said, and names started rolling out of his mouth.

Then Brad chimed in, and Ryan, and I was scribbling frantically to keep up. The guys even noted which Greek was which, so I wouldn't commit the egregious sin of calling a Phi Sig a Phi Delt or vice versa. Only Don remained aloof, silently letting the others finger their buddies.

By the time they ran out of steam, I had twenty-five new names in my notebook. Just a little something to keep Henry and Ellen busy, I thought.

While the guys were so talkative, I nailed down their alibis for Seth's murder. Seth had left the bar at last call, and his friends had soon followed. Brad and Dennis had gone home to their apartment; Ryan had gone back to the fraternity house ("My roommate will swear to it," he assured me); and Don had crashed at a friend's. I raised an eyebrow, he blushed, and I decided I didn't really need to push him for details.

I figured I'd gotten just about all I was going to get from these guys, so I started making moves to leave. I passed out cards to all of them, and tossed a dollar bill onto the table to cover my Coke. Didn't want the guys to think cops could drink free.

Don just happened to leave with me. He told the other guys he had to meet a friend. Brad and Dennis seemed to buy it, but Ryan shook his head like he knew better. I knew better, too, and wasn't surprised when Don trailed me through the bar and out to the parking lot.

"Look," I said as I pulled my keys from my pocket, "if you're worried about your alibi, it's okay. You don't have to tell me who she is."

"Hey," he said, all innocence, "who says she's a she?"

"You just did," I said, and unlocked the car.

He looked chagrined.

"Pronouns," I said, almost shaking a finger at him, "you have to watch your pronouns."

"That's grammar," he said.

"Yes," I said.

"Grammar sucks," he said.

"Especially when you get it wrong," I agreed.

We were standing in the parking lot at the back of the bar, and the sun was just beginning its dive behind the buildings that edged the next street. Don's face glowed a bright orange and he squinted painfully in the glare. I thought he was feeling guilty about his poor education. As it turned out, he had a different kind of guilt on his mind.

"The guys, you know, they like to boast," he said, trying to sound like such an urge had never troubled him.

I swung open the car door but I didn't get in. There was a nice breeze coming across the lot, and I wasn't anxious to shut myself up in my stuffy little car. I folded my arms across the top of the door, rested my chin on my forearms and waited for Don to spit it out.

"All that talk back there," he said, nodding toward the bar, "'bout how to sneak into the park and not get caught?"

I nodded.

"Just talk," he said.

"Oh?" I said, not particularly surprised.

Don pulled a cigarette out of his shirt pocket to busy his hands, twirling it through his fingers like a baton. "Truth is," Don said, "coupla guys did get caught."

"Seth?" I asked.

Don nodded. "Seth and another one of the brothers. It was no big deal. No arrest or anything," he assured me. "Just a coupla rangers caught 'em sneaking into the woods."

"No citations?" I asked.

"Nothing on paper," Don said. "Just a warning." He made a face over his cigarette. "Guess the warning didn't work so good."

"Seth went back anyway," I said.

"At least once a week," Don said.

So the rangers knew the guys were smoking up in the park, I thought. But with no citations, there was nothing on the record.

Now why hadn't my good buddies Joe and Ray, who were paid to prevent pot parties in the park, told me about the boys' adventures on the river?

And why was Don, who was sworn to defend his brothers, being so helpful?

"Because some son of a bitch raped Seth," Don said fiercely.

"He didn't just rape Seth," I pointed out. "He *killed* Seth."

Don shook his head. "Rape is worse," he said. "Believe me, for a brother, it's worse."

I felt my jaw drop. I'd thought we were past the days when rape was a fate worse than death.

But Don disagreed. "Someone's gotta pay for Seth," he said, jabbing the air with his cigarette for emphasis. "Someone's gotta pay for taking his manhood. It wasn't just the brothers who knew he'd be down in the park. It wasn't just the drunks in the bar. The rangers knew, and they didn't stop it. They're just as guilty as whoever killed Seth. They let it happen, and they oughta pay."

His logic was faulty but common. People needed someone to blame. If they couldn't pin the crime on the perpetrator, then they blamed the cop for allowing the crime to happen in the first place. No one knew who killed Seth. So the alternative was to blame the rangers who patrolled the park.

It was the quick and dirty solution.

It didn't occur to me until I had shooed Don away that sometimes quick and dirty is just right.

Chapter Twenty-Four

The parking lot at the trailhead was packed and a mob of gray-haired ladies in hiking shoes milled around the ranger station. So what if the sun was going down? So what if three people had been murdered on the trail? The ladies had signed up for an evening nature hike and, by God, they were going to take it.

Bradley had ordered the main trail sealed after Seth's body was discovered, but there was enough of a path to the new picnic shelter, still under construction, that the rangers had been able to salvage the hike (and appease many park donors). Extra rangers had been brought in on overtime to guard the hikers down an unfamiliar path and protect them from murderers. I spotted Ranger Larry trying to organize the ladies at the head of the line. Ray was roaming through the parking lot, rounding up stragglers. Joe was leaning in the doorway to the ranger station, looking like he wanted to be anywhere but on a hike with retirees. So I decided to distract him.

"Don't you ever wear the right shoes?" he asked.

I looked guiltily at my feet. I wasn't wearing heels, but the soles of my flats were too smooth for hiking. I'd slide onto my butt within the first ten yards.

"You'd better stay back," Joe advised, "or these old gals will stomp all over you."

"I wasn't planning on going along," I said.

"You want to talk to me," he said, "you'll have to." And his tone of voice said he wasn't looking forward to me or the hike.

I was mildly insulted. After all, I'd allowed the man to kill a deer with my gun—quite against the rules. So I let a little frost creep into my own voice as I suggested a private chat in the ranger station.

He made a face, but in the end, my badge was bigger. We ducked into the station just as Ranger Larry was launching into his official welcome. Several ladies, I noticed, tittered as he introduced himself.

The ranger station was a cabin divided into two large, boxy rooms—a public waiting room in front, where visitors could rest while reading park brochures, and an office in back, where the rangers did their paperwork. The walls were roughly paneled and the décor was rustic. I half-expected to find a moose head mounted on the wall. Instead, there were bulletin boards with work schedules and meeting notices and lists of rules and all the other things that normally get posted in an office.

Joe dumped himself behind a desk in one corner. He didn't specifically invite me to sit, but I took the desk across from his anyway. The station was super-air-conditioned, and I shivered a little as I noted the coffee maker plugged into the far wall.

Joe didn't take the hint.

So I asked him outright why he hadn't stopped Seth and his buddies from smoking in the park.

"Might as well ask why I don't make water run uphill," he complained.

"According to one of the fraternity brothers, you caught the dead boy sneaking into the woods for a smoke."

"Probably did," Joe said, nodding.

"But you didn't cite him."

"Probably didn't," Joe agreed.

"Why not?" I asked.

Joe folded his hands across his belly and eyed me speculatively, as though we weren't on the same side anymore. "Well, it's kind of hard to say exactly why since I'm not exactly sure which one of the dopeheads I rousted this summer is the dead kid. It's dark, they're high, they all start to look alike in the headlights, you know? Your source says someone on the night shift warned the kid to stay out of the park, then it must've been me. But it happens two, three times a night. I don't remember 'em all."

"Do you ever cite them?" I asked.

Joe sighed. "On what grounds?" he asked. "You see a boy and a girl drive by after dark, you know they're looking for a place to have sex. You can't prove it, but you *know* it. Same thing with drugs. You see a couple of guys drive by after dark, you know they're looking for a place to get high. Again, you can't prove it, but you *know* it. Either case, you stop the car, you can *warn* 'em about lots of things, but the best you can cite 'em for is trespassing."

"So do you ever cite them?" I repeated.

"Jesus, Jo," he said in exasperation, "you ticket every bad driver you see?"

"You aren't answering the question," I said.

He took a deep breath. Despite the overly industrious air conditioner, his face has flushed an angry red. Joe was losing patience with cops questioning him like he was a bad guy.

"I cite the repeaters," he said finally. "Most kids get scared off with a warning. That's all we want, anyway—scare 'em out of the park. Can't stop 'em from smoking dope, but it'd be better if they took their dirty habits somewhere else, you know?"

I nodded, more to keep him talking than to agree with his game plan.

"So if it's busy, I just warn 'em how I'm gonna wreck their lives if they even try to sneak into my park again," Joe said. "If it's slow and they're mouthy, then, yeah, I'll cite 'em. Or if I recognize 'em. This kid got killed last night? I don't recognize his name, so I probably never laid a citation on him."

"But you knew he and his buddies were coming out here," I said.

Joe sighed again. "Didn't I just say so?"

"I'm just trying to get a clear picture of what goes on here at night," I said.

"Nothing 'goes on,'" Joe snapped back. "Kids try to sneak in all the time to get high, but most get stopped by the rangers. Once in a while, someone gets lucky and gets through. Just because a kid sneaks in once in a while doesn't mean there's drug parties on the river every night."

"I never said there were."

"Coulda fooled me," he said, and his voice was definitely chilly.

"Fine," I said. "You didn't know *this* dead boy would be smoking dope in the park last night, but you could have made an educated guess that someone would be. Is that about right?"

"Yes, ma'am," Joe said. "Except for one thing."

There was always one more thing, I thought wearily.

"My shift ends at eleven," Joe said. "Your victim got himself killed after two. I was home in bed by then. Ask my wife." And he waved to the phone.

I ignored the offer. "Are all rangers off duty by eleven?" I asked.

"There's one man on an overnight shift, in case there's any kind of trouble, but most of the employees work a day shift or an afternoon shift, and the afternoon folks clock out at eleven."

"So *one* ranger could have run into the dead boy last night," I said.

"Could have," Joe said. "But he didn't."

"How do you know that?" I asked.

Joe's eyes hardened. "I know the men I work with. Some of them are a little strange, like Larry. Some are a little crude, like Ray. But none of them are killers. I *know* that."

If I had a dollar for every time a witness vouched for the good character of a criminal, I could retire to a summer home on the beach.

Instead, I went home to my stuffy old house in the city.

Chapter Twenty-Five

Agent Beck came back to town the next day with an FBI team trained in serial killings. No one officially took the case out of our hands, but there we all sat in City Council chambers, with the FBI on one side of the aisle and the local cops on the other, and Bradley and Agent Beck standing in front like they were both in charge. But it was Beck fielding all the questions and passing out the assignments while Bradley nodded approval and tried not to get too red in the face.

Part of me didn't really mind the intrusion. The feds had more resources, and their high visibility would take some of the heat off Bradley. Anyone who could divert the stroke lurking in Bradley's future was okay in my book. And who knew? Maybe the feds would actually catch someone.

But another part of me sat back with Henry in the last row and glared at the suits. We had been sent down to the minors. It was irritating, to say the least.

The feds were big on paper. They passed out profiles, case studies, maps and statistical analyses, and we balanced them awkwardly on our laps as one of the pros talked for the rest of the morning about serial killers. I didn't think it got us any close to *this* particular killer, but it did keep us all safely off the streets.

At noon, we sneaked down the street to the Farmhouse and let the newcomers figure out for themselves where to go for lunch.

The Farmhouse was a town bar and grill that specialized in red meat and grease. In deference to the more learned types from the university, the cook had added Caesar salad to the menu, and for an extra buck, he'd throw in a grilled chicken breast. But real cops went to the Farmhouse for hamburgers smothered in onions and steaks so rare, they mooed.

Even Ellen gave in to a cheeseburger and fries.

We spent the first half of lunch taking pot shots at the feds. Everyone had a horror story, and no one in the booth was above embellishment. By the time Henry had cleaned his plate and was swiping my fries, we had reduced the feds to a bunch of pencil-pushing geeks.

We could have sunk from there into some brutal self-analysis, but that would have required booze, and we were all on duty. So instead we bickered over the assignments we had been given.

"Carmen Martinez's track rivals," Henry groaned. "They're all over the country."

Berger simply grunted. He had Judy DeMarco's two sons.

"At least you can stay in town," Ellen complained. She had drawn the farmer who owned most of the land surrounding the park. The reasoning was he might have noticed someone getting onto park property by the back door.

I was supposed to check out former park employees. After my interview with Joe the day before, I could just guess how welcome I'd be at park headquarters.

"It's busy work," Henry said as he snagged my dill pickle.

"It doesn't appear to be a good use of resources," Ellen said diplomatically.

"They're fucking around with my computer," Berger said, in what passed as passion for him.

"Right," I said. "Like you don't have the good stuff stored away in some secret files."

"That would be an improper use of departmental software," Berger said.

"So how many secret files you got?" Henry asked.

"Six," Berger said.

"That you'll admit to," I said.

Berger sucked on his teeth and shut up. The department's computer system had been his creation. He had dragged us all kicking and screaming into the electronic age, and we were better cops because of it. But Berger had the highest security clearance in the department, even higher than Bradley's, and as a result, I kept nothing personal in the computer. I suspected Berger amused himself nightly by reading all our e-mail. But he knew better than to push his computer shenanigans too far around me. I controlled the budget.

"I think Bradley's lost his nerve," Henry said as he drooled after a waitress delivering mugs of beer to the next booth.

I was sitting beside him, and he felt me stiffen.

"No offense, Jo," he said quickly. "I know you and Bradley are pals."

I glared at him.

"Okay, ex-pals."

I gouged him in the shin with the heel of my shoe.

He winced and probably would have kept his mouth shut, only Ellen interrupted.

"Why do you think the chief has lost his nerve?" she asked. She was the only person in the booth who called Bradley the chief, and the sound of it hung strangely over the table.

Henry looked at her in consternation, as though it should be perfectly obvious. "He let the feds take the case."

Ellen nodded. "They have more experience in this kind of thing."

"But he let them *take* the *case*," Henry said.

"I thought the mayor called them in," Ellen said.

"The old Bradley wouldn't have let the mayor do it," Henry said. "The old Bradley would have threatened to quit first."

"Maybe he did," Berger said blandly.

We sat in silence and digested the thought of Bradley issuing an ultimatum—and backing down.

"No way," I said, slipping the check to Henry. "Bradley doesn't bluff."

Henry spread his hands. "The feds are here, aren't they?"

"Bradley didn't lose his nerve," I said stoutly. "We just didn't give him a suspect."

"Like it's our fault?" Henry said incredulously, even as he picked up the check because it was his turn.

"It isn't Bradley's," I said as I nudged him out of the booth.

Henry rolled his eyes.

Ellen looked at her watch. "You think I can get out to that farm and back before the sitter leaves at three?"

"Maybe the DeMarco boys have e-mail," Berger said wistfully.

Henry looked at me. "Who's hot on the track now that Martinez is dead?"

"Oh, for God's sake," I said, "you people are hopeless." And I shuffled Agent Beck's assignments so Berger could track down Carmen's rivals via the Internet, and Henry could have a heart-to-heart with Judy DeMarco's sons, and Ellen could cozy up to Ranger Larry for records on former park employees.

That left me tramping through the barnyard.

Bradley would have liked that.

Chapter Twenty-Six

The cornfields were wilting under a vicious August sun as I drove down a dusty driveway to the farmhouse. I'd checked out the county tax map and discovered that Mr. J.D. Hawkins had once owned all the land right down to the west bank of the river. But interest rates had been excruciatingly high some years back, and grain prices had been agonizingly low, and he had sold the strip along the river to the park district. I hadn't had time to hunt up the purchase price, but it must not have made Hawkins a rich man. The farmhouse sitting at the end of the lane looked solid, but it wasn't a mansion and it needed a fresh coat of paint. So did the barn and the other buildings sitting across the dirt yard from the farmhouse. The tractor just outside the barn was crusty with mud and, to my city eyes, looked well-worn. There was one cow, chewing in the shade of the barn, and she struck me as typical of the Hawkins farm—sturdy but getting on in years.

I parked in the dirt between the house and barn and, just in case the drive down the lane hadn't announced my arrival, I slammed the car door hard. Then I strolled over to the fence and leaned on it to watch the cow and await my welcome.

The cow was much better at waiting. She was in the shade and could flick away flies with her tail. I was in the sun and was tailless. But I had the might of the law on my side, and eventually J.D. Hawkins ambled out from the barn to see what the law was doing in his yard.

He was about fifty, lean and weathered dry like his work clothes. He was tall enough that I had to squint up at him, which isn't the best way for a cop to conduct an interview. But I had a skirt, which can get a man's attention even when a badge won't.

I introduced myself and his eyes flicked to the barn, then back to me. He smiled at the same time, and it was a very nice smile, but I had seen the eyes flicker just the same.

"Aren't you kinda far from home?" he asked. The question could have been belligerent from another man, but he had a quiet way of talking that wasn't threatening.

"City property's just over there in the woods," I said, pointing toward the river.

"Park property," he corrected.

I shrugged. "Same thing."

He looked at me in puzzlement. "You're a park ranger? I thought you said city police."

"I did," I said. "City police investigating the murders in the park."

"Ah," he said, and despite the word murder, he seemed to relax.

I couldn't understand why.

He started walking past the barn, toward a field separating us from the park, and since it was my interview, I followed him. But I hoped he wasn't planning to wander far. The glare out in the open was radiating right through my sunglasses.

He looked over his shoulder at me as we tramped along a narrow path from the barn into the field. "You got a maniac in the park," he said.

"You've seen him?" I asked.

"Don't need to see him to know he's a maniac," Hawkins said.

"So what are you doing about it?" I asked.

That stopped him short. I almost bumped into him. "Me?" he asked. "What makes you think I'm doing anything?"

I smiled innocently. "People getting themselves killed right next door, I'd think you'd be a little nervous."

J.D. snorted and resumed the march down the path. "First off, 'right next door' is relative. My land borders the park, but the trailhead's about a mile downriver from here, on the other side. It's not like in the city, where you can watch your neighbor's TV from your own living room."

I conceded that it was a good hike—and a swim—from his house to the trail in the park.

"Second, this maniac is killing people in the park." He looked back at me and he said deadpan, "I don't go to the park."

"I guess you're pretty well covered, then," I said, but I could see where he was coming from. The killer was picking off his victims in the park. As long as the park stayed open, it would continue to provide him with easy targets. The killer had no need to stray. All J.D. Hawkins had to do was stay home and he was safe.

It was a good theory. I could think of at least three people who'd be alive if they'd followed it.

We stomped over the stubble from last year's corn and mashed tiny yellow and white flowers that had grown up in its place. J.D. didn't seem to notice them. I wanted to pluck them out from under his feet, but then what would I do with them?

"You get many trespassers?" I asked.

"When the corn comes in, people try to help themselves." He gave me that over-the-shoulder look again. "I discourage them."

I decided not to pursue that.

"Anyone else?" I asked.

"Hunters sometimes."

"Poachers?"

He nodded gravely. "Yes, ma'am, if they're trespassing on my land, they're poaching."

"How about two nights ago? Anyone poaching then?"

"It isn't deer season," he said.

"It's people season," I reminded him.

He nodded and thought about it some. "Nope," he decided. "Nothing when that boy was killed."

"How about last May, when the first woman died?"

He thought about that, too, but nothing came to mind. Judy DeMarco's murder was a lost cause. He couldn't even remember when she died, so how was he supposed to remember strangers cutting across his land?

We had reached the end of the field and his property line. On the other side of the fence was a woods, hushed, green and owned by the park district. Two very narrow paths meandered from the field back into the woods.

"You must get some hikers back here," I said, pointing at the paths.

J.D. gave me a smile that was more pity than humor. "You don't get out in the woods much," he said.

"Walk my dog every day," I said stoutly.

He squatted to inspect a fence post. "Those are deer paths," he said, politely looking the other way so he wouldn't see me blush.

I chewed on my lip and felt like a boob. The interview was not going well, and I wasn't sure how to turn it around. With the FBI in town, I wasn't even sure I wanted to make the effort. It was hot, it was sticky, and it was guaranteed the feds would make the bust now. It was how things worked.

So I stood on the edge of J.D. Hawkins' land, wondering where to go next, and J.D. started talking—not about serial murders and broken necks, but about how the land used to be, back before banks and agribusiness got a stranglehold on small farmers. He was working on the wire fence, replacing a piece that had torn loose from the post, and his hands seemed to do the job without paying any mind to the history lesson pouring out of his mouth. He talked of Hawkinses farming five generations back, and I looked at the field and could see them there with their horse-drawn plows, breaking the ground for the first time. He talked of years when the river surged up out of its banks and swept over the fields in great muddy waves. And he remembered years when the river shriveled to a crooked, narrow stream and the land baked dry. He was a wonderful storyteller.

I just didn't understand what had unleashed his memories.

When he segued into the history of the local grange, I called it quits. J.D. Hawkins just didn't want to talk about current events. And I wanted an air conditioner.

He excused himself from escorting me back to the car. He wanted to finish the fence before supper. I said no problem, and trudged back over the field alone. As I hiked, I noticed two other houses up the valley, and thought as long as I was checking the back door into the park, I might as well check those houses, too. Bradley liked it when I was thorough.

I came up behind the barn and heard a lot of grunting inside. It wasn't grunting of the barnyard variety. It was definitely human, accompanied by the clank of metal on metal. I hesitated for a moment, wondering whether I really wanted to barge in on something kinky. Then I shrugged—my badge was my license to be nosy—and I strolled up to a door in the lower level of the barn.

The bottom half of the door was shut. I leaned over it to peer into the shadows of the barn. The noises were louder here and separated into distinct voices—at least two, maybe three, huffing in time with the metal.

I knew the sound, and it wasn't sex.

To my right was a stall, and through the slats I could see pieces of exercise equipment—weights and bars and other implements of torture. It didn't look like an extravagant setup, but it certainly was being used vigorously. Teen-age boys sweated and stretched and swore with conviction. One was spotting for his pals, but my shadow in the doorway must have distracted him. He looked at me in annoyance, then his eyes widened and he ducked down behind the slats.

I knew then why J.D. Hawkins had been reluctant to see me—why he'd dragged me out to the field to talk instead of standing in the barnyard.

He wasn't worried about murder of the human kind. He was afraid I'd come to arrest his boys for poaching on park property.

Some folks, I thought, just didn't have their priorities right.

Chapter Twenty-Seven

Poaching wasn't high on my priority list that afternoon. Neither was a confrontation with three sweaty teen-agers on their own turf. So even though I could hear Henry mocking me in my head, I left the boys to their instruments of torture and drove away from the farm as though I hadn't seen a thing. But by the time I reached the main road, a sound of another sort was mocking me—the memory of the labored, wet breathing of a gut-shot deer. So on the way back to town, I detoured to park headquarters.

Joe had the day off, but his partner Ray was just coming on duty. Joe must have told Ray all about our little chat the day before, because Ray was not the ornery young man who had taunted me with a midnight jaunt over a condemned bridge. He was decidedly frosty when I brought up the subject of poachers.

Ray acknowledged that he knew J.D. Hawkins and he'd heard somewhere that the farmer had some teen-age sons, but no, ma'am, he'd never had occasion to question them about hunting on park property. Didn't have any reason to.

"I *saw* them, Ray. At least one of those boys was out in the woods that night."

Ray stared out over my head and lazily scratched his jaw. "Well, beggin' your pardon, ma'am, but I've only got your say-so on that."

I felt the ranger ranks closing solidly against me, and my blood pressure shot up. "Fine," I snapped as I turned back to my car. "I was just passing along information—a professional courtesy. You don't want to act on it, that's your business."

Ray watched me climb into the car and almost grinned in appreciation when my skirt hiked up my thigh, so I knew he wasn't *too* pissed off. I gunned the engine and saw his lips move as I peeled out of the lot. He might have been telling me to have a nice day.

Or not.

*　*　*

There was great gnashing of teeth when I got back to the station, mostly of a jurisdictional nature. Beck and his experts had squeezed themselves into the squad room and it wasn't pretty. Berger was ashen. Strangers were hacking away at his computer. Ellen was pursing her lips as she packed her personal effects safely into a drawer while an eager young agent sat in her chair with his feet up on her desk and yakked into her phone. Herchek was alternately chasing other agents out of his supplies and hauling reporters out of Bradley's office. Henry hovered over the coffee pot with Beck, talking baseball as the coffee brewed, but you could see them jockeying for the first cup.

I had never been a good team player, not even in grade school, so when the Fed Ex guy arrived with the afternoon delivery, I grabbed the packages myself. I wanted first dibs on the preliminary lab work from the state techs handling Seth Schirria. But it wasn't there, and I moaned loudly enough to distract Herchek.

"Of course, it isn't there," he said as he took custody of the deliveries. "They're on strike."

I was appalled. "The *state*?"

Herchek's look was disappointed. "Don't you read the paper?"

I waved an arm around the squad room. "Does it look like I have time to read the paper?" It was a purely theatrical gesture. The chaos brought by the feds had nothing to do with my reading habits and Herchek knew it.

"The secretaries and clerks went on strike this morning," he said. "You won't get anything from the state until it's over."

I blew my bangs off my forehead in frustration. "My reports are hung up somewhere because there's no one to mail them. Is that it?"

Herchek nodded.

"That's stupid," I said.

He shrugged and smiled. "That's America."

*   *   *

Eddie Corrigan called from the university. "I hear the feds have landed," he said cheerfully.

The feds were so close, they could hear Eddie's end of the conversation. I scooted my chair back against the window behind my desk. "A battalion," I said.

"My boss hopes to meet them," Eddie said, adding diplomatically, "to compare notes."

I tried to picture Sarah Tate introducing herself to Agent Beck and suddenly felt sorry for the feds.

"I'll mention it to Bradley," I said.

Eddie grunted. He knew how much I wanted to do favors for Sarah. But at least now he could report to his boss that he had tried.

I asked him how the university was taking the latest death in the student body. He said it was a public relations nightmare.

"But that's why I called," he said. "I got a funny coincidence."

Coincidences always get my attention. I don't believe in them.

"Remember when you tipped me to the guy hanging out at the track?" Eddie asked.

"The one staring at the girls," I said. "I remember."

"It might've been Seth Schirria."

My brain suddenly felt scrambled. The stalker at the university track was supposed to be a suspect. How could he end up as a victim?

"I'm not following you," I said, shaking my head as though that would help.

"I know it's screwy," Eddie said. "But I've been watching the track ever since you told me, and I got it narrowed down to maybe three guys who fit the bill, and Schirria was one of them."

"*Maybe* fit the bill?" I repeated.

"I've never seen any of 'em do anything, bother anybody," Eddie said, "but they're all guys I've spotted at the track more than once. Guys who don't have any reason being there."

"That you know of," I said.

He agreed.

"Did you talk to Seth about it?" I asked.

"Naw," Eddie said. "I didn't even have a name for him until he got himself killed. It was all very tentative, Jo. I'd noticed him, but I hadn't seen him do anything, and no one had complained to me about him."

"Maybe because the girls he was bugging went home for the summer," I said.

"Maybe," Eddie said.

I rubbed my eyes to blot out the busy little figures scurrying through the squad room, but it didn't help sort the images knocking around in my head. Seth's body on the riverbank just didn't fit with the hungry eyes that Carmen Martinez's teammates had described to me. How did a man go from sexual predator to sexual victim in a matter of weeks?

"I told you it was screwy," Eddie said. "But so is the idea that this killer suddenly switched from attacking women to attacking men."

"It's not an idea," I said. "It's a fact."

"But are you sure the same person killed Schirria and the women?" Eddie pressed.

"Nothing proves it wasn't," I said, but I thought fleetingly of the lab reports hung up by a strike. Maybe I ought to just drive over and get them myself.

But another part of me was ticking off for Eddie all the reasons the murders were committed by the same man. "The cause of death is exactly the same—*exactly*. All the victims were attacked from behind. All were taken by surprise. All were killed before they were raped. All were killed in the park." I stopped for a moment and pictured the dead. "All were about the same size."

"Different ages, though," Eddie said. "Different sex."

"Same broken neck," I said.

"Maybe it's a good copy cat," Eddie said.

"Who's copying whom?" I asked. "We don't have a clue who killed Martinez. How can someone be out there copying him when we don't even know who *he* is?"

"It's a puzzle," Eddie agreed.

"A deadly puzzle," I said.

"And now there's Schirria," Eddie said.

I rubbed my forehead. I suddenly had a ferocious pain boring into my left eye. "Maybe Seth was killed in retribution for stalking the track team," I said without much enthusiasm.

"Could be," Eddie said, "but who was paying him back?"

"Maybe the girls," I said.

"Schirria was raped," Eddie reminded me.

"Maybe the girls have a boyfriend," I said. And Jesse Conklin's face popped into my head.

The day was starting to look better.

* * *

I caught up with Jesse Conklin at the student union. It was an awkward encounter. He was in a back booth, feeling up Carmen Martinez's viperous roommate, Lisa.

They scooted apart when they saw me—as though I couldn't figure out what was going on beneath the table. The last time I'd talked to Jesse, I'd been trying to arrest him for murder, so he wasn't quite sure how to handle me. He tried defiant, but he was blushing too much, so he had to settle for sheepish.

Lisa simply scowled at the interruption.

"Hi, guys," I said, and slid into the booth across from them.

Jesse mumbled something. Lisa tapped a cigarette out of a pack lying on the table.

I confiscated the ashtray. "If you don't mind," I said.

Lisa pursed her lips against a tart reply. She crossed her arms and let the unlighted cigarette dangle from her fingers.

Jesse slouched in the booth and looked like he wanted to slither away.

I smiled broadly at Jesse. "Isn't life funny? Last time I saw Lisa, she was calling you a pig."

Jesse's mouth dropped open, but before he could say anything, I transferred my smile to Lisa. "And he called you a bitch."

Lisa didn't flinch, but her eyelids fluttered.

"Of course, I suppose you were both in shock, seeing as how Carmen had just been found dead."

Jesse's blush deepened and he stared at his Coke glass in embarrassment. Lisa said nothing, but her eyes smoldered.

"Guess you aren't in shock anymore, huh?" I said, and I nodded as though happy for their adjustment.

"We haven't done anything illegal," Lisa said angrily.

"You *are* guilty of poor timing," I pointed out.

"This isn't Victorian England," Lisa said, demonstrating she'd learned a thing or two at college. "There's no required period of mourning."

"You're right," I agreed. "But it sure looks bad, doesn't it?" And I smiled again to show I sympathized with the fix they were in.

Jesse wisely said nothing. Lisa fumed.

I waited patiently for her to give in to the urge to justify herself. It didn't take long.

"Jesse was in pain," Lisa said, tapping her unlighted cigarette on the table. "I was in pain. We comforted each other."

And how.

"Even if it offends your sense of propriety, what business is it of yours?" she asked. "Everyone knows Jesse didn't kill Carmen."

I nodded agreeably.

"So?" Lisa demanded when I didn't go away.

I looked at Jesse. "You want to tell me anything about Seth Schirria?"

Jesse's eyes widened. "Oh, man, you aren't gonna try pinning that on me, too?"

I shrugged. "Give me a good reason not to."

"Don't answer that," Lisa said swiftly.

He looked at her in panic. "You don't know, Leese," he said. "You don't know what it's like to be hauled into a police station because some cop thinks you killed somebody."

"You didn't kill anybody, Jesse," Lisa said coldly. "Just shut *up!*"

My smile was becoming permanent. Jesse and Lisa might not be guilty of murder, but they certainly were guilty of *something*. I was enjoying myself immensely.

"Seth was a frat bum," Jesse said. "I had nothing to do with him."

Lisa shook her head in disgust, stuck the cigarette in her mouth and lit a match with a rasp that made Jesse wince. Something told me Jesse was going home alone tonight.

"So you *did* know Seth," I said.

"Hey," Jesse protested, "I saw him around. Partying, you know? Doesn't mean I *knew* him."

"Did you see him at the track?"

Jesse gave me a look that seemed genuinely confused. "You mean running? I didn't even know he was on the team."

"He wasn't," I said. "But he might have liked to watch."

"So what?" Jesse said. "Lots of people watch."

Lisa sighed dramatically as she tapped her ash into a Coke can. "She doesn't mean *watch*, Jess. She means *leers*."

Jesse pondered that for a moment. He was a little slow on the uptake.

Lisa wasn't. "That's what you mean, isn't it?" she challenged me. "Someone leering at the girls?"

I nodded.

"Well, we don't know anything about that," Lisa said firmly. "Carmen never said anyone was bothering her at the track. Did she, Jess?"

Jesse slowly shook his head. But I wasn't sure whether he was answering a question or just chasing the bugs out of his brain.

"So, you see," Lisa decided, "we can't help you."

"Can't or won't?" I asked.

Lisa finally blushed. "I don't see the point," she sputtered. "Even if Seth *was* watching Carmen and the other girls, what does it matter? He's dead."

"Don't you think it's odd that someone who was watching Carmen ends up dead, just like Carmen?"

Lisa inhaled a lung full of smoke, then spit it out at me. "I don't think it's odd," she said. "I think it just proves there is a God, and she has a sense of humor."

Chapter Twenty-Eight

It was the kind of hot summer night that only the Midwest could produce. For a while, it looked like a thunderstorm would sweep in and give us some relief, but Mother Nature was such a tease. She taunted us with the big, ripe thunderclouds, moaned lustily, and snapped a few bolts of lightning over out heads, then sauntered off into the twilight, leaving us in a stew of our own sticky juices.

There was a fan blasting in the kitchen, where Dave half-heartedly graded quizzes, and another in the living room, where Mother and Adam squabbled over the remote control to the TV, but neither one accomplished much. I had dragged home files to study, but couldn't find a single corner of the house where I could breathe. So eventually, I wound up at the picnic table on the deck, with a spotlight glaring down on my piles of papers and mosquitoes dive-bombing me.

There were stacks of notes representing each victim and stacks of notes linking one to the other, and even more notes that seemed to have no relation to anything whatsoever. I had a vague notion that if only I organized them all correctly, a brilliant pattern would emerge, but so far, I had created nothing but a psychiatric nightmare. An arrogant world-class runner raped and murdered by a spurned lover made sense. A beloved wife and mother raped and murdered because she went walking in the wrong place at the wrong time made sense. Even a careless voyeur raped and murdered in some sick form of retribution made sense. But the thought of all three of them raped and murdered by the same man just twisted my brain into knots. How could the death of Carmen Martinez logically lead to the death of Judy DeMarco, then to the death of Seth Schirria? How could they be tied together?

How could they not?

Adam slapped a Coke can down onto the table in front of me. "Any good pictures?" he asked.

I swept the Martinez and DeMarco autopsy photos under a notebook, but he snatched up the Schirria prints before I could stop him. They were standard morgue shots—utilitarian, precise and coldly impersonal. In some photos, the deceased was clearly recognizable. In others, the camera focused so closely on the wounds, the photos seemed to be barely human. Seth Schirria was reduced to a slab of meat.

Adam didn't flinch. Nor did he come up with a smart-ass remark. He simply slid onto the bench across from me and studied the photos as though they were surprisingly helpful visual aids from one of his classes.

I decided to ignore him and concentrated instead on police reports from the park for the last year. I had some notion of tracking which rangers were on duty when certain crimes occurred. Not that I suspected a ranger was our killer. I just wondered whether there was a weak link on the staff, a lapse in park security that the killer had discovered and used to his advantage.

It was just hard to keep schedules straight when I had to stop every ten seconds to swat at mosquitoes.

"Why isn't there more blood?" Adam asked.

"What?" I snapped. I'd just squished a fully gorged mosquito on my shoulder, and there was *plenty* of blood.

Adam slipped an autopsy photo across the table at me. It was a shot of Seth sliced open stem to stern.

"Why isn't there more blood?" he repeated. "You see it all the time on TV. Surgeons are always covered in blood."

"Surgeons are usually working on live patients," I said.

"So?"

"This 'patient' is dead. His heart isn't pumping."

"Ah," Adam said, and he took back the photo.

I stared some more at the park work schedules. Ranger Larry had dropped off the schedule for a large part of January. But then, so had most of the miscreants who hung out in the park. January had been especially frigid that year. Did it make any difference that the park's crime rate dropped while Ranger Larry was gone?

"What's this?" Adam asked, and he slid another photo under my nose.

I didn't have a clue. I sheepishly checked the pathologist's notes. "That's a crushed larynx."

"No kidding?"

"Really. It says so right here."

"Cool," Adam said.

And we both stared in fascination at the injury that would have suffocated Seth Schirria if the broken neck hadn't cut off all communication to his brain first.

"What's that?" Mother asked.

I jumped. I hadn't heard her come outside. But Adam wasn't so easily startled.

"That's a crushed larynx," he said.

"Really?" Mother said, and she adjusted her glasses for a better look. "Are those the vocal cords?"

"I think so," Adam said, and he scooted over to make room for Mother on the bench. They both bent over the photo, looking for anatomical landmarks.

"Why isn't there more blood?" Mother asked.

"Heart's not beating," Adam said smoothly.

"Of course," Mother said. "I should have thought of that."

I rolled my eyes.

There were other oddities in the park schedule, but none jumped out at me as significant. Ray and Joe seemed to have the best record for citing poachers. They were almost always working together on the evening shift when hunters were caught on park land. They weren't nearly as successful when teamed up with other rangers. So maybe they were just lucky, or maybe they were well-matched. Or maybe the other guys weren't so crazy about flying over condemned bridges in the middle of the night just to pick up a yahoo hunting out of season.

As I worked backwards, I saw that Ranger Larry had been absent for several weeks around Labor Day, too. That was about the time Mulhaney's flasher first appeared at the park, but for the life of me, I couldn't see how the two might be related. Would a pervert start dropping his pants in front of ladies just because Ranger Larry took a few days off?

"What's this?" Adam asked, shoving another print—a photo shot so close, it was nearly abstract—across the table.

I glanced at it and wrinkled my nose. "You don't want to know," I said, and tried to take it away from him.

"We've already *seen* it," Adam said as we wrestled over the photo. "What *is* it?"

"I should have never let you have it," I said primly.

Mother plucked the print out of our hands and flipped it over to read the pathologist's note. "Good Lord," she said, and the photo dropped out of her hands as though it were red hot.

Adam snatched it up again and read the note. I expected him to wince, but instead, he just nodded his head.

"Why," Mother asked, "would anyone need a picture of *that*? It's pornographic."

"It's evidence that Seth was raped," I said.

"I would think you could simply take the coroner's word for it."

I sighed. "Who's the coroner, Mother?"

She was silent for a moment. "Good point."

Adam turned the photo sideways, then upside down. "It's kind of artful," he said, "in a bizarre way."

"The only thing that's bizarre," Mother said, "is your sense of taste."

Adam just grinned. He was getting used to Mother.

Dave wandered out to the deck with a beer. "Everyone disappeared out here. What's up?"

"My daughter is giving your son a lesson in art appreciation," Mother said sternly, as though she hadn't been pawing through the pictures just as eagerly as Adam.

Dave looked at the pile of photos on the table and groaned. "Christ, Jo—"

"*I* didn't ask anyone to come out here," I said as I shoveled the prints back into a folder. "You all *had* to butt in."

"Just trying to help," Adam said. "You're the one who brought your work home with you."

"She *always* brings her work home," Mother sniffed. "As though she can't get enough murder and mayhem at the police station."

"Oh, please," I said as I tried to refile my stack of notes in some kind of order. "Dave brings his grading home. You and Adam bring your schoolwork home. Why's it so awful if I bring a picture or two home?"

"Dave's quizzes don't turn people's stomachs," Mother said.

Adam chuckled. "That's not what his students say."

Dave cuffed him on the back of the head, but he wasn't entirely displeased.

"You were *fascinated* with the photos," I said. "Don't even *try* to deny it."

"Of course, I was fascinated," Mother said. "Everyone is *fascinated* by mortality. That doesn't mean murder is healthy after-dinner conversation."

Dave took a long swig of beer and belched. Mother frowned. Adam drained his Coke can and did a masterful imitation of his father. I frowned, just like Mother.

"Why," Dave asked, "are we spending a gorgeous summer evening ogling autopsy photos?"

"Number One," I said, a shade defensively, "it is *not* a gorgeous summer evening. It *stinks*. Number Two, I was *not* ogling. I was studying my case files, which happen to include a few graphic photos."

Adam grinned. "I think we ought to frame that—um—you know—"

"Over my dead body," Mother said.

"Don't tempt me," I muttered.

Adam snorted.

"I'll rephrase the question," Dave said, and he swallowed some more beer to help redirect his thought processes. "Why are you spending your precious time off duty obsessing on this case?"

I swallowed some of my own beer. "Why are you spending your precious time outside the classroom obsessing over some quizzes?"

Dave was silent for a moment, then nodded. "Touche."

And we clinked beer bottles.

Adam looked at Mother. "Did I just miss something?"

"I believe they just had a disagreement," Mother said, "and settled it amicably."

"Wow," Adam said. "Interpersonal relationships are something, aren't they?"

"Take a psychology class next semester," Mother advised. "You'll find it enlightening."

Dave propped his bad leg up on the bench and grunted a little at the effort. "So what are you looking for?" he asked me.

I spread my arms wide. "A brainstorm."

"From us?"

"Why not?" I countered. "The FBI certainly hasn't had any."

"Aha!" Mother said.

I turned on her. "Aha?"

"As in, 'Oho!'" Dave chimed in, positively beaming.

Adam was beside himself. "*Now* what did I miss?"

"I don't even want to know," I groaned.

Mother ignored me. "Jo," she informed Adam, "is spending her precious time off duty obsessing on this case because the FBI has swooped into town."

"And," Dave added, "she's pissed."

"So she's trying to break the case herself," Mother said.

"So she can shove it up the FBI's ass," Dave said.

"Delicately put," Mother said.

"I thought so," Dave said.

I just held my head in my hands.

"All right," Dave relented. "You want real ideas?"

I grunted without looking up.

"Okay," Dave said, and suddenly he switched into his teaching voice, the one that had been honed over the years to snag his students' attention and make them think. "You've been focusing on the who—the killer and his victims. Who was Carmen Martinez? Who was Judy DeMarco? Who was Seth Schirria? And who wanted them dead? Are you with me?"

I reluctantly peered out at him through my bangs. "So far."

"What if the who is irrelevant? What if the important fact is the where?"

"That's easy," Adam said. "The park."

"Why the park?" Dave asked.

"Because it's an easy place to catch his victims alone," Mother said.

"And get away when he's done," Adam said.

"Both good points," Dave said. "Easy opportunity and easy escape. But what if those are merely secondary considerations?"

I squeezed my eyes shut. Pieces of the case were starting to shift around in my head, and I was afraid if I looked too hard, they would stop.

"What if the main purpose isn't killing those particular people, but killing them in this particular park?" Dave asked.

"If people keep dying in the park," I said, more to myself than to anyone else, "the park will change. The trails will be closed because they aren't safe. The number of people coming to the park will drop because the park won't be as useful. Financial support will be eroded. Jobs will be cut. The park could close."

Dave smiled broadly. "There you go."

"But who could possibly want to close the park so badly, they'd kill for it?" Mother asked.

Dave shrugged. "I don't have a clue. Ask her."

Mother turned to me. "Well?"

"Well," I said slowly, watching the pieces in my head slide into new configurations, "budgets are tight. If the park closes, the money used to run the park could be shifted elsewhere." And I thought ungenerously of Berger's incessant campaign for new computer pieces and parts.

"That doesn't seem big enough to justify killing three people," Mother said.

"Oh, I dunno," Adam said. "How much money are you talking about?"

"Maybe a million a year, give or take a hundred thou," I said.

"I could kill for a million," Adam said.

Mother glared at him.

"Theoretically," he added hastily.

"What about developers?" Dave asked. "Does anyone want to turn the park into a mall?"

I chewed on that a bit. The closest mall was a thirty-minute drive up the interstate—not very convenient for the student body. "But it's a flood plain," I said. "And it isn't zoned right. Even if a developer could get his hands on the land, there'd be a ton of red tape to change the zoning, and how would he get the financing or insurance in a flood plain? You can't legislate Mother Nature."

"No, but you can pay people off to ignore her," Dave said.

"He has a point," Mother said.

Adam was spinning his Coke can around the table, spraying Mother with a sticky Coke residue. "My biology prof said the river is home to an endangered species of salamanders."

Mother snatched the can off the table. "I'm surprised you remember."

"It was kinda cool," Adam said, not the least bit offended. "You think of exotic animals as being endangered, but a salamander? Right here in our own ecosystem?"

"Ecosystem?" Dave mouthed to me.

I shrugged.

"I saw that," Adam said.

Dave might have blushed behind his beard.

"So," I said to Adam, "you think a raving scientist wants to shut down the park to save the salamanders?"

"Why not?" Adam asked. "Makes as much sense as killing people off to appropriate the park budget."

Dave couldn't help himself. "*Appropriate?*"

"Your college tuition at work," Adam said smugly.

Before Dave could come up with an adequate reply, two fat raindrops plopped down on my notes. Off to the west, Mother Nature teased us again with a rumble of thunder. Mother Ferris, always the pragmatist, started grabbing my files off the table.

"Now wasn't that nice?" she said brightly. "We've given Jo lots of ideas, so she can stop bringing her work home." And she shoved the files into my arms and shooed us all indoors.

Dave grudgingly returned to his quizzes. I staggered to the dining table, trailing photos and reports behind me. Adam obligingly followed, picking up the pieces.

"Dad had a good idea," he admitted as he handed over an overexposed shot of Seth Schirria on the autopsy table. I winced. Dave was right. I really shouldn't bring such things home. "You mean the park angle?" I asked as I tried to find the right folder for the photo.

"Yeah," Adam said. "That was smart."

Out in the kitchen, Dave raised his head in surprise.

I smiled. "Your dad's pretty sharp," I agreed.

"For an old guy," Adam amended. He knew his father was listening.

"For an old guy," I said, perfectly aware that Dave was listening, too, "your dad rocks."

Adam hooted, and Dave buried his head in his papers, his ears burning.

I gave up on the filing. It could wait till morning. Adam, however, had other ideas. Both he and Barney followed me down the hall to the bathroom. I knew what Barney wanted. He was on a perpetual hunt for food. Adam was another matter.

"Yes?" I said, my hand planted on the bathroom door.

"I just had a goofy idea," he said.

"Goofier than salamanders?"

He dismissed that with a wave of his hand. "I was just yanking your chain."

"Imagine that," I said.

"Made you think, though, didn't it?"

I crossed my arms and tapped my foot. "Adam, I came to the bathroom for a *reason.*"

He peered around me at the toilet and grinned sheepishly. "Okay, gotcha. You want me to hurry up. So here it is: When I heard about this third guy, killed in the park just like the others, you know what I thought?"

"I have not begun to fathom the depths of your thoughts."

He hesitated for a moment, considering whether that was a compliment or an insult (it was both), then plunged ahead. "I thought, this looks just like a hazing."

I forgot my bladder. "You mean, like a fraternity?"

"In a sinister sort of way," he added.

"Seth, or all of them?"

"All of them—absolutely."

"Hazing's illegal," I said automatically.

Adam was dead serious. "So is murder."

Chapter Twenty-Nine

Two days later, I took Gene Emery, the editor, to lunch to pump him about local development plans. Actually, Gene makes more money than I do, so he paid. But I was the one who issued the invitation.

We met at a little vegetarian restaurant that catered to the university crowd. I hadn't abandoned meat, but Gene had celebrated Christmas with a double bypass, so hamburgers at the Farmhouse were out. That was okay by me. Too many people would notice the editor and a cop having a pleasant chat at the Farmhouse.

Gene was pushing retirement age, but he enjoyed owning a small-town newspaper too much to give it up. He'd forsaken red meat for salads and hard liquor for tea on his doctor's orders, but he wasn't ready to step down from his place in the local hierarchy. His newspaper would never win a Pulitzer Prize for investigative journalism, but the power brokers in town preferred to stay on Gene's good side. A damning editorial from Gene could still sting at the polls.

Gene and I had kissed and made up since our spat over the DeMarco case. I knew he was just looking out for one of his employees; he knew I was just trying to nail the son of a bitch who killed Judy DeMarco, so there were no hard feelings. Besides, he played poker every week with Bradley, and I figured if Gene had any real problem with me, Bradley had smoothed it over.

Normally, I would have gone to Bradley with Dave's thoughts about people who might want to shut the park down. But Bradley was too distracted with the feds in town *and* the mayor and City Council on his back. It would only inflame his ulcer to hear I was toying with the idea of a developer resorting to murder to get his hands on park land. That was just bad for taxes.

But talking to Gene behind Bradley's back was touchy, too. I might be able to talk Gene into keeping our conversation out of the newspaper, but I'd never be able to persuade him to keep it from Bradley. It was bound to come out at the next poker game.

So I wasn't quite sure how to bring the conversation around to murder.

The state strike had bumped Seth Schirria's murder off the front page, and Gene was quite willing to talk about *that*. So far, the strike involved only clerical employees who worked directly for the state, but it was the same union that represented employees at the university, and if they walked out, too, our town would be hurting. There wasn't a family within the city limits that wasn't linked one way or another to the university. If the university shut down, the town would, too.

So as we studied the menu, Gene was lecturing me on the delicate relationship between town and gown, and how the state's refusal to give clerks in the highway department anything more than minimum wage ultimately would sabotage my own pay raise. It was enough to put me right off the $10.95 pasta entrée of the day.

If I were the cynical sort, I'd point out to Gene that it was hypocritical to harangue the state for its abominable wage policies when his own employees worked dirt cheap. But it was a matter of perspective. Half of Gene's staff was made up of students, and from their point of view, the money was damned good. In return for the experience, they worked their butts off, and the town got a newspaper free of the impersonal evils of big chains. It was a nice deal all around.

The waitress (who I thought was much too plump for a strict vegetarian diet) derailed Gene's train of thought by sliding two nice cups of herbal tea onto the table. I sipped tentatively while they debated the merits of the breaded eggplant vs. the green curry on a sweltering summer afternoon. By the time she jollied Gene into the curry (I opted for a safe bean sprout salad), his tirade against the state had run out of steam and he was ready to ask what I really wanted.

"A crash course in local economics," I answered.

He looked at me warily. "You aren't planning to become a junk dealer, are you?"

In my wilder moments, I did occasionally fantasize about opening my own shop and stocking it with my auction finds, but I assured Gene I had no immediate plans to go into business.

"Good," he said. "Republicans are in the White House and the economy stinks."

"I wasn't really looking for the national view," I said.

"Same thing locally. Walk down Main Street. More empty storefronts every day. Downtowns can't compete with the malls. America lives in the suburbs, and that's where the stores have gone."

"But we still have the university," I said.

"And the students, God bless 'em, are what keeps most of the remaining businesses open."

"So you don't see a mall in our immediate future?" I asked as I flipped the napkin off a basket of warm bread that the waitress had slipped onto the table. It smelled so good, it made my nostrils twitch.

"Immediate, as in next year?" Gene asked as he helped himself to more butter than was healthy. "No. Five years down the road? Maybe."

I nibbled on my bread. Murder now for a payoff five years later seemed contradictory. If a person were passionate enough to kill, would he be patient enough to wait that long for the benefits? It didn't seem to fit.

"Why not now?" I asked.

"Location," Gene said. "The optimum location would be near the interstate interchange on the east end of town, but so far, no one is in control of enough land around there to make it work. There've been different developers over the years who've tried to piece together a tract big enough to support something like a mall, but too much of the land out there is owned by the university, or it's actively farmed by guys who aren't ready to park their tractors yet. But someday, they will."

"And no other locations around town would work?"

"No other location has an interstate. You need access, Jo. A state highway can't bear the same kind of traffic as an interstate. Any developer who tried to build on the south end of town, for example, would be starting out with a big strike against him because the roads through there weren't built to handle the kind of traffic needed to sustain a mall."

I chewed on that while the waitress delivered our meals. The bean sprouts didn't look nearly as appetizing as I'd imagined.

"What about residential?" I asked. "Any big developments in the works?"

Gene poked at his curry. The color didn't seem to be what he'd imagined, either. "There's always new housing going up in a college town. You don't need the same kind of expensive infrastructure to support an apartment building as you do for a mall." And he proceeded to rattle off four different housing projects that were in various stages of development around town.

"None of those is on the west side," I said as I forked up what looked to be some day-old lawn clippings.

"'Course not," Gene said. "The park service owns most of the vacant land on the west end."

"Of course," I said.

We played with our food for a while. I tried to pretend mine was a cheeseburger. Gene loaded up on more bread.

"There *is* a development going in to the west, beyond the park," Gene said. "Upscale housing, the kind that top administrators at a university can afford. There's very little housing in town to match the kind of salaries a dean or a vice president makes these days."

That got my attention, but I tried to look more interested in my salad than the conversation. I unearthed a tomato beneath the greens and was ecstatic. Gene had excavated through his veggies and was digging into a lump of rice. Lunch was so healthy, I felt like jogging back to the station.

"This upscale development," I said, "is it going to be big?"

"It's just one farm being divided into very big lots," Gene said. "You can't do too much out there with so much land tied up in the park. Plus the market for that kind of housing isn't very big."

"If the park weren't there, would it be an attractive site for developers?"

Gene carefully laid down his fork and gave me his full attention. "I'm not a blithering idiot, Jo. It's flattering to go to lunch with a younger woman, but you haven't charmed me so much that I've forgotten I'm an editor. Do you really want to take the conversation in this direction?"

"Not officially," I said honestly.

"You think I won't go back to the office and put a bug in my best reporter's ear about development and murder on the same side of town?"

"No comment," I said, and speared some tasty-looking dandelion leaves.

Gene sighed and went back to his soggy green rice.

We finished our lunch in silence. Gene was no doubt wrestling with First Amendment issues. I, meanwhile, was pondering the difference between taking a "younger" woman to lunch vs. a "young" woman. I didn't think I appreciated the distinction.

The waitress stopped by to peddle some dessert. She was particularly fond of the "forest berry" pie. I opted for the passion fruit sorbet with a nice sprig of mint.

"What do you really want from me?" Gene finally asked over a fresh cup of tea.

"Background on park opponents," I said.

"That'll require a history lesson," Gene said, loosening up a little. He couldn't resist the opportunity to expound on local history, even to a cop who was holding out on him. "Thirty years ago, there *was* no park—just a picnic area out by the main trailhead."

"I remember," I said, nodding. "My parents used to take my sister and me there in the summer. My dad would go fishing and my sister and I would pick berries." And poison ivy, I thought.

"It was a nice spot," Gene agreed, "but it lacked certain amenities."

"Like restrooms."

"I was thinking more of parking and maintenance, but, yeah, restrooms have been a nice addition." He swallowed a hunk of pie and waved his fork at me, lecturing. "The county formed a park district, bought up a couple of secluded spots like the old picnic area, then went to the voters for a levy to develop them. That generated a *lot* of opposition—on two levels."

I looked at him quizzically. "Two?"

"One—" and he held up a finger—"among property owners, especially farmers with big tracts of land, who didn't think they should pay a big new tax just so city folks could go play games in the country. Their opposition was enough to defeat the levy four times. Unfortunately for them, the city folks finally outvoted them on the fifth try."

"And two?" I prodded.

"Local government—the townships where the parks were eventually developed. Land taken over by the park district was removed from the tax base—meaning the townships could no longer collect taxes on those properties. So their tax base shrank while the demand on services—road maintenance, fire and rescue and the like—rose because of the influx of park visitors."

"And the biggest, most successful park has been the one down by the river."

Gene nodded. "Much of the opposition there has died down over the years. People learn to live with the monster in their midst. But there's still some bitterness among the old-timers."

"You mean old farm families," I said, spooning up the last few drops of sorbet and deftly avoiding the mint.

"Depends on which farmers you talk to," Gene said. "Take the river park—the park district used the initial levy to buy up a lot of land to the south of the old picnic area to create the trail. The farmers who owned that land got a good deal. You don't hear *them* bad-mouthing the park. But farmers who weren't lucky enough to sell out are dedicated park opponents."

I frowned at my empty bowl. "Farmers to the south made a killing, while farmers to the north just got saddled with an extra tax levy."

"More or less," Gene said.

"J.D. Hawkins' place is to the north," I said, more to myself than to Gene. But Gene hadn't finished his narrative. "J.D.'s father was a big park opponent. He operated a private fishing camp on the side, but the park blocked his access to the best parts of the river, so he eventually shut down the camp. He went to his grave condemning the park."

"And J.D.?"

"J.D. was a big opponent, too. Said the park helped kill his dad. But about four years ago, the federal government came through with a development grant for the county park district, and part of it has gone into an expansion of the river park to the north."

"I've seen the construction," I said.

"J.D. sold a big tract to the park district for the expansion. A deal like that kind of softens a man's opposition."

I thought of J.D.'s hot, dusty farmyard. "I've been out to the Hawkins place. It looks like it's just this side of bankruptcy."

Gene signaled for the check. "If I were J.D., I'd have used the money to pay off my loans, not to paint the barn."

I sighed and tossed my napkin onto the table. Finding someone who wanted to shut down the park had seemed like a great idea over the picnic table at home, but it wasn't looking so promising under the restaurant's lights. Maybe if lunch had been a little more substantial, I'd have been more encouraged.

Gene signed the receipt and sent the waitress away with a bigger tip than the food deserved. "Why's Bradley wasting your time on park opponents?" Gene asked. "He's already gone down this road."

I was startled, and it showed.

Gene was amused. "He didn't tell you?"

"It must have slipped his mind," I mumbled as I kicked around beneath the table for my purse. It had migrated to the next booth.

"He brought it up at poker weeks ago—right after Judy was killed," Gene said. "Wondered whether anyone was so desperate to close the park, they'd kill for it. We pretty much decided it was unlikely."

Oh, well, I thought as I snagged my purse with my shoe, if Bradley's poker buddies thought it unlikely, then that was that.

Gene was still chuckling as he led the way out of the restaurant. I was starting to fume. Bradley was the chief of police, for God's sake. *He* was supposed to deal with politicians. *I* was the one who chased criminals.

Gene escorted me to my car and thanked me for the "date." I thanked him for the information, such as it was.

He shook his head in parting. "I really am surprised Brad didn't tell you about the poker game. I thought he told you *everything*."

I fretted about *that* all the way back to the station.

Chapter Thirty

It was probably inevitable that the feds would decide to set up a decoy operation in the park.

They spent a week reinterviewing everyone the home town team had contacted since Carmen Martinez had died, and they stirred up enough excitement in the process to get the murders back on Page One, but when the week was through, they wound up sitting around the squad room just like the rest of us, swilling the same coffee and hashing over the same tired theories. Their profile of the typical serial killer was just dandy, but without a name, it was as useful as a wart.

Bradley and Agent Beck spent another two days debating the effectiveness (and cost) of decoys, and the argument appeared to be going against the idea, but then there was a scare on the other side of the county that decided the debate for them. A teen-age girl jogging at twilight down the road from her home reported that she was grabbed from behind and nearly choked to death before a lucky kick disabled her attacker. He hobbled away and she ran home to the phone.

Agent Beck mobilized his entire team, and there were officers swarming all over the eastern half of the county, looking all night for an athletic young white male with an unexplainable limp. But then Ellen caught the victim contradicting herself on little bits of her story, and by morning, it had all unraveled. Instead of a victim who had miraculously fought off a stone-cold killer, we had a sorry little girl who had fabricated an attack to make her boyfriend jealous. Agent Beck wanted to throw the little trollop in jail. Bradley prevailed with a referral to a family psychologist.

But the uproar was enough to convince the mayor that Something Had to Be Done, and he pushed Bradley into a decoy operation with the feds.

It wasn't small, by any stretch of the imagination. The park trail was only five miles long, but by the time Beck and his agents finished strategizing, there were nearly a hundred officers of some stripe or another assigned to the park.

The operation was on such a grand scale, even Sarah Tate from the university was drafted for the festivities.

The plan was to stake out the park on Monday evening, two weeks after Seth Schirria was killed. Agent Beck commandeered the VFW hall on the west end of town as a staging area. I thought that was a brilliant move right there. Shutting down the VFW hall was sure to keep the operation a secret.

Everyone involved (and by my count, that was half the Western Hemisphere) was ordered to the VFW hall Monday morning for a briefing and to pick up their assignments. I thought that was a brilliant move, too. Nothing would ever leak out in the six hours between the briefing and the sting.

"For Christ's sake, Jo," Bradley groused as I methodically pointed out the flaws in the planning, "just give it a rest, will you?"

We were sucking up the coffee that the ladies of the VFW had cheerfully provided (another flaw, I noted) while we waited for the masses to assemble. There was a small platform at the front of the hall, where Agent Beck had set up a large map of the park. A table to the side of the platform was stacked with folders—our assignments, I presumed. With the exception of the ladies of the VFW, no one without a badge was allowed into the hall. After all, this was a secret operation.

"I'm just saying, we want to lure the killer out to the park, not scare him off with an army." I thought I was making a reasonable observation.

Bradley thought I needed to be more of a team player. "Get with the goddamned program," he grumbled, and lumbered off to join Agent Beck on the platform.

I made a face at his back and settled into the last row of folding chairs, between Henry and Ellen. Sarah Tate, I noted, was sitting in the front row.

Henry was grinning as I sat down. "You and Bradley have a little spat?" He didn't miss a thing.

"We had a slight difference of opinion over the deployment of resources," I said stiffly.

Henry nodded. "You had a *big* spat."

"That's an oxymoron."

"My wife often says I'm a moron," Henry said agreeably as he helped himself to my coffee, "but even *I* know not to piss off the boss before an operation like this."

I snatched back my coffee and pouted. Because, of course, he was right. Bradley was in a tight spot. He didn't need me sniping at him, too.

And I *had* been sniping, ever since my lunch with Gene Emery. I told Bradley he had no business opening—and closing—a whole line of *investigation* without letting his *investigators* know about it. He glared and said pretty much the same thing about me. We hadn't been good buddies since.

Agent Beck mounted the platform and the room slowly quieted. The air conditioning had been shut down to make it easier for us to hear, and the sour stench of too many people drinking too much coffee crept in like the fog. The metal chair was already making my butt ache. While Agent Beck droned his introduction, I distracted myself with thoughts of Dave and a new bottle of massage oil. Ellen took copious notes. Henry fingered the pack of cigarettes in his pocket. Berger stroked his laptop.

Eventually, Agent Beck turned the briefing over to his second-in-command, who would actually coordinate the operation from the park rangers' office. Despite ourselves, we perked up as he laid it out for us.

The plan was to stake out a two-mile stretch of the trail and send out four decoys—all female—who would hike from six o'clock, when it was still plenty light enough for the rest of us to take our positions, until ten, which the feds figured was about as late as they could expect the decoys to stroll through the woods without making the assailant suspicious. (The fact that Seth Schirria was killed between two and five a.m. was dismissed as a fluke.) The decoys would be spaced a half-mile apart, and they would be wired.

Teams of officers would be hidden off the path at eighth-of-a-mile intervals. Each team would have one FBI agent, one local officer and one park ranger. The ranger would be there for background purposes; only the cops would be armed.

I forgot to be a team player and shook my head. By my count, the plan called for planting forty-eight officers along a two-mile stretch of what was supposed to be a deserted woods. All would be linked by radio. And we didn't expect the killer to **notice**?

More agents and rangers would patrol the opposite bank of the river, watching for anyone trying to sneak into the park. Other teams would roam the parts of the trail we weren't staking out, just in case. And another jolly group would be picnicking at the trailhead, monitoring the comings and goings in the parking lot.

Just so the parking lot wouldn't be jammed with cruisers, most of us were to be bused into the park from the VFW hall. The trail would be shut down at five-thirty, so we could get into position. Some folks argued that the trail should be closed all evening so there would be no hapless civilians getting in the way. But Bradley pointed out that if we shut out the public, we'd be shutting out the killer, too.

"Unless he's one of us," Henry muttered.

I looked at Henry in surprise. It was an uncharacteristically insightful observation.

Agent Beck made it clear that the feds were running the operation. If anyone suspicious appeared on the trail, the feds would decide whether to close in. If anyone threatened the decoys, the feds would respond. The locals were there merely for backup.

There was a lot of grumbling among the locals as our assignments were passed out. I reminded Henry that he really needed to be more of a team player. He curled his lip at me.

Our assignments weren't that bad, all things considered. Henry and I were both staking out the trail. Ellen was picnicking at the trailhead. Berger was patrolling on the other side of the river. I warned him to stay off condemned bridges.

I assumed all the decoys were federal agents. And I was almost right. Agent Beck made them stand and face the crowd so we'd know whom we were protecting, and three of them were, indeed, agents who looked to be in their thirties. The fourth was Sarah Tate.

The home team was stunned. Even Ellen gaped, and Henry was shocked into speechlessness. I looked at Sarah as she stood at the front of the room and stared fiercely at the assembled cops and couldn't believe what I was seeing. The feds had picked a woman with absolutely no street experience to play a key role in a sting to catch a serial killer. Were they *nuts*?

"Beck likes her looks," Bradley said calmly when we accosted him after the briefing.

"Man's got no taste," Henry said as he lit up.

We had surrounded Bradley in the parking lot before he could get to his car. Normally, he would have barked at us to shut up and get back to work. But since we were on the brink of a delicate operation, he felt obligated to soothe our nerves.

"Beck thought she looked innocuous enough to appeal to our assailant," Bradley said.

"Innocuous?" I repeated. "She's as *innocuous* as a tank."

"Big as one, too," Berger said.

"Judy DeMarco wasn't dainty," Bradley reminded us.

"Judy DeMarco was a nice lady," I said. "Sarah Tate is *not nice*."

"Our killer won't know that," Bradley said. "All he'll see is a middle-aged woman walking alone on the trail. An *out-of-shape* middle-aged woman. I think she'll look pretty defenseless."

Henry rolled his eyes.

Berger snorted.

Ellen, as usual, was practical. "She hasn't had the proper training, Brad. She could compromise the entire operation with a silly mistake, or even get herself hurt."

Bradley raised his hands to placate us. "Hey, I hear what you're saying, but it's a done deal. She's the campus security chief, and in Beck's book, that makes her qualified."

I sniffed.

Bradley clapped me on the back. "Could be worse, Jo. *You* could be the decoy and she could be covering *your* ass."

I shuddered.

Bradley glanced over his shoulder to make sure no federal types were eavesdropping. "Look, guys, I know it stinks, but we've got no choice here. It's the feds' operation, and we've got to make it work." His face was suddenly grim. "We've got to stop this bastard."

We all looked at our shoes in embarrassment. In the heat of our turf war, we'd forgotten why we were there in the first place.

Bradley surveyed his troops. "No fuckups tonight, right?"

We made noncommittal noises.

"I didn't hear you."

"No fuckups," I said obediently, and the rest mumbled more or less the same thing.

"Good," Bradley said. "Now get out of here. Grab some lunch. Take a couple hours off. Be back here at five."

And he pulled his keys out of his pocket and ambled over to his car.

The others scattered, but I thumbed through my notes, stalling. I'd caught a look from Bradley, and eventually followed him to his car. He rolled down his window and I leaned into it. "What?" I asked.

"Ellen's right," he admitted. "Sarah Tate hasn't been trained for this. She's a smart woman, but it's all book smarts. She doesn't know the street."

"So stop it," I said. "You're the chief. Beck will listen to you."

Bradley sighed. "I gotta live with this woman, Jo. I can't go to war with the campus security chief."

I saw where he was headed and didn't like it one bit. "You want me to cover her butt."

He nodded.

"She tried to get me *fired*," I reminded him.

"Sometimes you oughta be fired," he countered. "But tonight, I want you to keep an eye on her."

Across the parking lot, Sarah Tate marched purposefully to her car. She was wearing a bright summer pantsuit in electric green and orange. It was hard *not* to keep an eye on her.

"God, Brad," I whined, "why pick on me?"

He smiled wickedly as he reached back into the slogans of my past. "Sisterhood is powerful, Jo," he said, and he raised a fist.

I scoured my own memory banks. "You're a male chauvinist pig," I finally spat at him.

He thanked me as he drove away.

Chapter Thirty-One

At five-forty-five, we took our positions.

By five-forty-eight, we were being consumed by mosquitoes.

The stakeout started a mile from the trailhead. My team was another mile down the path, right in the middle of the operation. My team "leader" was a solemn young agent who took his responsibilities very seriously—so seriously that I began to worry that this was his first stakeout. Fortunately, we were accompanied by the ranger Ray, who was so excited by the operation that he momentarily forgot he was pissed off at me. Ray, at least, could be counted on for a little comic relief.

We were camped in a wooded section of the trail about ten yards from the river. Our "leader," identified only by the last name Mohler, had wisely positioned us on the river side of the trail, so no one could creep up behind us. Mother Nature had conveniently deposited several boulders on the spot during the retreat of the last Ice Age, and more recently, she had added a nice locust tree, with a very wide trunk, providing us natural camouflage. We were only three yards off the trail, but if we hunkered down behind the boulder and the tree and stayed absolutely still, we were barely noticeable.

Of course, it's hard to remain absolutely still when mosquitoes are feasting on your precious bodily fluids.

Ray had come equipped with insect repellent and was cheerfully willing to share. But Mohler was afraid the smell might repel murderers, too. Ray assured us his spray was odorless. It turned out to be pretty ineffective, too.

The afternoon had been muggy, but I had dutifully dressed in long sleeves and long pants. At five-forty-eight, it was still sweltering, and I was simmering in my own juices. Sundown couldn't come fast enough.

I sat against a boulder with my back to the trail and peered through the underbrush at the river. It was low and sluggish this time of year. Sand bars had appeared in areas that in the spring were swamped with water. Ray said that if we were quiet, we'd probably see deer come down to the riverbed for a nightcap.

Ray had appropriated the other boulder. Since he was not encumbered with weapons, he had carried along a backpack that promised to produce all sorts of earthly delights. So far, he had pulled insect repellent and a really nice set of binoculars out of his magic bag. I was curious to see what other goodies he had brought along for our amusement.

Agent Mohler didn't seem to appreciate how a few amenities—like, say, a Thermos—stashed in a backpack could make or break a stakeout. I pegged him to be about Ray's age—meaning he was significantly younger than I—but whereas Ray was a cowboy, Mohler was striving for cool and efficient, an American James Bond. He had the looks—hell, if I hadn't had Dave waiting for me at home, I might have even tried flirting with him—but his intensity set off a little alarm in my brain. He struck me as a man who would perform admirably if everything went by the book. I just wasn't sure he could improvise.

We had all been outfitted with earpieces so we could hear the main radio traffic, but only Mohler had been entrusted with a transmitter. What I lacked in electronic gear, I had made up for in weaponry. I had one gun holstered in the small of my back and another strapped to my ankle, which was twice as many guns as I normally carried, I'd brought along Mace and a stick, and I counted my teeth and fingernails as lethal. If I sweated much more, I was going to be pretty lethal in that department, too.

I wasn't in favor of the feds' plan, but as we crept closer to six o'clock, I felt myself getting psyched. We had no reason to expect our man to be in the woods that night, and if he was, I had no reason to expect he'd go after anyone on my little stretch of trail. But despite what I saw as major flaws in the planning, there had been a buzz building as we gathered at the VFW hall, and it only intensified as we set up our positions. I turned away from the river and squinted hard at the trail. I patted my guns to reassure myself that they were there and ready. I took a deep breath. The game was on.

Dave would never understand it.

But his son would.

*   *   *

The park reopened at six o'clock, just as the first decoy—an agent—was launched down the trail. The decoys had been told to walk like Judy DeMarco, not run like Carmen Martinez. The idea was to present themselves as vulnerable to attack, but not to tip our man off by obviously loitering on the trail and begging for it. They were supposed to act like they were familiar with the woods and knew where they were going, not to behave like sightseers. They had to keep enough distance between themselves that no team would ever be watching more than one decoy at once. And they had to keep up the pace for four long hours.

As the first decoy left the staging area, Ray positioned himself with the binoculars. I thought he was a tad premature—the woman was still a mile away—but it kept him occupied and quiet. It also left me relatively free to weigh the merits of Agent Mohler's ass versus Dave's.

The park was unusually quiet, even though it was harboring a hundred assorted police officers. Six o'clock on a summer evening was normally a busy time for the trail, but since the park had been shut down while we were bused in, the woods were empty of the usual conglomeration of parents and kids. There were no voices laughing and shouting and screeching through the trees. There were no gears shifting as cyclists pedaled around the bend. There were no pants and grunts as joggers pounded down the trail.

In the absence of human noises, I could clearly hear the river gurgling as it rounded a gentle curve. A squirrel scampered through dead leaves and made enough of a racket to visibly tense Agent Mohler's shoulders. The whine of the mosquitoes was thunderous.

"Shouldn't she be here by now?" Ray asked anxiously.

Mohler gave Ray a severe look.

I put my finger to my lips to shush him.

And belatedly screwed my earpiece in place.

The transformation was as deafening as the mosquitoes. An agent stationed in the ranger's office was coordinating the radio traffic, catching the transmissions from the field and relaying the information to the rest of us. His voice was deep and hammered into my brain. I wished I could turn the volume down.

The first decoy (creatively pegged Alpha) had safely passed the first checkpoint (creatively pegged Team 1) and was being handed off to the second team down the line. We were Team 8. We had a long time to wait before we saw any action. I wasn't sure Ray would make it.

The picnickers reported that civilians were slowly returning to the parking lot, and before the first decoy reached us, two bicyclists shot past our position. If they spotted us, they gave no sign. Agent Mohler said nothing, but I could tell from the tense frown as he watched them pedal down the trail that he didn't appreciate the extra traffic.

Alpha wasn't very peppy, and even I was feeling antsy by the time she was handed off to the team up the line from us. By then, the second decoy was in play, too, and keeping the radio traffic straight was becoming a little more challenging. The radio guy seemed to have a pretty good handle on it, but I had to wonder how clear-headed he would be when all four ladies were out here, hiking from post to post. And whatever would he do when they reached the end of the stakeout and started backtracking each other? The possibilities made my head swim.

But not so much that I was hallucinating. When the radio guy announced that Alpha was being handed off to our team, I looked expectantly up the trail.

And she wasn't there.

I squinted at the spot where the path curved away from the river and out of sight, back toward Team 7, and all I saw was trees. There should have been a woman in khaki shorts and Nikes, with little pink pom-poms on her white ankle socks, but nothing moved on the trail. I blinked rapidly to clear the sweat from my eyes, but it didn't help. The path was still empty.

I looked at Mohler. He seemed to be watching the trail quite calmly—if you didn't count the muscle twitching in his clenched jaw.

Ray, on the other hand, was ready to jump out of his skin. "Where *is* she?" he demanded, and in his agitation, he started to stand.

I yanked him back and shot Mohler a look that basically demanded the same thing.

He ignored me.

In my ear, the radio guy asked for confirmation that we had picked up the decoy.

Thirty seconds had passed since the handoff. Mohler was making no move to go rescue our decoy. I had been right. He couldn't improvise.

But just as I decided to charge out of hiding, there was a flutter of color up the trail, and Alpha, with all her limbs intact, walked into view.

My eyes darted to Mohler, who was talking quietly into his transmitter, then to Ray, who was grinning in relief, then back to the decoy. In my ear, the radio guy boomed that Alpha had been safely handed over to us.

Safely, my ass. She had been out of sight for more than thirty seconds. Carmen Martinez's neck had been snapped in less time than that.

I watched Alpha hike confidently toward us, but I was really straining to hear what Mohler was saying into the radio. Any second, I expected the radio guy to order the decoys to halt. We had a major blind spot in the stakeout. It was imperative that we regroup.

But the order never came. Alpha kept up her pace as she approached us, and I even imagined she was smiling in the direction of our position. The radio guy was droning her location and the progress of the next decoy in decidedly bored tones, and Mohler was no longer whispering into his radio. His eyes were fixed on Alpha.

Ray raised his eyebrows at me. He knew something was wrong.

I shook my head at him and waited. Waited while Alpha passed silently within a few yards of us, waited while another pair of cyclists ripped along the trail and veered around her, waited while she brushed their dust off her shorts and continued down the path, waited until she was just a colorful dot in the distance. And just before she faded out of our sight, the radio guy reported that she had been spotted by the next team down the line.

I turned to Mohler. "We have a blind spot."

He tried to shush me.

"We have to tell them," I said, and I didn't even try to speak softly.

Mohler winced at the sound of my voice.

"We have to *abort*," I insisted.

Mohler glanced swiftly up and down the trail. There wasn't a soul in sight. He sighed and motioned me toward the river.

We left Ray standing guard behind the boulders. We slipped quietly through waist-high weeds, and clouds of gnats swarmed up into our eyes and noses. I bit back a mighty urge to sneeze and followed Mohler down to the edge of the river, where the sounds of the water just might mask our voices.

Mohler kept his back to the river so he could see me and monitor Ray at the same time. "We will not abort," he said quietly.

"But we have a blind spot," I repeated.

"I know."

"Did you report it?" I demanded.

Mohler's face reddened. "Yes," he said tersely. We were speaking in whispers, but there was enough anger boiling around us, we might as well have been shouting.

"You *told* them we have a blind spot, and they didn't call those women back? They didn't order us to find a new position?" I was incredulous.

"If we move," Mohler said reasonably, "we'll just compromise the position of the next team down the trail."

I planted my hands on my hips and blew the bangs off my forehead in frustration. "Did anyone even survey the trail beforehand? When they decided our positions, didn't anyone check for blind spots?"

"The trail isn't straight," Mohler said. "There are several positions where the line of sight isn't optimal."

"*Several*?" I hissed. I was no longer incredulous. I was horrified.

"It was agreed that the risk was acceptable," Mohler said.

I snorted. Bradley sure as hell wouldn't have found it acceptable. Or had the feds decided Bradley didn't need to know about little things like blind spots?

"What about the decoys?" I asked. "Do *they* know we can't cover them?"

"The decoys are trained federal agents. They understand the risks."

"Sarah Tate is *not* an agent," I reminded him.

"Tate was fully briefed on the operation," he said, but his eyes wouldn't meet mine.

I opened my mouth to protest, then snapped it shut. I could just picture Sarah Tate shrugging off the risks. She was a big, tough woman, and she was the campus security chief to boot. No one was going to tell *her* the job was too dangerous.

The silly bitch.

"I want to talk to my chief," I said.

Mohler just shook his head. "No unauthorized radio traffic."

"I want to report to the chief of police," I insisted, and I held out my hand for the radio.

But Mohler quickly stashed the radio in his hip pocket. "Can't do it. You'll compromise our position. You'll compromise the entire operation."

I stared in exasperation at the river. A family of geese was waddling single file down the opposite bank for an evening swim. Below us, a turtle climbed out of the water and up onto a rock to sun itself. Above, a blue heron swooped along the river toward its nest downstream. It was a gorgeous, peaceful summer evening on the river. And any minute, a monster could come charging out of the woods. I was no longer sure we could stop him.

"This sucks," I told Mohler.

But I followed him back into position.

* * *

The feds weren't as incompetent or as cavalier as I liked to imagine. Agent Mohler and others had reported three blind spots along the trail, and as soon as the locations were nailed down, the decoys were directed to report in whenever they passed through one. I was not mollified, but my vote didn't count.

Sarah Tate, code named Charlie, huffed into view at six-forty. I gave her credit for a 20-minute mile (I was faster) and she scored points for appearance. She'd traded in her electric pants suit for a white T-shirt, denim shorts and sensible shoes, and though the sweatband across her forehead was a shocking pink, it did keep her hair out of her eyes and her vision unobscured. She clutched a water bottle in one hand (it was already half-empty) and the well-worn bird guide that she carried in the other hand was a nice touch. She even paused once to consult her book, then peer quizzically up into an oak tree.

Ray snorted when he saw her, and even though it was an ungentlemanly comment, I had to agree with the sentiment. Even with the pasty thighs dimpled with cellulite and the cheeks red with exertion, she didn't exactly come across as a vulnerable target. There was a fearsome air to her stride, and a look that said, "Don't fuck with me, buster." Unless our killer was out looking for a challenge, I just couldn't picture him zeroing in on Sarah. There were other, much tastier morsels strolling through the park.

Like the sweet thing who came around the bend just behind Sarah. I guess she could have been called a jogger, but she wasn't exactly blazing down the trail. She had the uniform, all right—short shorts that showed off slim, tanned legs, and a halter top that bounced prettily in the golden sunlight, and a ponytail that swung saucily in the breeze—but her form was all wrong.

Well, at least it was to me. Ray's eyes followed her as though she were Olympic caliber. Even Agent Mohler allowed himself to be distracted from Sarah.

I quietly cleared my throat, just to bring the boys back to attention.

Ray grinned unapologetically.

Agent Mohler glared at me for breaking silence.

The girl sidestepped Sarah and pranced past us. Sarah shot a sour look at the girl's backside. I wondered whether the girl had made an ungenerous comment in passing.

Two cyclists sped down the path in the opposite direction. They didn't stop to gawk, but they were distracted enough that one of them nearly veered into Sarah. She barked, the cyclist swerved in surprise, and both he and his partner slid toward disaster. They recovered just in time, and shot on toward the trailhead, but not before Sarah blistered their ears with unkind speculations about their parentage.

It was my turn to grin at Ray. Sarah Tate was a pain in the ass, but you had to admire her command of the language.

* * *

At seven o'clock, Ray passed out candy bars. They were dark chocolate (not my favorite) and sticky from the heat, but we gobbled them up. It's hungry work sitting perfectly still on stakeout.

At seven-fifteen, another jogger pounded into view. He was more my age than Ray's, and I realized in surprise that he was the computer guy, Nieman, who had placed Jesse Conklin in the trailhead parking lot the night Carmen Martinez had died. Part of me acknowledged that I ought to point him out to Agent Mohler, but Mohler *had* been shushing me all evening, so I primly kept my mouth shut. Besides, it wasn't all that surprising to see Nieman on the park trail. It was the only good path off campus for a guy like Nieman to fight the battle of the bulge.

But I made a mental note to drop in on Nieman sometime soon, just to make sure he was behaving himself. I occasionally do believe in coincidences, but only after I've ruled out all other possibilities.

A little later, I caught myself zoning out on the radio guy. With four decoys in play, he was like a symphony maestro, conducting an unwieldy quartet in mad four-part harmony while an orchestra of officers chimed and tooted in the background. His voice was the baton that marshaled them all together, and I marveled at how calmly he directed us. Other minds may have come up with this plan, but he was the one who orchestrated the score, and I caught myself ignoring the trail and listening instead to the radio as he smoothly directed

Alpha and Delta to cross paths in front of Team 4, launched Beta on her second tour and admonished Charlie (aka Sarah Tate) to pick up the pace.

I shook my head and forced myself to concentrate on the trail. It was pleasant to hear Sarah at the receiving end of the feds' marching orders, but *my* orders were to keep a clear head and secure my little strip of the path. So I shut out the radio guy's soothing voice and counted civilians instead.

It was the evening rush hour in the park world, and despite the earlier closing, the trail was busier than I had ever found it on my morning hikes with Barney. There were youngsters wobbling on training wheels, followed by moms huffing over the weight they'd pick up since they'd last ridden a bike. There were dads with one or two babies stashed in the carriages they towed behind their bikes. An older couple pedaled serenely down the trail on a tandem. A gang of young teens tried to shoot through the woods on skateboards and kicked up enough dust to gag us. And in between all of the bikes were joggers and hikers, mostly in pairs, but a distressingly high number of them out in the woods alone. Hadn't Carmen and Judy and Seth taught them anything?

It was tough to stay perfectly hidden with all of that humanity weaving in and out of the trees around us, and two of the teams were, indeed, discovered by civilians during that hectic hour before sundown. I was hoping maybe *that* would pull the plug on the operation, but the feds were resilient. They sent the curious back to the trailhead with ringing lectures on patriotism, followed by stern warnings to keep their mouths shut or else.

I figured that would keep things under wraps for—oh—another ten minutes.

At eight-fifteen, there was a flurry of excitement in our neck of the woods when a cyclist pulled out to pass a jogger and clipped him with his handlebar. They both fell to the ground in a tangled heap of legs and spinning bicycle tires.

Ray wanted to run out and help them, but I held him back. It was a good thing, too, because they came up swearing and swinging, and neither one seemed too concerned about any bystanders who might get in their way. It was a dandy fight—I thought the cyclist's helmet gave him an unfair advantage, but the jogger made up for it with creative oaths—and they scrambled to get at each other over the fallen bike.

But then a fatherly type pedaled around the bend, and being the upstanding sort, he put a stop to their shenanigans. I was kind of sorry to see it end. I thought it was the best show of the night.

As it turned out, I was wrong.

Chapter Thirty-Two

The woods were melting into blue twilight when Sarah Tate passed us on her second trip back toward the trailhead. She still struck me as distinctly unapproachable, but after two hours on the trail, she was starting to sag. Her hair was wet with sweat, and her shirt clung damply to her back. The look on her face was grim, and she was no longer taking the time to pose with her bird guide. She was limping, as though she had a blister or two swelling on her toes, and she was definitely off the pace. Delta was only one team behind her.

The radio guy ordered Delta to take a five-minute breather so she wouldn't wind up on Sarah's back. Sarah must have heard the order, too, but she didn't react visibly to the indirect rebuke. She plodded doggedly up the trail, and we just as doggedly watched her. As she was fading into the shadows, Agent Mohler reported to the radio guy that we were handing her off.

Sarah was in the blind spot, and we silently counted off the seconds until the next team could pick her up. At thirty, I wasn't too concerned. She should have radioed her location, but she was obviously walking slower and perhaps didn't realize she was out of our sight. At forty-five seconds, I frowned. At sixty, I looked questioningly at Mohler. The trail was empty of civilians at that point. The next team should have had no trouble picking her up.

The radio guy asked for Sarah's position. Nobody had her.

And Sarah wasn't transmitting.

Ray was fixated on his watch and had lapsed into counting off the seconds out loud.

Mohler's fingers were twitching over his radio.

At ninety seconds, I shout out from behind the boulder.

"Maintain your position!" Mohler hissed.

I gave him credit for using the right terminology, but Bradley's order to keep an eye on Sarah was ringing in my head and I was out of there.

I was stiff after crouching for more than two hours behind a boulder, but I forced my legs to move, and all those mornings hiking with Barney paid off. I tore up the trail toward the spot where we had last seen Sarah. The woods were becoming murky with shadows, but the path was clear, and I made it to the bend in the trail in seconds.

There was no sign of Sarah around the curve.

The trail behind me was empty, too. Mohler hadn't followed me.

I pulled my gun from the holster at my back and ripped the radio receiver from my ear. I couldn't concentrate with the radio guy booming into my head.

I stopped and forced myself to breathe slowly while I listened to the forest. There were no sounds of thrashing in the underbrush, but there were no comforting animal sounds, either. Something had startled the birds and the humming insects into silence.

I stepped off the dusty trail into the quieter growth along the edges, and slowly moved forward. The trail ahead of me was still empty. If anyone from the next team up the line had come out to investigate, he was much too stealthy for me to pick him out.

As I crept forward, I peered through the deepening gloom for scuff marks on the trail or flattened weeds that might reveal where Sarah had left—or had been dragged—off the path, but the undergrowth seemed undisturbed. Sarah had simply vanished with the sun.

I shivered. We *couldn't* have lost her that fast.

I slowly turned around in a full circle, scanning the woods, the trail and back again. Nothing but trees and weeds and rocks and more weeds—

And a flash of white.

A head-high clump of Japanese knotwood sprouted ten feet off the trail, and through its broad green leaves, I could see a flutter of white like Sarah's T-shirt. I was too far gone to wait for backup. Whoever was wearing that white shirt was on the ground.

I quietly parted the leaves and slithered through the stalks gun first, and caught Sarah with her pants down.

Literally.

"What in hell are you *doing*?" I barked.

"What in hell does it look like?" she groused back as she squatted in the weeds. "You wouldn't have a tissue, would you?"

"Jesus Christ," I sputtered, but her request had been a command, and I fumbled for a Kleenex in my pants pocket. "Why haven't you called in your location?"

Sarah balanced precariously with one thick hand muffling the wire on her chest. She grabbed the Kleenex with the other. "I didn't care to share my business with the rest of the world."

"The rest of the world," I reminded her angrily, "is out here covering your ass," which, at that moment, was way too much in evidence.

"I couldn't wait any longer," Sarah said simply.

Behind us, footsteps pounded belatedly up the trail.

Sarah tugged one-handed at her shorts and finally looked troubled. "We can keep this between us girls, right?"

Oh, right, I thought. My career had just gone in the dumper, but Sarah and I were going to keep her overactive bladder to ourselves. Sure.

"Jo?" Ray called from the trail. "Where are you?"

I shook my head in exasperation. It was amateur hour on stakeout.

And Bradley's order was still hanging over my head. Take care of Sarah.

"Radio your location," I snapped at her. "I'll handle this."

Sarah was still fumbling with her zipper.

"*Now*," I said, and plunged back through the weeds.

Ray jumped when I emerged, and his eyes bugged out. I still had my gun out, and it was pointed right at his gut.

"Sorry," I said sheepishly as I stuffed the gun back in its holster.

Ray was panting. "You okay? Is she dead?"

I made a face. "We're both okay. She just wandered off the path."

Ray looked skeptically around the trail. "It's not *that* dark."

"She thought she saw something and she left the trail, okay?"

"But how—" Ray started, then Sarah stumbled out of the weeds, still tugging at her shorts, and he grinned at me. "Oh, *I* get it."

"She thought she saw something and went off the path to investigate," I said sternly.

Ray winked at me. "Gotcha."

"Must have been a bear," Sarah said, getting into the act.

"Deer," Ray corrected.

"Right," Sarah said. She turned to me. "I radioed my location. You're clear to go back."

"I'll just wait here till you're farther up the trail," I said stubbornly.

She shrugged. "Suit yourself. I gotta make up for lost time." And she squared her shoulders and marched up the trail.

I screwed my earpiece back in and we waited until the radio guy confirmed that the next team had spotted her. And then we waited another half-minute, just to be sure. She was just a wavering white splotch in the shadows by the time we turned for the hike back to our hiding spot.

Ray warned me confidentially that Agent Mohler was pissed. I didn't care. I'd take an angry FBI agent over an angry chief of police any day.

*　　*　　*

Mohler was, indeed, threatening hell and damnation as we slipped back behind the boulders, and he wasn't buying any story about Sarah being lured off the trail by a suspicious deer. I was inclined to let him vent, but then his observations got a little too personal, and Ray jumped in to my defense, pointing out it wasn't my fault Sarah had to answer a call of nature.

Mohler was outraged. He was too well-trained to raise his voice on stakeout, but he made it clear that my flaws and Sarah's were going in his report. Ray squirmed guiltily for revealing the sordid truth, but I patted him on the shoulder to reassure him, then turned my sweetest smile on Mohler.

"Breathe one little *word*," I said calmly, "and I'll tell your boss how you stayed behind when Sarah Tate disappeared and refused to back up your partner."

Mohler's mouth dropped open.

"I swear to God," I said, "that's what I'll tell him."

Mohler stared at me as his reputation flashed before his eyes.

I stared back.

And the big bad FBI agent blinked.

Just like I knew he would.

*   *   *

Bradley was not as easy to bluff.

The stakeout was halted at nine-forty-five, when it got so dark that one of the decoys twisted her ankle on the trail. The other decoys were game for another round, but there was no moon and no way for us to adequately protect them. So Agent Beck shut us down, and we pulled out our flashlights for the hike back to the trailhead. In nearly four hours, none of the teams had gotten so much as a nibble.

I tried not to gloat.

Back at the VFW hall, the ladies' auxiliary had come through with more urns of coffee, platters of sandwiches and plates of cookies. Henry was inhaling food, and Berger was right there with him, shoving cookies by the handful into his mouth. There was almost a festive air in the hall, as officers and agents shook off four hours of enforced silence and slapped each other on the back and told outrageous lies. The fact that we hadn't accomplished anything didn't seem to bother anybody.

Well, except for Bradley, who was standing alone in a corner and glowering over a sandwich at the proceedings. I backpedaled to the restroom before he spotted me.

And found Sarah Tate leaning over the sink, splashing water over her sweat-streaked face.

I just nodded and ducked into a stall. I did **not** want to rehash the night with her.

But she was still there, vigorously scrubbing her face with a paper towel, when I re-emerged. She stepped aside to give me room at the sink, and I busied myself at the soap dispenser.

"I've asked Agent Beck to reassign me," she said abruptly.

I looked up in surprise, and our eyes locked in the mirror. The harsh light of the restroom was not kind to either of us. We both looked every one of our forty (or more) years, and the picture was not flattering.

She turned away first. "I am not a good decoy," she admitted as she balled up the towel and tossed it into the trash can. "I am a good administrator and a good coordinator, but I am not a good decoy."

I hadn't expected such brutal honesty from her and felt an uncomfortable urge to console her. "The bird guide was a good idea," I said lamely.

She brightened for a moment. "Yes, it was, wasn't it?" Then she shrugged. "Perhaps I'll give the book to one of the other girls." Then she fluffed her frizzy hair with her fingers, pronounced the results satisfactory and marched out to mingle with the bosses.

I shook my head in bewilderment. Had Sarah Tate just revealed herself to be human? And had I responded in kind? Dave would never believe it.

I ran into Berger and the ranger Joe hanging outside the restroom door and telling their buddies how they had chased away two poachers who sounded to me like J.D. Hawkins' kids. Ellen was sitting at a folding table next to them, commiserating with one of the lady agents over breastfeeding and diaper rash. Henry was still planted firmly in front of the food, joking with some deputies about a certain stocky decoy huffing and puffing down the trail. I surprised myself again by feeling somewhat irritated by his tone of voice.

I'd chowed down on two of Ray's candy bars during the evening, so I allowed myself only one cookie. Bradley caught up with me as I was grabbing a cup of coffee to wash it down.

"You got any idea how much this fiasco is costing us in overtime?" he complained.

"It wasn't a fiasco," I corrected him. "It was a waste of time."

"Same difference," he said, and appropriated my coffee.

I sighed and turned back to the urn for another cup.

"We're doing it again tomorrow," he said.

I groaned.

"The mayor thinks it's brilliant," he said.

"Remind him of that when he gets the bill," I said, and we nursed our coffees while we surveyed the crowd.

"You're being reassigned," Bradley said after a while.

I raised my eyebrows at him.

"You're on Beck's shit list. He wants me to reprimand you."

"So noted," I said stiffly.

"Well, what'd you expect?" Bradley demanded, finally losing the tattered leash on his temper. "You left your goddamned post."

"There was a blind spot," I snapped back at him. "We lost our decoy. What was I supposed to do?"

"*You* weren't supposed to do anything. It was the agent's call, not yours."

"The agent was an idiot," I protested.

"And maybe his partner was, too," Bradley shot back.

We abruptly turned away from each other and glared at the festivities. I was furious with Bradley for personally saddling me with Sara Tate's welfare, I was furious with Beck for hauling me off surveillance, and I was *really* furious with Mohler for reporting my shortcomings to his boss. I'd been bluffing when I'd threatened to squeal on him. Now I was seriously contemplating following through with it.

"Are the feds doing anything about the blind spots?" I asked when I could finally trust myself to speak.

"They're changing the plan," Bradley said, still without looking at me. "They're gonna limit the stakeout to two decoys and a one-mile section of the trail. No blind spots."

"Why'd they change plans?"

"Because I told them I was pulling my guys out if they couldn't protect the decoys."

"The mayor would never allow you to do that," I told him.

Bradley shrugged. "Beck doesn't know that."

I drained my cup and turned around to toss it into a waste basket. Bradley fired another shot from behind. "I'm putting Ellen in your place."

Normally, I would have clawed his eyes out for that. But I was still so angry over other insults to my delicate psyche that I shrugged that one off. "Fine," I said wearily, "Ellen and Mohler will be a perfect match."

Bradley looked disappointed that I hadn't snapped at his bait. He was in such a foul mood, he wanted to keep the fight going.

I just wanted to go home. And I was actually digging through my pockets for my car keys when Sarah Tate reappeared.

"Chief Bradley," Sarah announced loudly, "I want you to write this woman up." And she waved a chubby finger in my direction.

Sarah's voice carried over the crowd and conversations halted all around us. Curious eyes darted our way, expecting a catfight. I was caught off guard. What had happened to all the warm and fuzzy feelings in the restroom?

Bradley, for his part, suddenly looked very uncomfortable. "What's the problem, Sarah?" he asked cautiously.

"I lost radio contact and wandered off the trail in the dark, and this woman," she said sternly, still pointing at me, "this woman was the only officer who had the presence of mind to go out and find me before I could fall into the river and drown. I want you to write her up."

Bradley was perplexed. "Write her up—*how*?"

"Put a nice note in her personnel file," Sarah said. "Give her a day off. Hell, give her a raise."

I gaped.

Bradley looked stunned. After all, this was the same woman who'd demanded my badge just a few months ago. And now she was my best buddy? "I'll keep it in mind," Bradley managed, and he fled without saying goodbye.

Sarah chuckled as she watched him duck into the safety of the men's room. "That oughta fix *him*," she said. Then she nudged me in the ribs with her elbow. "We girls gotta stick together."

And she plunged happily back into the crowd, fighting over the last of the cookies.

I watched in awe as she flicked Berger aside, and felt an old rusty urge to raise my fist in salute.

Sisterhood was full of surprises.

Chapter Thirty-Three

W e descended on the park the next night with fewer officers but fortified once again by the ladies of the VFW. There were some awkward moments when I joined the picnickers at the trailhead—they had really liked Ellen—but then I produced a box of Mother's brownies and I was welcomed warmly into the gang. We spent a jolly evening nibbling on snacks, tossing a Frisbee, playing cards and—yes—watching the people driving into and out of the park. I spotted two runners from the university (both male) and the young cyclist who had been on the trail when Carmen died, but no one else was even remotely interesting. By the time we packed up at ten, I was exchanging phone numbers with my fellow picnickers and promising to keep in touch.

Except for two high school kids who had crept down to the river to study human reproduction, there was no trouble on the trail that night. No one harassed the decoys or any other hikers. The operation was a bust.

The next night, it poured, and since no one wanted to sit in the woods during a thunderstorm, the stakeout was temporarily suspended. The rain continued relentlessly for two more days, and by then it was the weekend, so the feds left town for a little R and R. But Agent Beck vowed to be back on Monday.

In the meantime, I dropped in on the jogger, Ken Nieman, and we had a pleasant chat. He was much more comfortable talking to me in the privacy of his office. When I mentioned Judy DeMarco and Seth Schirria, he quickly volunteered that he had been home with his wife both nights, and he offered me his home phone number, just in case I wanted to check with her. Spouses are notoriously bad alibis, but I took the number anyway. His answers to my questions didn't set off any alarms in my head, and neither did his wife when I called her later that day. Except for some mild irritation at being hassled by the police (his wife's words, not mine), they both seemed relatively secure in their belief that Nieman had nothing to do with the murders in the park.

I also got back to the cyclist who thought both Nieman and I were ancient. I tracked him down at his home, where he was doggedly trying to patch a tire in between my pesky questions. He was much more focused on his bike than he was on me, and if he hadn't been prancing around the garage in his shorts, I would have been irritated by his behavior. He'd been working out, and he was a pleasure to watch even if the words coming out of his mouth weren't particularly useful. I left him feeling much as I had after questioning Nieman. Only coincidence had brought them into Carmen's world the day she died, and there wasn't even coincidence to link them to DeMarco and Schirria.

Monday dawned clear and hot, and I rolled into the station with another box of Mother's brownies, fully expecting to spend the evening picnicking at the trailhead. But there wasn't a single federal agent in the squad room—no suits usurping my desk, no one molesting Berger's computers and no one hogging the coffee pot. There wasn't even a reporter peeking at the overnight arrest sheets. The station was dead.

I warily approached Bradley's office, expecting to find Agent Beck in residence, but it was only Bradley sitting behind the big mahogany desk, scowling as usual at a pile of reports.

"What?" he grumbled without looking up.

"It's awfully quiet around here," I said, stealing a glance behind his door, just to make sure Beck wasn't lurking in the shadows.

"So?" Bradley said as he scrawled his signature across the payroll sheets.

"So, where *is* everybody?" I asked tentatively, half-afraid they'd launched a major sting without me.

But Bradley just grunted. "Gone."

"Gone?" I repeated inanely. "Gone *where*?"

Bradley finally deigned to look at me. "Gone to the next crisis," he said.

"Naw," I said.

"Oh, yeah," he said, and for a moment, he lost the dour look of a man immersed in paperwork, and a boyish grin almost crinkled the corners of his mouth.

I plopped into a chair and broke out the brownies. "Tell me everything."

And he did, in between mouthfuls of chocolate. I was sprayed with a lot of crumbs, but I still got the essentials. Someone had tried to kidnap a senator's daughter, and Beck had been ordered back to Washington in the dead of night. His troops had been pulled out with him. No one was saying that Carmen Martinez was no longer a top priority, but a dead track star didn't have the same urgency as a living, breathing teen-ager.

"So the feds left town?" I asked. "Just like that?"

Bradley nodded as he reached for another brownie.

I slapped his hand away.

"And what are we supposed to do?"

"Beck had some suggestions," Bradley said as he dolefully eyed the thick frosted brownie I had been saving for myself. "He thought maybe we should run a single decoy through the park at odd hours, with just a jogger or two as backup. He thought Ellen might be attractive."

I made a face. "Oh, yeah, Ellen and her baby stroller would be *very* attractive."

Bradley's face reddened. "I wouldn't send her out with the baby. Give me *some* credit."

I sniffed and closed the box of brownies.

"I'm not sending anyone out," he said as he resigned himself to only two brownies. "The decoy operation didn't do anything but bust my budget."

"Made the ladies of the VFW happy," I said.

"Then they ought to hold a bake sale for us. Our overtime account is shot." And we both thought glumly about explaining *that* little problem to City Council.

Bradley tossed the payroll sheets into his out basket. "You got *anything* to follow? It'd be nice to shove an arrest up Beck's nose when he comes back."

I pondered my options. "There's the flasher."

Bradley rolled his eyes.

"Or we could squeeze the panty thief again." But that image was so nauseating, we both grimaced.

I sighed. "What I'd really like is the forensics on Schirria."

"What's stopping you?" Bradley asked.

I pointed at the newspaper on his desk. "State strike is still on. Says so right there. Our reports are gathering dust on some striker's desk."

"So go get a copy yourself," Bradley said practically. "You *do* still drive, don't you?"

I blushed. "It's an hour away," I said in feeble defense.

"It's on the city clock," he said. "What do you care?"

"The city could be raped and pillaged in my absence," I pointed out.

"We still got Berger," Bradley assured me.

"Dear God," I said. But I went anyway.

*   *   *

The forensics lab, which served ten counties in our corner of the state, was tucked behind a cornfield in a location that was convenient to no one but a handful of law-abiding farmers. It was a dandy site for a barn. A four-story brick and stone office building with an acre of mostly empty parking spots was wildly out of place. But it was blissfully air-conditioned. My car was not.

The pickets razzed me a little as I crossed their line, but there were only two of them, and the sun had broiled the contrariness right out of them. I smiled and nodded pleasantly at their half-hearted chants about scabs and ducked into the lobby. I figured if I spotted a Coke machine inside, I might treat them to a drink on my way out.

There was no one at the reception desk and no secretaries in the offices, so I wandered around until I stumbled upon a guard, who threatened to frisk me. I flashed my badge instead, and he blushed and escorted me to a lab where a harried technician eventually unearthed the Schirria report, along with a dozen others that had been piling up for us. I thumbed through the stack and noted bloodwork from a traffic fatal that Henry had been trying to clear for three weeks, a fiber analysis on a rape that had been haunting Ellen and a brilliant report on a hunting "accident" that Berger had been steadfastly ignoring. And at the very bottom were two DNA reports, one labeled Martinez and the other, DeMarco.

I frowned. "I thought you already gave us the reports on Martinez and DeMarco."

The technician just shrugged. "DNA takes longer."

I opened the Martinez folder, but it was gibberish to me. "What's this mean?"

The tech sighed. I was keeping him from some really fascinating hemp samples. But he took the folder and scanned the results. "It means the semen sample we took from Martinez came from a white male, not a relative."

"That's it?" I asked. "No names?"

The tech shrugged again. "Our database is still pretty small. There were no matches."

"What about DeMarco?"

The tech resigned himself to my ignorant questions and thumbed through the DeMarco folder. "Same thing. White male, not a relative. No matches."

"Except to the Martinez perp," I said.

"Well, sure," the tech said. Then he frowned and reread the Martinez results. Then he went through the DeMarco folder again.

"Well, no," he said uncomfortably. "They don't match, either."

"That can't be right," I said as my brain suddenly cramped up in knots.

The tech looked just as confused as I felt. "They don't match," he repeated helplessly.

"You're saying two different men killed these women?"

"Two different men had sex with these women," the tech corrected me. "Same person might have killed them."

"Well, shit," I said, and I desperately reread the reports, as though somehow I might have the smarts to spot a flaw in the findings.

The tech edged away from me, hoping I'd take the troublesome DNA results away with me. But I wasn't ready to let him off the hook. "What about Seth Schirria? Are there any matches for him?"

"There were no semen samples with Schirria," the tech reluctantly reminded me. "No DNA to analyze."

"So," I said with exaggerated patience, masking the frantic gearshifts in my head, "you're telling me two different men raped Martinez and DeMarco, but you don't know whether either man raped Schirria."

"You got it," the tech said brightly.

"Jesus Christ," I muttered as I restacked the reports. How would I ever explain *this* to Bradley? We'd focused our entire investigation on the premise that one man was the killer. Even the FBI had assumed that only one monster was roaming through the park. How could we have been so *wrong*?

I absently hoisted my purse to my shoulder and scooped up the reports in my arms. My brain was racing through the names of all the men we had questioned, weighing and discounting all sorts of combinations of killers and victims, and it didn't register with me until I was fumbling for the doorknob that the tech was telling me to wait.

He was slipping some more papers into a fresh folder. "You might as well take this one, too. It came in over the weekend."

I was having a hard time tracking. "We didn't have any fatals this weekend."

"It's a suicide," he assured me. "The sheriff's office caught the call. I thought if you were heading to Doc Sweitzer's office anyway . . . ."

I sighed and let him slip the folder on top of the stack in my arms. "You're sure it's a suicide?"

"Man hanged himself," the tech said firmly. "Nothing for you guys to worry about."

My eyes crossed as I scanned the folder under my nose. The name on the tab seemed familiar. Morbid curiosity prompted me to drop my armload of reports onto the counter and open the fresh folder.

My frazzled brain screeched to a full stop.

The face staring out of the autopsy photo was Ranger Larry.

Chapter Thirty-Four

"**I**mpossible!" Bradley bellowed.

"Illogical," Ellen agreed.

"Un-fucking-believable," Henry said.

And they were all three right.

It was early evening by the time I got back to the station, and everyone was gathered in the squad room, either coming or going, so I just dropped my bombs all at once, without any preamble.

I had stopped at the coroner's office first to accost Doc Sweitzer. He acknowledged that a dead ranger from a park where three other people had died violently was a tad suspicious, but when I berated him for not telling us, he blustered his way out of it by blaming the weekend shift. "I'm the goddamned coroner," he grumbled. "I don't work weekends."

"So we lost forty-eight hours," I snapped back at him as I paged through the autopsy report. "Thank you very much."

"Doesn't matter," Doc Sweitzer said. "It's a *suicide*."

He had me there. Ranger Larry had lived alone in a rented farmhouse several miles north of the park (squarely in the sheriff's jurisdiction). He had called off sick Saturday morning, but that hadn't raised any alarms at the park. Ranger Larry frequently called off sick. But when he failed to show up at a family party in town that evening and didn't answer his phone, a brother had driven out to the house and had found him hanging from a rafter in the barn. He'd been dead several hours by then.

There had been no signs of a struggle, and a stepladder was found lying on the dirt floor beneath the body, but the sheriff had called in the state techs anyway, and their preliminary findings indicated that Ranger Larry's death was exactly what it appeared to be—a suicide by hanging. No one had unearthed a reason yet for the man to be so depressed, but none of his family or friends seemed particularly surprised, either. Doc Sweitzer speculated that a skeleton would pop out of Ranger Larry's closet sooner or later.

"There's a reason he did it," Doc said wisely. "We just don't know it yet."

"How about guilt?" I sniped.

"Guilt manifests itself in many forms," Doc intoned.

I gagged and went to the station, where I promptly ruined everyone else's day.

Bradley paced the squad room like a very testy bear, and his skepticism sounded pretty much like my own reaction at the lab. "Let's see if I got this right—we got three victims, all killed exactly the same way in exactly the same location, and you're saying three different perps did it?"

Bradley is not above killing the messenger, so my stomach was churning as I corrected him. "The DNA says two different men raped Martinez and DeMarco. Maybe one of them did Schirria, too. Or maybe a third perp raped him."

"So maybe one guy killed them all, but at least two guys raped them. Is that about right?" And the look he leveled on me was blistering.

"Right," I said bravely.

"And maybe one of these guys was the ranger, who got up Saturday morning and decided to hang himself out of remorse, right?"

"Well, maybe," I said.

Bradley stopped in his tracks. "*Maybe*?"

"We don't know *why* he hanged himself," I said. "It might have nothing to do with the murders."

"Yeah, right," Henry said. He'd just stopped in to pick up some baseball tickets from Herchek. Now it looked like his night shift was going to start five hours early.

Bradley suddenly took aim at Ellen. "This ranger has been your buddy. What the hell's going on here?"

Ellen nearly jumped out of her chair. At first, she had been fretting because her babysitter was on overtime. But when I told them about Ranger Larry, she had gotten very pale, and she had been deep in her own thoughts as Bradley sparred with me. Bradley's sudden charge rattled her. "I—I'm shocked," she admitted. "He always seemed so upbeat, despite the murders."

"Maybe he was upbeat *because* of the murders," Mulhaney offered quietly. He was still officially on sick leave and had just wandered in for some gossip. He got a lot more than he bargained for.

Henry nodded as though he liked Mulhaney's idea, but I wasn't entirely sold. "Maybe he did DeMarco and Schirria, or maybe he did Martinez and Shirria," I said, "but he couldn't have done Martinez and DeMarco."

"Not so fast," Berger said from behind his computer screen. "The DNA says two different guys raped 'em. Doesn't mean one guy didn't kill 'em."

"Bullshit," Henry complained. "You think this guy just happened to stumble on random rape victims in the park and snapped their necks before they could recover?"

"Actually," Berger said, unperturbed, "I was picturing it the other way. Different rapists stumbled on the bodies and had their way with 'em before we got there."

"Doc Sweitzer *did* say they were killed first," Bradley admitted.

"Like Doc Sweitzer is some kind of authority," I sniffed.

"You got a better idea?" Bradley demanded.

"You mean something better than murderers and rapists tripping all over each other in the dark?" I retorted.

Henry grinned. He loved a good fight. Berger and Ellen hunkered down behind their desks. They had more sense. Mulhaney just sighed. "You two would get a whole lot farther if you weren't hauling around so much baggage."

Henry hooted.

Ellen blushed.

Bradley and I simply glared at Mulhaney.

But illness had stripped Mulhaney of lots of inhibitions, and he didn't even flinch. "Quit snarling at each other and focus on the *case*."

Bradley wanted to tear into Mulhaney. I could almost see little blood vessels popping in his head. But he drew the line at beating up on sick old men. "What exactly do you suggest we focus *on*?" he asked, straining to lower the volume to simply ear-splitting.

"You got two possibilities," Mulhaney said, and he held up two fingers still puffy from chemotherapy. "One, you treat each death as a separate case. Different killers, different motives, different suspects, different alibis. Open up a new investigation into each one. Don't let 'em overlap."

"And two?" Bradley asked with exaggerated patience.

"It's a gang bang," Mulhaney said.

"A *what*?" Ellen asked.

"A gang bang," Henry repeated helpfully. "That's when a bunch of guys—"

"I know what a gang bang is," Ellen interrupted, though some of us doubted her. "Define 'gang.'"

"Multiple killers acting in concert," Mulhaney said promptly.

Henry shot me a look over Mulhaney's head. "In *concert*?" he repeated. I bit back a smile. Mulhaney had been watching too much TV.

"You mean, like a club?" Bradley asked.

"The ladies' auxiliary," Henry snickered.

"A fraternity," Berger said, but he wasn't snickering.

"Something like that," Mulhaney agreed. "Maybe nothing so formal, with rules. But a *group*."

"A group of killers," Bradley said, and he stopped pacing while he thought it over.

"Why would a group kill?" I asked. "What's the purpose?"

"Initiation," Berger said, hanging onto the fraternity idea.

"Bonding," Ellen agreed.

"Survival," Bradley said. "That's a pretty strong motive."

"Money," I said. "Even stronger."

"Sex," Henry said.

Mulhaney raised his hands. "All of the above."

"So what group of people would kill as an initiation?" Bradley asked.

"A fraternity," Berger said doggedly. "Schirria was in a fraternity."

"It wouldn't have to be *his* fraternity," Ellen said. "The university has dozens of them."

"Oh, hell," I said. "You might as well throw in the sororities, too."

"You're forgetting the little problem of semen," Henry chided me.

"I'm sure a sorority could draft some donors," I said.

"But they probably didn't," Bradley said, clearly disappointed in me. "Forget sororities. Who else would be bonding?"

"The track team?" Ellen asked. "Athletes can be pretty intense."

Bradley nodded, getting into it. "But don't limit it to the university. High school runners have popped up in this investigation, too."

"There are the rangers," Mulhaney offered. "They work together as a fraternity of sorts."

"And one of them just offed himself," Henry added. "Maybe he was the weak link—the first one to crack."

Ellen nodded sadly.

"Who else?" Bradley asked.

"Other people use the park regularly," Mulhaney said. "Bicyclists, hikers."

"Okay," Bradley said. "Add bicycle and hiking clubs to the list. What about money as a motive?"

"That takes us back to developers. But we ruled them out," I said diplomatically.

"It's a brand-new investigation," Bradley said, dancing just as carefully around the I-told-you-sos. "We should look at developers again."

"And farmers," I said. "The park has cost some of them lots of money."

"That leaves sex," Mulhaney said cheerfully.

That sounded kind of funny coming out of Mulhaney's mouth. He looked so frail, I could have knocked him over with a whisper. But there he was, grinning like a schoolboy with a copy of Playboy stashed in his locker.

"Sex as a motive is a little more difficult," Ellen said. "Why would a group pick *these* victims for sex?"

"They had nothing in common," I admitted.

"Except location," Berger said. "They were all in the park."

"Still," I said, "two women and one man, two young victims and one middle-aged—if it's a gang looking for sex, why didn't they prey on the same type of victim?"

"Maybe that's why there's a different rapist for each victim," Bradley said. "Different tastes, different victims."

"So if it's a gang," Berger said, "there's gotta be at least one member who likes boys."

"And one member who has a fixation on his mother," Henry said.

I looked at him in some awe. I didn't necessarily agree with him, but he sounded like he'd actually read the FBI's profile material. It wasn't like him at all.

"Sex as the main motivation is still problematical," Ellen persisted. "What *group* has to resort to attacks in the park to get sexual release?"

"Teenage boys," Mulhaney said promptly.

"Married men," Berger said ruefully.

Even Ellen managed a small smile.

"Maybe it's a mixed group," I said. "Martinez and DeMarco for the guys and Schirria for the ladies."

"That would explain the lack of semen," Bradley admitted.

"Yeah," Henry said, "but what did the 'ladies' shove up his ass?"

And we all sort of shuddered as we thought about it.

Bradley wearily rubbed the back of his neck, working out the kinks, both physical and mental. "Okay, we start over. Share what you find, but I went Ellen to concentrate on Martinez. You're the youngest," he said to her. "See if you can squeeze something out of her teammates, her classmates. Go back to the boyfriend."

Ellen nodded, satisfied with the assignment.

"Berger gets DeMarco," Bradley said.

Berger raised his eyebrows.

"You're the right age," Bradley said. "Talk up the husband. If these *are* separate killings, the spouse is the likeliest suspect for DeMarco."

Berger sighed. Judy DeMarco was going to cost him serious computer time.

Bradley didn't particularly care. "Henry, you get Schirria."

"I *am* working nights," Henry delicately reminded him.

"What better time to investigate a frat boy?" Bradley countered. "Work on his brothers. Dig into the bar where he was last seen. Who wanted this boy dead?"

"You should talk to Eddie Corrigan," I said. "He thought Seth might have been bothering the girls on the track team."

"Yeah," Henry said. "I'll call Eddie first thing." But I knew Henry would take his good old time before he'd call Eddie about anything.

"What about me?" I asked. "Everyone has a case but me."

"You?" Bradley asked, and he suddenly looked wicked. "You get the gang bangers."

Henry patted me on the shoulder. "All right, Jo!"

I snarled at him.

"We won't tell Dave," he added solemnly.

I slapped his hand away.

"That's an awful lot for one person," I objected. "I get the fraternities, the track teams, the athletic clubs, the developers, the rangers, the farmers—did I miss anyone?"

"How about the poachers?" Ellen asked helpfully.

"I was being facetious," I said.

Ellen didn't get it.

"Someone's gotta take the broad view," Bradley said.

"I could do broad," Henry offered.

Bradley ignored him. "The other guys focus on single murders—you work on linking them with multiple perps."

"We need to bring back the feds," I muttered.

"And clear up this suicide while you're at it," Bradley said. "Make sure it really *is* suicide."

"Christ," I groaned.

Bradley glanced at Mulhaney. "Did I leave anything out?"

"Nope," Mulhaney said, nodding heavily. "I think you got it covered."

Bradley looked at the rest of us, still parked behind our various desks. "Did I mention I want status reports from all of you first thing in the morning?"

We were out of there.

Chapter Thirty-Five

I stopped by the house to change clothes and decided Barney might be a handy partner when I braced the rangers. He didn't object.

It was nearly eight-thirty when I parked at the trailhead. The air was still stifling, but the sun was barely clearing the treetops, and the parking lot was bathed in a sticky orange sunset. The lot was surprisingly empty—maybe it was just too damned hot for biking and hiking—but I disappointed Barney by keeping him on the leash. There were still a couple of families straggling through the parking lot, and I didn't want Barney barreling over toddlers.

I found only a volunteer in the ranger station, and she wasn't sure whether Joe and Ray were on duty or not. They had both clocked out about seven for Ranger Larry's calling hours.

I made sympathetic noises, but the volunteer wasn't inclined to gossip. So I said I might just hike down to the river and let Barney play in the mud while we waited. The volunteer took me literally and said dogs and humans weren't allowed in the water. But she grudgingly agreed to send the rangers my way when they checked in. She implied it could be hours.

Undaunted, Barney and I tramped through the woods to the first bend in the river, close to where Seth Schirria's body had been found. Barney whined to get off the leash, and since I was the only law around, I indulged him. He dived joyously into the river and promptly terrorized a family of ducks.

I was sitting on a boulder, dangling my feet in the water, when Joe quietly came up behind me about ten minutes later. I wasn't particularly alarmed. If Joe made any threatening moves, I figured I could swim away while Barney mauled him.

Joe frowned at me and the dog. "You're in violation of at least two city ordinances and a half dozen park regulations," he said, nodding at the empty leash on the riverbank.

I squinted up at him. "You could cite me."

For a moment, he looked like he was going to pull his ticket pad out of his back pocket. Then he grimaced. "Ah, hell, Jo, I don't want to cite anybody." And even though he was still in his dress uniform, he slid onto the rock beside me and watched unhappily as Barney bolted up the bank to chase a rabbit.

"Funeral tomorrow?" I asked eventually.

"Yep," he said without looking at me.

"You gonna be a pallbearer?"

"Yep."

"Had much practice?"

"Too much."

"That sucks."

"Tell me about it," he said, and he scooped up a handful of pebbles to flick across the river.

When he'd relaxed enough that he could skip a stone five times before it rattled onto the opposite bank, I asked him why he hadn't bothered to inform the cops that Ranger Larry had killed himself.

"Why'd I want to do that?" he asked. "You fixin' to send a sympathy card?"

"It would have been helpful to know that a ranger involved in a murder case hanged himself," I said.

Joe's mouth twisted as he flung another pebble across the river. "First off, Larry wasn't 'involved' in a murder case. He just happened to work in a park where some people got killed. And second, *you're* good buddies with the coroner, not me. I don't see where I was under any obligation to 'inform' the police of anything. Didn't your coroner do that?"

"He was a little slow sharing the information," I admitted.

Joe shrugged. "Not my problem."

Barney tore out of the woods and splashed into the river in front of us. I thought it was rather refreshing. Joe swore.

"You want to cite us yet?" I asked.

"I'm getting there," Joe said, and he delicately brushed beads of water off his pant leg.

"A man kills himself during a murder investigation," I said after a while, "the police tend to wonder whether the two events might be related."

Joe nodded. "I can see how you might think that. But Larry didn't kill himself over those women or that boy. I know that for a fact."

"How can you be so sure? He didn't leave a note."

"Didn't have to," Joe said firmly. "Larry had other problems, and they had nothing to do with your murders."

I waited for him to elaborate, but he sank into another mournful silence. I looked at him in the deepening twilight, and his jaw was clenched tight. "Would you care to share those problems with me?"

"No, ma'am," Joe said. And he purposely turned away to stare at Barney's antics in the river.

I sighed. "Maybe you'd like to come downtown to share your thoughts with my chief."

"Wouldn't care much for that, either," he admitted.

And we sat some more in silence. I was feeling my frustration grow with the darkness. Joe and Ray had seemed like pretty decent guys that first night, when we had gone chasing poachers. Ray had even been mildly helpful during the FBI fiasco in the park. But the longer the investigation stretched out, the more the rangers clammed up, and it was leading me to do the unthinkable—doubt a fellow officer.

Barney trotted up to us and plopped his dripping chin on Joe's knee. I expected Joe to growl—after all, he had to wear those trousers to a funeral in the morning—but instead, his tight face softened, and he scratched the damp fur behind Barney's ears. The dog simply drooled.

"I like dogs," Joe said. "They're honest. They like you, they show it. They don't like you, they bite you in the ass. You always know where you stand with a dog."

"Unlike cops."

"Especially cops," Joe said as he reached for the leash and smoothly looped it around Barney's neck. The dog happily let him.

Part of my brain noted the fact that with Barney on the leash, I was somewhat defenseless, alone in the woods with a man who could be a murder suspect. But Joe made no moves toward me. He was staring across the river again.

"Larry was gay," Joe said.

I reached down for my shoes to hide my surprise. "Are you sure?"

"It wasn't a secret around here. Larry didn't broadcast it, but we all knew. Made no difference to us. He was just—Larry."

"Larry flirted shamelessly with Detective Graham," I said as I fished my socks out of my shoes. "That doesn't sound gay to me."

Joe nodded. "That was Larry's public face. He didn't want the superintendent thinking he was hitting on guys in the park, so sometimes he overcompensated."

"And did any of the ladies reciprocate?" I asked as I squished into my shoes.

"Naw," Joe said. "He wasn't very good at it."

"Ellen thought he was cute."

"But you didn't," Joe pointed out.

I thought that over. "No," I finally said, "I was put off by it."

"There you go," Joe said as he handed me the leash.

Barney leaped up the bank, dragging me off the rock. I yelped and scrambled after him. Joe actually smiled.

We scrambled back to the trail, which was quickly disintegrating into varying shades of charcoal and silver in the moonlight. Barney stopped to sniff the breeze, then bounded off toward the trailhead. I stumbled after him, swearing mightily as an errant branch swooped across my cheek.

Joe sighed as he took the leash from me and Barney automatically heeled.

"No treats for you," I grumbled.

"I wasn't expecting any," Joe said.

And we plodded up the trail in silence as I pondered the significance of *that*.

The parking lot was empty except for my car and Joe's pickup. The ranger station was nearly dark—just one bulb burning over the door. I should have been wary, alone in the park at night with a man who had more control over my dog than I did, but no alarms were going off in my head. Underneath his irritation with me, I detected only sadness in Joe.

I might have been more nervous if there hadn't been a gun riding on my hip.

I opened the passenger side door and Barney obligingly hopped in. He wiggled around the bucket seat until he found just the right spot, buried his nose in his paws and pretended to go to sleep. Mud dripped from his tail.

I walked around to the driver's side, playing with my keys. "So you're telling me Larry killed himself because he was gay, is that about right?"

"It isn't an easy life," Joe said.

"But you said the guys here didn't care," I reminded him.

"Others did," Joe said.

"His family?"

"Oh, yeah," Joe said. "His family cared a *lot*. But it wasn't just them. Even in a university town, which folks say is *supposed* to be more liberal, a gay man is a target. Larry spent his whole life torturing himself because he was different, because he didn't fit in. I think Saturday night, he just said to hell with it. He wasn't going to put up with it anymore."

"He didn't have to kill himself. He could have just moved away," I said.

"Is it any different anyplace else?" Joe asked.

I got his point.

I slid into the car, which was already steaming with the smell of hot damp dog. I cranked down the window and gulped in the fresh night air. Joe was already halfway to his truck.

I got a sudden thought. "You feel comfortable with a suicide ruling?" I called out to him.

Joe stopped and looked back at me over his shoulder. "What—you think it's some kinky sex thing?"

"Autoeroticism is a dangerous pastime," I said.

"Jesus," Joe said, shaking his head in disgust. "The man wasn't *weird*. He was just gay."

And he climbed into his truck, as though glad to be rid of me.

I started the car and drove cautiously out to the road, ever watchful for deer. But even as one part of my mind focused on the mechanics of driving, another part was toying with the macabre possibilities of death by hanging. By the time I reached the comforting lights of the city, I had settled on three scenarios.

Ranger Larry had killed himself—either in guilt or despair.

Or he had died accidentally, the victim of a sad sexual game.

Or he had been helped along by his murderous accomplices.

In my line of work, gay never meant cheerful.

Chapter Thirty-Six

It was another hot Saturday night at the Farmhouse, the last weekend before the start of the fall term. The bar was packed with university types intent on one final binge before buckling down to the irritating business of dealing with students. Dave was especially hyper, talking nonstop as he geared himself up to face yet another semester of slackers, dimwits, bleeding hearts and clowns. He put on such a lively performance that I didn't think once of Ranger Larry dangling from the rafters or Judy DeMarco lying dead among the wildflowers.

At least not until my new best friend squeezed herself into the booth beside me and introduced herself to Dave.

Dave had drunk a little too much and was uncharacteristically gallant. Normally, he would have glared at anyone who invaded our space, especially someone who was almost a cop. But he aimed a smile at Sarah Tate that was so dazzling, she quivered. It made me wonder crankily whether he had had so much to drink, he wouldn't live up to my expectations for later in the evening.

Sarah had dressed for the heat in a gauzy shapeless shift that allowed her to dispense with such annoying items as bras and nylons. I didn't care much for such clothing either, but I was about forty pounds lighter. I gave her credit for not giving a damn. It was her night off, too.

She signaled the waitress for a pitcher, which neither Dave nor I needed, but it would have been impolite not to partake. I was wondering madly what the three of us could possibly talk about—Dave was not well-versed in celluloid Santas—but I had underestimated Sarah. Instead of talking shop with me, she talked shop with him, bringing up a salacious grading scandal in the university history department. Dave snapped at the bait, and they were off and running. I sank back into the corner of the booth and nursed my beer, unexpectedly ignored, while they debated the decline of academic integrity.

Ah, but Sarah was sly. She let Dave score with a convoluted argument that was either brilliant or the byproduct of alcohol, and while he toasted himself with another beer, she turned on me. "You gonna make an arrest before the FBI comes back to town?"

I jerked to attention. "Who says they're coming back?"

Sarah couldn't help herself. She smirked. "One of my fellowships was in federal law enforcement. I have contacts."

Contacts that plopped her right in the middle of a decoy operation where she didn't belong, I thought in some irritation.

Dave watched us in amusement. Despite drinking vast quantities of beer, he still knew exactly what I was thinking.

"The little problem of the senator's daughter has been cleaned up," Sarah said, dismissing it with a wave of her hand. "Beck is coming back."

I groaned. "Does Bradley know that?"

Sarah's smirk was becoming permanent. "He does now."

I felt Bradley's ulcer as if it were my own.

"So," Sarah said, resting her forearms on the table and leaning in conspiratorially, "what do you say we just wrap this up before Beck gets here?"

Dave raised an eyebrow over "we," but I was suddenly listening hard. "How much time do we have?"

"Beck has some formalities to attend to—like an arraignment—but he'll be here by midweek," Sarah predicted.

"We aren't that close."

"We're all intelligent people," Sarah said, including Dave in the compliment. "Maybe if we put our heads together . . . ." And she let the offer dangle out there over the table.

"Why do you care?" Dave asked, voicing the question that was bouncing around my own head.

Sarah forgot she was trying to flirt and shot him a blistering a look. "You mean besides the fact that some son of a bitch is killing my students?"

Dave graciously backed off. "Point well taken," he conceded.

Sarah pulled back her claws. "It's also in the university's best interests if the city makes an arrest before the FBI does," she admitted. "The local publicity is already hurting us. A federal case is going to seriously damage our recruitment nationally. At least that's what my boss thinks."

"You disagree?" Dave asked.

Sarah shrugged. "I don't think there's any way around the PR hit, no matter who makes the case. Carmen Martinez was a big-name athlete, and the national media will follow the court case right down to the verdict. But my boss thinks the publicity won't be as widespread if it's a local arrest."

"Your boss has his head up his ass," Dave said.

"My boss happens to be your boss, too," Sarah reminded him.

"He still has his head up his ass," Dave declared, and he helped himself to more beer.

"We aren't close to an arrest," I repeated morosely.

"Sure you are," Sarah said. "You just don't know it yet."

I felt my eyes crossing. It had nothing to do with the beer.

"You just have to prioritize," Sarah said. "Quit wasting time on your marginal suspects and focus on the viable ones."

Prioritize? Marginal? Viable? I looked at Dave in panic, but he was nodding solemnly at Sarah. She was talking his language.

"Number one," Sarah said, counting on her fingers, "these aren't separate killings. No copycat is that good. At least not multiple copycats. Number two, the evidence says the victims were raped by at least two different men, so you've got at least two men working together. Number three, to get away with it this long, only a tight group of men, a tight *brotherhood*, could have pulled it off. Only one group of people in this case fits those criteria."

I stared glumly at the pitcher. I did not like where this was going at all. "You're talking about fellow officers," I said stiffly.

"I'm talking about stone-cold *killers*," Sarah said forcefully.

Dave suddenly decided that he needed a trip to the bathroom. I glared at him as he abruptly excused himself and slid out of the booth. Dave had a bladder the size of an elephant's. He was simply removing himself from the line of fire.

Sarah zeroed in on me before Dave was decently out of earshot. "I'm all for professional courtesy, Jo, but it's time to haul those rangers in for some serious questioning."

"We have no evidence implicating the rangers," I said stubbornly.

"One of 'em just hanged himself," Sarah reminded me. "That reeks of guilt to me."

"He didn't kill himself over the murders," I said. "He killed himself because he was gay."

"Says who?" she demanded.

Joe, I thought, and I felt myself blushing.

"Who's had easy access to all the victims?" Sarah asked as she poured herself another mug of beer. "The rangers. Who's *found* all the victims? The rangers. Who's been the rangers' best alibis? Other rangers. Good God, woman, get some warrants and get some DNA samples from these guys. How can you *not* suspect them?"

"They *have* had the best access to the victims," I admitted.

"It isn't just access to the victims," Sarah said. "They've had access to the *investigation*. They've been treated like cops instead of suspects, and as a result, they've been all over the crime scene. They've been all over the witnesses. They were even players in the FBI's decoy operation. Is it any wonder that whole exercise failed?"

I bit my tongue. There were quite a few reasons the decoys hadn't work out, and one of them was sitting beside me.

Sarah had the good grace to blush. "Okay, maybe that isn't the best example, but you get my point."

"It's true no one's ever been attacked when the park has been under surveillance," I conceded.

"And as long as you keep the rangers in the loop, nobody will," Sarah said, and she sat back, crossed her arms beneath her substantial chest and nodded decisively.

I picked at the pretzel crumbs littering the table and thought of Ray, sharing candy bars on stakeout, pictured Joe scratching Barney behind the ears, remembered Ranger Larry making eyes at Ellen. They were all *nice* guys. How could they be a gang of killers?

I shook my head to clear the buzz of alcohol. The images that leaped into focus were no more comforting—Larry sneaking peeks at Carmen Martinez's body while Ellen questioned him; Ray tugging Judy DeMarco's body out from under the bushes, compromising the crime scene; Joe letting dopers like Seth Schirria skip out of the park with just a warning; all of them there in the background as we collected evidence and interviewed witnesses and set up decoys.

Was there any part of the investigation they *hadn't* touched?

"But why?" I protested, more to myself than to Sarah. "Why would they do it?"

"It doesn't matter why," Sarah said. "All that matters is you lock the bastards up."

Dave would have frowned at her attitude, but he was still skulking around the men's room. I shoved my half-empty mug to his side of the table. I was no longer in the mood.

"I'll talk to Bradley," I said without much enthusiasm.

"When?" Sarah pressed.

I felt the sweating, drunken bar crowd closing in around me. The big clock above the door was nearing midnight. "Now doesn't seem the right time."

"Right," Sarah said. "He's probably home in bed."

I didn't care for that picture, either, and tried to shake it off.

"But you get with him first thing Monday morning," she warned.

I tried to focus on her, but my eyes were crossing. "Or what?"

"It's your case, Jo," she said as she pried herself out of the booth, mug in hand. "But the feds are coming back. You don't go to Bradley soon, I will."

And I swear to God, the woman winked at me as she bellied up to the bar.

Chapter Thirty-Seven

I prowled around the house all day Sunday, nursing a hangover and fretting over Sarah's theories. I didn't want the rangers to be the perps, but the more I thought about it, the more I realized we'd let them skate. We'd questioned them after Carmen was killed, but then we'd homed in on Jesse Conklin, and we'd never given the rangers' alibis a hard second look, not even after Judy DeMarco was killed. Sure, I'd cornered Joe at the park after Seth was murdered, but my irritation then had been focused on his lackadaisical enforcement of the drug laws, not the murders. And even after Ranger Larry hanged himself, I had gone to Joe hoping he'd give me a reason *not* to pursue the rangers. And he had obliged. Larry, he told me, killed himself because he was gay.

And I had been happy to believe him.

But what if Larry hadn't killed himself at all? What if Joe's revelation that Larry was gay was just a story? What if Larry had been silenced, either because he had discovered what his fellow rangers had been up to, or because he was a player and was cracking under the pressure?

So after Sunday dinner, as Dave and Adam squabbled over the dishes, I called Bradley at home. I was rotating to the night shift on Monday and decided Sarah's warning shouldn't wait until the next time he and I happened to pass in the squad room.

I expected him to bitch at me for interrupting his ballgame, but the return of the feds had been weighing on his mind, too. So we chewed over Sarah's conclusions and decided Henry would be just cranky enough from the abrupt switch to the day shift that he should haul the rangers in for a long overdue session in the interrogation room. Technically, that meant Bradley was taking the main thrust of the investigation out of my hands, but I didn't mind too much. (Maybe if it had been Ellen instead of Henry, I would have squawked.) Neither of us mentioned that it had been a while since Seth was killed and the murderers could already be stalking their next victim. But we both felt time running out for us.

So I promised to turn my notes over to Henry and I crawled into bed that night with a clearer conscience. The burden of proving or disproving Sarah's conjectures had been passed onto Bradley and the day shift. Henry would get to play the heavy. And no matter how it played out with Joe and Ray and their fellow officers, it wouldn't be my fault.

*   *   *

I complain about the night shift just like everyone else. The world just doesn't cater to people who work all night and sleep all day. Even something as mundane as refilling a prescription or stopping at the car wash becomes a major hassle when your internal clock is turned upside down. But the wicked truth was, since my household had expanded to include my mother, then Dave and then his son, I took a secret delight in having the house all to myself during the day—at least at the beginning of the month, before the weariness has a chance to creep into my bones.

Monday morning, when Dave's alarm went off at seven, I simply burrowed under the pillows and purred while he stumbled out of bed and dragged himself to class. It didn't even register when Mother and Adam hustled off to campus, either. I slept soundly until ten and was so astonished by my good fortune, I rewarded myself with another hour in bed.

The morning was warm, but not nearly as humid. Summer was loosening its grip on campus and the town. When I finally forced myself awake and peeked out the window, I even noted a few yellow leaves dotting the trees. It was a brilliant, clear day, and there wasn't a single thing I *had* to do until my shift started at eleven. So I indulged myself with a late breakfast on the deck and a few hours with a book, and didn't think once about checking in with Henry to see how the interrogations were going.

My generosity knew no bounds. I had dinner waiting on the table when the gang got home, and they were so strung out after their first day of classes, I even volunteered to do the dishes, too. But when I slid the last plate into the cupboard, it was still only seven o'clock—way too early for even me to show up at the station.

Mother and Adam were studying, and Dave was trying to read ahead for his new class in election statistics. No one wanted to play with me.

Except for Barney, who had been laying a guilt trip on me all day for not devoting quality time to him.

"You know, the cats never ask me to take *them* for a walk," I informed him as I pulled the leash out of a drawer.

Barney just yelped in glee and galloped to the back door.

"Don't take him to the park," Dave warned automatically, without looking up from his book.

"No park," I agreed, and kissed him on the top of his head.

He just grunted.

He needn't have worried. The last thing I wanted to do was run into Joe and Ray.

Instead, I drove out beyond the park, up the road past the Hawkins farm to an abandoned apple orchard about five miles out of town. One of the patrols had told me there was an old path from the orchard down to the river, and I figured there was just enough daylight left for Barney and me to get there and back.

Technically, we were trespassing, but judging from the tire tracks in the dirt off the road, we weren't the first. I parked in the shade of the first row of trees, firmly attached Barney to the leash and marched into the woods to explore.

"Path" was too generous a word. A slight crease in the vegetation was more like it. But Barney nosed valiantly ahead, and I stumbled behind him, sidestepping branches and brambles. Eventually, we found the river, and it was a soothing sight, so soothing that I lost track of the clock in my head. When we finally turned around to climb back uphill to the car, I was surprised at how much daylight we had already lost. By the time we reached the orchard, the world was turning gray, and the breeze under the trees was unexpectedly damp and cool.

I was wiping mud off Barney's paws when my radio crackled to life. And even though I wasn't on duty yet, it was the dispatcher asking for my location.

I frowned at Barney and told her where I was. There was a moment of silence, which I used to shoo Barney into the back seat, then Bradley's voice rumbled over the airwaves.

"We got another victim in the park," he said. "I need you there *now*."

"I'm five minutes away," I assured him and started the car.

"Make it sooner," Bradley said. "This one's alive."

*   *   *

A ranger had found her unconscious north of the trailhead, near the construction site for the new picnic shelter, and had radioed for help. That was all Bradley could tell me. I was north of the trailhead, too, but on the wrong side of the river. I could drive back into town to cross over on a real bridge, but Bradley had been emphatic. He didn't want the victim alone with the rangers while they waited for EMS. So I sped south past cornfields and barns and scoured the darkening fields for the rutted lane that would take me to the condemned bridge where Joe and Ray had tried to scare me silly.

I would have missed it if a buck hadn't darted across the road and trotted up the lane. I kicked up a cyclone of dust as I squealed into the turn and followed the white tail into the gloom. Barney bounced around the back seat and sprayed my neck with slobber.

My little car wasn't made for abandoned farm lanes, and it screeched and howled as I pushed it deeper into the woods. A branch came out of nowhere and cracked the windshield. I swore but drove on. Barney yipped in excitement.

The bridge popped up suddenly about fifty yards off the main road. It hadn't weathered the summer well. I could see real holes in the deck, and new concrete barriers had been erected at both ends.

"Well, shit," I said, and slammed on the brakes. The car slid to a stop inches from concrete.

I would have to hike in.

I grabbed my gun from the glove compartment and pushed open the door. Barney scrambled over me and out into the woods before I could stop him. I swore again, but didn't waste time trying to catch him. He'd just have to take care of himself.

I stepped around the barricade and scooted out onto the bridge. There was a little more light over the river, but that only showed me what a truly sorry state the bridge was in. The wood was rotten, and the metal supports were flaking with rust. Fortunately, the river was at its end-of-the-summer low. If the bridge collapsed around me, I might break a leg, but I wouldn't drown.

Barney raced past me as I was sidestepping a man-size hole and leaped onto the opposite bank. I swear, the bridge shuddered. So I grit my teeth and ran after him, and made the jump onto solid land before the bridge could disintegrate beneath my feet.

Barney disappeared into the woods with a lusty yelp. I ran in the same general direction, but much more quietly.

Park crews had roughed out a trail on the old roadbed, and I ran along it, raking my flashlight along both sides, looking for the crime scene. Bradley hadn't been very specific, saying only that the woman had been found near the construction site. If I remembered my geography right, that could be as much as a half mile to the south.

The faint wail of a siren drifted through the trees. EMS was closing in, too, but the paramedics would still have a rough hike from the trailhead, and they would be hampered by their equipment. I forced myself to run harder, praying as I panted that I wouldn't overshoot the victim.

A shadow flashed ahead of me, and I froze, gun extended. It was a cyclist, pedaling like hell toward me. I yelled at him to stop, but he skidded around me, spraying my feet with pebbles and dirt.

"Gotta get help!" he shouted over his shoulder.

It was the same guy who had been on the trail when Martinez had died. His eyes were wide and panic-stricken, and I didn't think my gun even registered with him. He just pumped furiously up the lane toward the bridge, and the smell of his sweat swirled behind him.

I didn't like the coincidence. But he *said* he was going for help, and I needed to find the victim. I let him go and ran.

The roadbed curved away from the river and deeper into the trees. The light from my flash was almost as treacherous as no light at all, bouncing as I ran and popping black shadows on and off the path. I veered around tree limbs that weren't there and raked my ankles on brambles that really were, and wondered what in hell this victim was doing on an unimproved section of trail at sunset.

I pushed on till I'd gone what I guessed was a quarter mile from the bridge and didn't hear or see anyone else. I stopped and tried to hear something above my own gulping breaths. I could have shouted out, but the tone of Bradley's call held me back. If an antsy ranger heard me coming, would that be good or bad for the vic? I decided bad, and kept my mouth shut.

And heard what could have been voices, up ahead and off the roadbed to my right.

Barney heard them, too. He must have been amusing himself at the river, because he suddenly charged across the roadbed about five yards ahead of me and plunged into the woods toward the voices. I didn't know whether to holler at him or let him go. I heard him galloping through the brush, then there was a boisterous bark like the kind that greeted me whenever I came home, and then the night cracked with the unmistakable shot of a gun.

My stomach pitched in despair.

There were real voices then, shouting frantically at each other. I shakily doused the light and crept into the woods toward them.

I had covered more ground than I had thought. About ten yards off the path, the woods opened into a clearing where the construction crews had dumped their materials. There were mounds of dirt and gravel and piles of timber and rock, and lying in the middle, a heap of fur, oozing blood.

Joe and one of the Hawkins boys were aiming shotguns at each other a few feet beyond Barney, and in their raw panic, neither one heard me coming. They were yelling, and the barrels of both guns were bouncing wildly as they shouted.

I crawled up a pile of dirt and leveled my gun at Joe. I could have safely popped them both, then sorted it all out later, but that's not what I'm trained to do. So I blocked Barney out of my mind and yelled at them to drop their weapons.

They froze, and their guns froze with them, each aimed at the other's chest.

"Drop them *now*!" I ordered.

The ranger's eyes flicked toward my pile of dirt. "Jo?" he said, and his voice was ragged with the strain. But he didn't lower his gun.

Neither did the kid. He was dressed for poaching, but there was something wrong with the way his clothes were hanging. I didn't have time to analyze it.

"Put your weapons on the ground and back away," I said.

"No fucking way!" the kid yelled. "He's gonna kill me!"

"You're gonna kill both of us!" Joe shouted back, and his fingers tightened ominously on the gun.

"Anyone shoots, you're both dead," I said, and I wasn't bluffing.

"He's fucking crazy!" the kid yelled.

"You're a fucking killer!" Joe shouted.

"Shoot him! Shoot him now!" the kid screamed at me.

Joe squinted down his sights. "He killed your dog, Jo."

"*He* did it! *He* did it!" the kid shrieked.

They both pulled back to fire.

I sucked in my breath.

And shot the kid.

Chapter Thirty-Eight

"**W**hy the hell did you wait so long?" Joe fumed at me.

"Why the hell didn't you drop your gun?" I grumbled back. "I had you covered."

Joe just harrumphed, and we hunched together on my pile of dirt while Bradley barked orders at the techs and the patrols swarmed around the clearing.

The victim—not dead—had been whisked away to the hospital. EMS had found her still unconscious at the construction site, with Ray grimly guarding her. He'd heard the shots in the woods, but Ray the cowboy had surprised me. Instead of charging to the rescue, he'd done the smart thing and radioed for more backup. The paramedics thought the victim might pull through.

The Hawkins boy would, too. I'd shot him in the leg, splintering bone, and he had gone down hard. I hadn't hit an artery, though, so despite howling in pain and bleeding all over Joe and me, he was still very much alive when the paramedics broke through to the clearing.

Henry came up behind them and razzed me for shooting to disable instead of shooting to kill. I didn't mind. I'd sleep with a clear conscience that night, and the Hawkins kid could hobble around prison for the rest of his life for all I cared. I thought it was a fair trade.

Joe and I stayed out of the way while other officers took over the scene. We were both in for a long night of questioning—Joe as a witness and me for firing my weapon. I'd take some bureaucratic shit for shooting a civilian, even though the said civilian had been involved in at least four attacks in the park. I might even be suspended while the department investigated. That was just the political climate these days. I wasn't too concerned. It was one of the hassles that came with the job.

I sketched what had gone down for Bradley. He looked speculatively at Joe, wondering whether I'd got it all wrong, then shrugged and sent Henry and Berger to pick up the Hawkins kid's brother. Ellen and Herchek went after the kid on the bicycle. Maybe he was just a victim of coincidence, but I didn't think the Hawkins boys were in it alone. I flashed back on the group working out in the barn the day I questioned J.D., and I remembered the cyclist's freshly toned arms and chest the last time I talked to him, and I figured it was worth trampling his civil rights to haul him in for some hard questioning, too.

There were enough cops on the scene for a convention, and two of them took Barney away when I wasn't watching. I refused to think about it. The goddamned impetuous dog.

Bradley sent Joe to the station so he could start giving his statement. It was full night by then, and the air was cool. I was shivering—not entirely from cold—and Bradley commandeered a Thermos from one of the rangers. My hands were trembling as I held the steaming coffee to my lips.

Bradley sat beside me and made me go over it again—from the time I took his call until I shot the kid—only in more detail. He grunted when I finished.

"What?" I said, keenly aware of the nuances in a grunt.

Bradley picked up a rock and flicked it at a wheelbarrow. The sharp ping on metal startled the techs, and they looked at us in irritation. Bradley ignored them.

"You waited kinda long to fire," he said finally. "They could have blasted each other while you were jabbering at them to drop their guns."

"Yeah, they could have," I admitted.

"They could have taken you out, too," he said without looking at me.

"Yeah," I agreed, pleased that he'd noticed. "But I was pretty well shielded."

"Except for your damn fool head," he said, and he looked at the dirt pile in disgust. In retrospect, the pile seemed rather puny.

"You could have shot the ranger instead of the kid," he pointed out.

"Yeah, I could have." And the image made me shiver again.

"The rangers were our main suspects. We questioned 'em all afternoon, on *your* say-so. When you found the ranger and the kid waving shotguns at each other, you *should* have taken out the ranger."

"Yeah," I agreed.

"So why didn't you?" he asked.

"Two things," I said, remembering the split second before I took my gun off Joe and aimed at the kid. "One, the boy's fly was open."

"Good of you to notice," Bradley said wryly.

I felt myself blush. "One of 'em had just been interrupted while attacking a woman. I figured the boy hadn't had time to zip up."

"What if he'd just been taking a leak when the ranger found him?" Bradley countered.

I carefully put my coffee on the ground and stood. "Well, that leaves point Number Two," I said.

Bradley looked up at me. "And that is?"

"Joe wouldn't have been afraid of Barney. They were buddies."

Bradley gaped at me. "*That's* why you picked the kid?"

I shrugged. "The son of a bitch shouldn't have shot my dog."

And I wearily trudged back toward my car so I could go dispose of Barney.

Chapter Thirty-Nine

I found Jesse Conklin and Lisa Spuhler in the same booth at the student union. They weren't nearly as cozy as last time. In fact, they seemed to be cautiously avoiding physical contact, sitting stiffly on opposite sides of the table while Lisa's cigarette burned unnoticed in an ashtray and ketchup congealed on Jesse's fries. A newspaper lay on the table, folded back to a story about the Hawkins boys' latest appearance in court. I wasn't surprised.

It had been a week since the boys had been arrested. (I called them boys, but they were all seventeen or eighteen, and all had been charged as adults.) There were four of them altogether—the two Hawkins brothers, the cyclist and a fourth classmate who had never even been on our radar. But once we hauled in the other three, they quickly gave up their buddy. There wasn't much loyalty in this pack.

They'd started out simply as a bunch of boys working out together. They all played one or another high school sport and they just fell into the habit of hanging out at the farm, turning a corner of the barn into their own private gym. J.D. thought it was a healthy thing—kept the boys away from town and out of trouble—and he even coughed up the money for some pretty expensive equipment.

And if the boys sometimes ventured into the park at night to take out some deer—well, the deer were playing hell with J.D.'s crops. The boys were just protecting their land.

That was how it started, at least. But then hormones kicked in, and the talk during their workouts somehow got twisted from simply raunchy to frightening and perverted. The older Hawkins boy had a girlfriend and occasionally got laid, but the other three were bursting with need and greed. They were good-looking boys, and their fanatical workouts had sculpted them until they were lean and mean, but the stuff that spewed out of their mouths turned most of the girls at school off. The few who went out with them didn't make the same mistake twice.

As their frustration grew, one of them got the idea of flashing at the park, and it was such a blast watching the sickened look on his target's face that they all got into it for a while, taking turns standing guard while they each got their kicks. The Hawkins boys knew the park so well, they had no trouble steering clear of the rangers and later Mulhaney. If they would have been caught, they would have passed themselves off as poachers, because they already had the rep. And poachers didn't go to jail; they just got fined.

As the weather cooled, so did the excitement over flashing. The boys went into hibernation in the barn, but their fantasies didn't. They just got uglier. By spring, the boys had made a sick and deadly pact. They would prey on women together, and each would have his turn.

It was supposed to be just a rape, but the boys underestimated their strength. Carmen Martinez's neck snapped, and it was such a rush, discovering the power of death, they didn't think twice about killing the next time out. Judy DeMarco never had a prayer.

J.D. couldn't fathom why his boys devolved from God-fearing young men to cold-hearted predators. I caught him watching the boys as they were arraigned, and the look on his face was one of sheer horror. I wanted to feel sorry for him, but I felt worse for John DeMarco, who was in the courtroom, too, silently weeping. J.D. still had his boys, monsters that they were, but Judy DeMarco was gone forever.

The last victim did, indeed, live. She was a freshman, new to the university and the town, and she had wandered out to the park to explore, ignorant of the murders and the danger that lurked there. Although the boys couldn't kill her, there was serious damage to her spine and years of therapy and perhaps surgery ahead of her before she would ever walk unassisted. But she wasn't blind or intimidated. She picked the younger Hawkins boy out of a lineup without so much as flinching, and she vowed to me from her wheelchair that she would *walk* into the death house the day the boys got the needle.

DNA targeted the older Hawkins boy for Martinez and the cyclist for DeMarco, leaving the fourth boy as the presumed killer of Seth Schirria. But whereas the boys simply smirked when charged with Martinez, DeMarco and the last woman, all four protested mightily when the Schirria charges were read. They denied ever touching him every time his name was brought up, and they were still squawking when they were arraigned. That bothered me some.

Henry told me not to sweat it. They boys just didn't want to go to prison tagged as sweet.

I still didn't like it. Which was why on a rainy Tuesday afternoon a week after the arrests, I was standing in the student union instead of sleeping off the night shift.

Neither Lisa nor Jesse was thrilled to see me. I slid into the booth beside Jesse and he slithered as far away from me as he could get. Lisa picked up her neglected cigarette and blew smoke in my face.

I smiled brightly and tapped the newspaper with my finger. "Good to see young people keeping up with the news," I said.

"You're very condescending," Lisa said as she stubbed out her cigarette. "Did anyone ever tell you that?"

"Repeatedly," I said agreeably. "So, you guys must be relieved, huh?"

"Why would we be relieved?" Lisa asked sharply.

"Because we arrested Carmen's killers," I said innocently. "It must have been torturing you, knowing they were out there, free and unpunished."

Lisa gave me a hard stare as she weighed her response. Jesse tried to disappear into the wall. "Well, yes," she conceded. "It has been—difficult."

I nodded sympathetically. "All those weeks going by—Carmen dead and no one in jail. You must have been frantic, thinking we'd never make an arrest."

"If you expect us to thank you," Lisa said tartly, "you're wrong. If you'd done your job sooner, those other people wouldn't be dead."

"Judy DeMarco," I agreed. "Seth Schirria."

Jesse flinched. Lisa darted a vicious look at him.

"I forgot," I said, turning toward him. "You knew Seth."

"Not hardly," Jesse mumbled, and he crossed his arms and stared out the window. He wanted me to go away.

"There's something bothering me about those boys we arrested, though," I said, looking back at Lisa. "Know what that is?"

"I'm sure I don't have a clue," Lisa said, and she reached purposefully for her pack of cigarettes.

I smoothly slid the pack away from her. "If you don't mind . . . ."

"I *do* mind," she said angrily.

"So do I," I said, and flicked the pack toward Jesse. Lisa waited expectantly for him to pass the pack back to her. He didn't dare.

"Those boys were pretty hyper when we brought them in," I said, drawing Lisa's attention reluctantly back to me, "but they haven't said much since they lawyered up. They haven't admitted killing Carmen, but they haven't denied it, either. Same thing with Judy DeMarco and the girl last week. They haven't admitted those attacks, either, but they haven't denied them."

"I'm sure their lawyers told them not to," Lisa said haughtily. "It's what they all do, isn't it?"

"Well, that's the funny thing," I said. "Every time we bring up Seth Schirria, they go ballistic—despite what they lawyers tell them. They can't yell long enough or loud enough that they never touched the boy. They stonewall us on Carmen and the other women, but they deny emphatically that they killed Seth. Now why do you think that is?"

"They don't want to be labeled queer," Jesse said unhappily.

Lisa glared at him to shut up.

But I turned to him, pleased to include him in the conversation. "That's what my partner says. But I think it's more than that." I paused to make sure I had their attention, then lowered my voice to force them to lean in to hear me. "I don't think they killed Seth at all."

"That's ridiculous," Lisa said quickly. "Of course they did. They killed Carmen and that other woman and Seth. You have proof."

I shook my head. "We have proof they killed Carmen, and we have proof they killed Judy DeMarco, and the girl last week picked one of the boys out of a lineup. But we don't have a shred of forensic evidence that any of them ever laid a finger on Seth."

"They **must** have killed him," Lisa insisted. "He was attacked in the park, just like everyone else. His neck was broken, like everyone else. He was even raped. Of course those maniacs did it."

"I don't think so," I said.

Lisa had grown a bit pale. "Why would someone else kill Seth?" she asked, but her tone wasn't quite as defiant.

"Because someone else—you two, actually—thought he killed Carmen."

Jesse might have moaned, but I was focusing on Lisa. She was a tough little piece of work, and she just laughed in my face.

She should have been scared.

"This is what I think happened," I said, happy to explain it for them. "Carmen's death threw you two back together—it's understandable; you'd both suffered a terrible loss and you'd been close once—but instead of consoling each other, you just fed each other's anger. You desperately wanted someone to pay for Carmen, but the police weren't cooperating by making an arrest. How does my story sound so far?"

"Absurd," Lisa said, but she wasn't laughing anymore.

"You thought we got sidetracked by Judy DeMarco and weren't paying enough attention to Carmen, so you did some nosing around yourself, and discovered that some guy had been creeping out the girls on the track team. That was pretty smart detective work—but then you should have come to me or another cop about it. We could have told you we knew about this guy and were checking him out."

"You never arrested him," Jesse sulked.

"Because we never had a reason to," I said. "He never quite broke any laws. But you two fixated on him. You decided he killed Carmen, so you nosed around some more and discovered his name and where he lived and where he worked and because he was alive and free and Carmen was dead and buried and it didn't look like the police were going to do anything to him any time soon, you two decided to kill him yourselves."

"That's preposterous," Lisa hissed at me.

"Yes, it is. Seth Schirria never did a thing to Carmen but maybe leer at her out on the track, and for that, you two killed him. You lured him out to the park when he was drunk, you broke his neck, just like you thought he broke Carmen's, and then you abused his corpse, just like you thought he abused Carmen. You copied Carmen's murder almost perfectly. It would have been exquisite revenge if the poor boy hadn't been innocent."

Lisa looked like she could really use a cigarette, and I almost told Jesse to give her one. But, hell, she didn't deserve an ounce of my sympathy.

"You must have been pretty proud of yourselves, thinking you'd figured it out before anyone else and then avenging Carmen's murder. I bet you were horrified when you discovered you'd killed the wrong man."

This time, Jesse *did* moan. I patted his arm. "Makes you sick just thinking about it, doesn't it? Why, I bet you two can barely stand to be in the same room with each other now, knowing what you did."

Jesse shrank away from me. Lisa's left eyelid twitched madly.

I glanced at the clock on the wall. It was just past three-thirty, and I had a very important appointment at four.

"You don't have any proof," Lisa rasped.

I slid out of the booth. "Proof? No, I don't have *any* proof." Then I smiled wickedly. "But I will."

And I left them sputtering at each other in panic while I went to the vet's to pick up my dog.